"Why don't you wait until the rain lets up. It won't take that long for the storm to pass," Amari coaxed, watching her as she held onto the door that led outside. Her next words had him raise his eyebrows questioningly.

"I better run."

Raven opened the door and ran out into the rain. She was completely drenched after just a few seconds. The sight would have made Amari laugh—if he hadn't been so shocked by it. She was practically running away from him, leaving him in the Center all alone!

Who was going to lock up? Was she crazy? Surely she would come back!

He watched, incredulous, as she got into her car and inserted the key to start the engine. Lightning brightened the doorway followed by deafening thunder. In the lot, the "Old Baby," coughed and sputtered but its engine refused to kick alive.

Was she really going to just drive away? Amari heard the car make a scratching sound that sounded very much like an elephant dying and then, after a while, he realized that she had given up on her car.

About time too, Amari thought smugly. It served her right for running out on him as if he were trying to assault her or something!

SHOW ME THE SUN

MIRIAM SHUMBA

Genesis Press, Inc.

INDIGO LOVE STORIES

An imprint of Genesis Press, Inc.
Publishing Company

Genesis Press, Inc.
P.O. Box 101
Columbus, MS 39703

Copyright © 2009 Miriam Shumba

ISBN: 13 DIGIT : 978-1-58571-405-6
ISBN: 10 DIGIT : 1-58571-405-4
Manufactured in the United States of America

First Edition

Visit us at www.genesis-press.com
or call at 1-888-Indigo-1-4-0

DEDICATION

This book is dedicated to Gabe Shumba,
Agnes Denenga, Nathan Denenga,
and my little miracle.

ACKNOWLEDGMENTS

My first acknowledgement is to my Lord and Savior Jesus Christ who gave me the desire to write and to share his love with others.

I am grateful to the publication community at Genesis Press for all their help.

There are many people who have supported me through this writing journey by reading my work, encouraging, and inspiring me. First, I want to thank my love, my husband Gabe who is always there with encouragement and ideas. My sisters and brothers who believed in me and supported my dream—you know who you are! I am grateful to my friends from high school to adulthood who read my short stories and drafts: Joyce, Tendai, Stella, Maureen, Nellie, Vera, Maryam, Tanesha, Angela, Angelica, Nura, Madeline, Chaka, and Natsai. I am also grateful to those in my critique book club who are willing to listen and motivate: Marylyn, Carmen, Nicole, Oluwa, and Alyson. For help with my research on social work I would like to thank Celeste Butler for her enthusiastic answers to all my questions.

I want to thank my mother, Agnes, who sent my comic books to publishers when I was ten years old. I didn't even know what publishers were then! This is for you.

PROLOGUE

Raven shifted uncomfortably in her chair. She wished she could be anywhere but here, sitting in front of this kind, beautiful woman with warm, understanding eyes. She didn't want her sympathy, or pity, or anything. She just wanted a divorce. Quickly.

"Raven," Janice said softly, leaning forward on her pristine desk and clasping her piano player's fingers on it. Raven noticed her exquisite diamond rings and a picture of her perfect-looking family, a handsome husband and three children. They were studio shots and they all looked like models, happy and perfect.

"I would really like to help you if I can. I know this must be very difficult for you."

Raven nodded, not yet able to find her voice while trying to hide her resentment. She had wanted a family, too. She had wanted one that belonged to her. Her own family to love her and for her to love. Finally, she wanted to accept that it was not to be.

She had walked in the office and declined a cup of tea or water and greeted Janice before settling down in the over-stuffed but comfortable chair.

Raven was only here because her father had insisted, had set up the appointment and driven her there. She had resisted, and even now as she sat there with her back straight and shoulders held back by sheer willpower, her body language spoke volumes. What screamed loudest to Janice was that this woman was fragile, and if she said the wrong word, Raven would break into a million pieces.

"Would you like to tell me what I can do for you?" Janice asked, her kindness seeming to be an endless well. Her gentleness flowed to her like rain, but Raven didn't let it enter her heart.

Raven pursed her lips harder, feeling the headache and the tension in her shoulders again. All the pain of the last few weeks was collected right there, almost stopping her circulation.

"I really don't need counseling," Raven began, the tears coming into her eyes. She didn't trust some of these church folks. This counselor was associated with her church, and she feared that what she would say would be heard by everybody she knew. She was already the subject of gossip and whispers, and she didn't feel like spilling any more to a woman she barely knew, kind or not.

"I think it's good to talk to someone, don't you think?"

"I'm all talked out, Ms . . ."

"Call me Janice."

"Janice. I have nothing more to say."

"It must be hard having all your life plastered in the media, but have you yet talked about reconciliation with your husband? Have you given it some thought?"

Raven just shook her head and wiped the stray tears running down her cheeks. She wondered where they were coming from, because she had already cried oceans.

"We usually like to try every other avenue before taking the drastic measure of terminating a marriage. Is there anything we can do to help you and your husband reach a new conclusion? Maybe counseling . . ."

"No, Janice. I've made up my mind. I only came here to appease my father. As far as I'm concerned my marriage is over. Now I'm just waiting for the papers, the formality, but in my heart and physically we are already divorced."

Janice didn't know what else to say. Raven seemed determined to end a marriage that had once been the talk of the city. A marriage that was now falling apart in appalling scandals and national media coverage.

"Is there nothing that you can think of that can save it? Think back to how you met, how you felt then. If there is a sliver of any of that emotion, then maybe you should reconsider," Janice insisted, though her voice remained patient and calm.

Raven glanced behind Janice's desk, at the beautifully framed copy of Charles Sebree on the gold textured walls. The whole room was peaceful, tranquil, like Janice Francis. Warm colors, structured and well lighted. The tranquility didn't reach her at all.

Yes, she could remember how it was when she met him. It wasn't so long ago, but it seemed like twenty years instead of two. How things had changed. How trust had been destroyed so cruelly. Meeting him, marrying him, had made her feel like finally, she would be accepted, finally she could hold her head high. How naive she had been. Now she was worse than an outcast. No, she was the laughingstock of Detroit.

CHAPTER 1

"Oh no," Raven muttered under her breath, as she looked in the review mirror and saw the flashing red and blue lights. "Stupid cops. Oh, God forgive me. I know he's just doing his job, but I'm so late! Why did he have to stop me?"

Raven stubbornly continued to drive, and then turned right onto a side street. How fast had she been going, and what was the speed limit? She angrily put her ancient Mini Cooper into park and sat back, taking deep breaths and trying to calm her beating heart. Only when she heard a knock on her window did she roll it down manually and stare at the officer, a tall, dark-skinned man dressed in the black uniform. Raven had never been good with authority, and cops were on her list of people she had little patience for. God was working on her, but right now she wished that the ground would just open up and swallow the man whole and his white marked car.

"License and registration please, ma'am," he said in a deep, authoritative voice.

"Oh, yes," Raven responded, looking for her purse. She was late and didn't even know if she had put her wallet in her oversized bag. Digging around her bag she pulled out the files from her social work office and then the binder from the Philips Center, where she was about to go to and have an important meeting with one of the Pistons. Their star, the point guard Amari Thomas. Her father, Pastor Philip Davies, had stressed how important it was that they impress this Piston guy so the center could get more exposure and funds. This was the second time the meeting had been set up. The last time Amari Thomas had called and cancelled, deepening her dislike of all athletes.

The officer impatiently stood by her window while she searched. She knew that she should apologize for the delay but couldn't bring herself to do so. *He can stand there and freeze. Didn't he have something better to do?*

Raven gave a sigh of relief as she pulled out her wallet and then started digging through the various credit cards and gym memberships to find her driver's license. Without looking at the officer she handed it to him, and then began the arduous task of putting her things back in the bag.

"Raven Davies," the officer said as if tasting her name on his tongue. "Are you related to Pastor Philip Davies? Of Calvary Church?" Raven nearly rolled her eyes, but instead she nodded.

"I thought I had seen you somewhere before."

"Please just give me the ticket so I can go. I'm really late for a meeting."

"I'll just let you go with a warning, ma'am. Any child of Pastor Davies does not deserve a ticket. In fact I have seen you there before. I see your beautiful sisters more, but I certainly know you."

"Thank you," Raven said, then reached out for the license. Officer Derek Johnson was taken by surprise at her lack of excitement that he had not given her a ticket.

He gave her back her license and walked back to his car. She wished she could see his face as she pulled into traffic and sped away from him as fast as her beat-up car could go.

Raven loved the heart of the city of Detroit and didn't even mind seeing some of the run-down buildings mixed up with the tall Renaissance Center that gleamed in the early morning sun. Detroit was like an old lady who was now going for plastic surgery one part of her body at a time. Starting with the nose, then the eyes, and slowly working her way towards the breasts and stomach. Though sections were falling apart the facelift would be completed soon, and a new and gorgeous city was about to emerge. Raven could already see the beauty in the delightful Campus Martius Park with live bands, exotic waterfalls in summer and skating and drinking delicious hot chocolate in the winter. She could see hope in the people that walked to work with brisk paces and smiling faces. She could taste the city's future in the air and it filled her with excitement. Maybe Detroit will one day shake off its negative image of being crime-ridden, poor and ugly.

When she arrived at the center, Raven looked in the mirror and didn't like what she saw. Her skin seemed darker and her full lips too shiny and dark. She wished her hair was thinner and easier to manage. Some mornings she tolerated the way she looked, but not this one. How many women wished they looked a little different.

As her mother, Clare, would say, "The world unfortunately is a beauty pageant. You are always being judged by what you wear and how you look whether you want to be or not." Clare Davies always dressed like she was in a pageant, but Raven refused to compete. What was the point?

The Philips Center for Children was located in the downtown area, a few blocks from Comerica Park and not even five minutes from her apartment, but somehow Raven had attracted the wrath of that early morning officer. Raven found parking in the street and made her way towards the front of the building. The entrance wasn't that appealing, but the main concern for the center was raising money for kids, not for appearances. That would come later, but after many other important needs had been met.

"Raven!" Kendra greeted her with a smile. Kendra's early morning eagerness was contagious. Kendra's smile was like the sun itself. Raven felt gaudy standing next to her. Even her dress was a lovely colorful blue number which showed a little bit of cleavage that begged for attention. She knew that any of the Pistons players would enjoy meeting Kendra.

"Hey, Kendra," Raven said. "I guess our benevolent basketball players haven't arrived yet."

"Actually they are here. *He's* here," Kendra said with a gleam in her eye. The last time Raven had seen Kendra this excited was when she had won five thousand dollars at the Greek Town Casino. Raven was surprised and annoyed at the same time.

He's already here? Before me? She knew she was being unreasonable. If he was late she would have still been irritated.

"He's in the office," Kendra continued, gesturing towards the only office in the building. Raven straightened her formal jacket and entered the office.

A tall man stood up when she opened the door. Raven reached her hand out to shake his and was so bothered at the effect the man had on her. His looks startled her more than anybody ever before in her life. He was so gorgeous she almost didn't find the words to start her greeting as she looked into his soft, brown eyes.

"Good morning. I'm Raven Davis," she finally said, wanting to take charge.

"Amari Thomas. Pleasure to meet you." Raven decided the only way she could get through the day was if she found him annoying. Why was he smiling like that? Did he expect her to fawn over him and ask him for his autograph or something? Hell would freeze over before she ever asked any celebrity for an autograph. To her that was the most demeaning thing to do.

"I understand you would like to help our program? What made you interested in this center?" she asked, gesturing for him to sit down and taking her place behind the desk.

"My cousin goes to the church that started this. I thought it was a great idea, and I want to be a part of what you'll are doing here."

Raven didn't want to say it was her father's church that started the center. "It's not an easy job to do. We work with very difficult students who are not motivated in school. It's a place where they can get tutoring and after-school activities in a safe environment for free."

"I know. I read the plan, and I'd like to do more than just donate money. I want to get involved and bring awareness to the program."

"Fine. But I thought your team has its own initiatives?"

"This is my own project. I don't always do things with the team. I'm an individual, and the team is just my job." They looked at each other. Raven could see Amari was getting a bit put out, and she knew she was being unreasonable. She had never seen anybody who just did things without wanting something in return, and she certainly didn't trust Amari. Nobody that good-looking could be that good a person. It would be unfair.

"Well, I have some time to show you around. I volunteer here, too, as do most of the staff here. What in particular would you want to do?"

"Maybe some coaching and tutoring in math," Amari replied as they left the office.

"That's good. We always need more math tutors. I struggle in math myself, so I can't help there," Raven said.

"Do you need tutoring?"

Raven stared at him like he had lost his mind. "Are you for real?"

"Sorry. Just a joke." Raven didn't even crack a smile as they walked to the classrooms and then to the gym.

Amari shook his head and whistled and got another frosty look from Raven.

"This building used to be a preschool," Raven explained.

"It has potential. Where do the kids play basketball?"

"We have a court outside. The vision is to build an indoor gym and also build a library, computer room and a cafeteria."

"You have a wonderful vision," Amari said.

"It's not my vision. It's my father's," she said, then covered her mouth as if she had let out a secret. "If you don't have anything else, I have to go to work. Kendra can answer the rest of your questions. She's the only full-time staff here."

"That's all, Ms. Davis," he said, holding out his hand. She shook his hand then walked away, leaving him alone in the hallway. Amari felt more relaxed when he saw the gorgeous Kendra walk towards him with a smile.

"So when is your next game, Amari? I watch you play all the time," she gushed, taking him by the arm.

CHAPTER 2

Amari drove back home in his black Escalade. He had never seen a woman respond so coldly to him. Ms. Raven Davis was as cold as the North Pole. He had a good mind not to work with her center and find people who were more enthusiastic, but he liked their vision and the accounts he heard about them, all the wonderful things they were doing in Africa and in the inner city of Detroit with the Philips Center. The center was a spiritual haven for lost children who could find hope and inspiration from various successful people in Detroit.

Now Kendra's response to him was exactly what he was used to. He had experienced firsthand women slipping their numbers in his hand or waiting for him outside his hotel or writing obscene letters to him. He didn't like it, but he was getting used to it. He now saw tossing the slips of paper aside as part of the job. Money and fame brought their own set of troubles.

His life took a turn just last year when the Pistons signed him. He was surprised at how quickly the season had gone by and the incredible things that happened in that one year. He was now back in his hometown after not being drafted initially and playing a few years in Europe. To him it was like he had been roaming around in the wilderness and now he was enjoying his Promised

Land, too. His mother wisely called the time of empti-
ness God's way of making sure he didn't get too much
success too soon. Gloria liked to say, "God said he would
give us little by little lest the horses go wild." There were
a lot of wild horses in the NBA.

God had fulfilled all his dreams beyond what he
imagined, even though it had taken a long time. He
heard that God can restore in a day what was stolen in a
lifetime, and this was the first time he had seen it first
hand in his own life.

Amari's phone rang just as he entered the highway. A
quick glance at the caller ID showed him that it was his
best friend and agent, Dan.

"What's up?" Amari asked.

"Have you ever considered taking acting classes?"

"What?"

"Well, I'm just talking to a few casting agents. I know
you did some acting in high school and college so I was
looking at some cameo appearances . . ."

"I don't know, man. Maybe. I went to that center I
told you about."

"Oh. I thought we should wait on that and get you in
some high-profile charities that can get you on TV and . . ."

"We can do that, too. I like this one," Amari insisted.
"It just seems more like what God wants me to do."

There was silence on the other side. Amari knew that
Dan was very uncomfortable whenever he mentioned
God, Christianity and Jesus.

He had been there. He totally understood.

"I'll go to church, Ma, but I don't really believe all that stuff," Amari had told his mother when he was entering high school. By the time he was sixteen he was using work and basketball as an excuse not to attend church. He didn't want to hear all the rules that were so hard to follow.

Don't do this. Don't drink. Don't smoke. Don't sleep around. Don't watch this. Man, there were too many rules. And some of the people who went to his ma's Baptist church were the ones who were sleeping around and doing all that stuff. He didn't want to be a part of that hypocrisy. His ma, Gloria Crystal Thomas, had continued to go to church alone, waking up early to catch the eight o'clock service so she could make it to work by three.

Amari didn't see it improving their lives. They were still poor. His ma had to work at a phone company during the week and in a nursing home during the weekends just to keep them in their tiny house. Just to keep Amari in the best basketball shoes, taking him to basketball camp and providing tutors even when he didn't need them. Yep, his ma had worked hard just for him. So he knew where Dan was coming from. He'd been there, knowing what God had done for him but still refusing to truly accept him.

"Can't argue with God." Dan's voice was laced with humor that Amari didn't miss. "So what's the center like?"

"Small. The lady I spoke to wasn't all that friendly."

"A lady not friendly to Amari Thomas. That's a first."

"One of those men haters, I think. I didn't do anything to her but she acted as if I ran over her dog or something."

"Could be a sign that you shouldn't get involved with them."

"Nah. I won't let her nasty attitude deter me."

"Is she hot?"

Amari didn't answer as he pictured Raven, bringing to mind her rich-hued coffee skin and big, brown eyes. He wouldn't call her hot. Kendra was hot in the usual way. Light skin, straight, dark hair falling below the chin and tight sexy clothes. Raven was not hot, but she was interesting.

"She a' right," Amari said. "Just cold. By the way, the center is in the beginning stages and needs a lot of capital. I'm thinking of building a gym for them soon."

"Slow down, Thomas. This year has only just began and we need to focus on getting endorsements that can make you more money."

"I know, Dan. But God doesn't work that way. You give in order to receive."

"Sounds like a scam to me."

"Nah. It's a natural law. The law of reaping and sowing."

"You gonna preach to me, man?"

"No, just explaining to you what's what. Ask Oprah Winfrey. That's why that woman's rich. She keeps on giving and her money gets to multiplying. Look. I better run. I'll talk to you later."

"Yeah. The movie business, man. That's the next place to go."

"We'll talk." Amari cut the phone and focused on the road. Raven's unfriendly face came to him, and he blasted his music to wipe it out of his mind.

After work on the day she met Amari, Raven decided to go to her father's church for the midweek service. She arrived at Calvary Worship and was once again amazed by the church that her father headed. Calvary Worship had been in existence for over twenty years, though it had started humbly in her father's living room. She was ten years old when Philip Robert Davies told his family at dinner that God had told him to start a church.

"I don't know how I'm going to do it, but I know that with God all things are possible," Philip explained as his wife and four children looked on. He left his job as manager of a car dealership and began the church by faith. There were many challenges along the way, but Philip always knew that he was doing the right thing. Now, twenty years later, he headed one of the biggest churches in the country and had planted another similar church in New York City. Raven knew that her father was becoming an example for many churches to follow in Detroit. He was impacting more than just their church family by encouraging investors and setting meetings with other church leaders to build businesses in Detroit and making a difference in the whole city. He always said, "As long as you are in line with what God wants, then anything is possible."

The new building for Calvary had been standing for five years and Raven was always impressed by the beauty of the architecture and the heart of the people who gave their earnings so that they could have that building.

Raven parked her car on the slowly filling parking lot and locked it with a key. She walked into the foyer and was greeted by smiling door greeters who stood by the door over an hour before the mid-week service began. She was once again amazed by the number of people who volunteered their time and talents to work at the church. Doctors, musicians, teachers, accountants. Everybody had a part to play in that glorious church. Raven walked past the bookshop, coffee shop and other offices and finally arrived in her father's office. Her younger sister, Tahlia, greeted her first.

"Rave!" Tahlia cried, hands reaching out for her sister. Somehow the gesture reminded Raven of Tahlia as a toddler, following Raven everywhere. Raven hugged her sister and looked into the room over her shoulder. When Tahlia stood back, Raven realized she had interrupted an important family meeting. The whole family was there, besides her, of course.

She could see the slight annoyance in her mother's beautiful face. She glanced at her brother but he smiled happily. Philip Junior, mainly called PJ, was always happy to see her. Esther smiled, too, but the best smile of all was the one her father beamed at her. It was filled with the love and tenderness that she always craved.

Right now his warm eyes took away her doubt and insecurities.

"Raven. It's good to see you. Come and join us," Philip Senior said. Raven walked towards him and he kissed her cheek. "Sit. Sit."

"How are you, Raven?" Clare greeted her oldest daughter. Raven smiled at her shyly. If anybody could make her feel like a little girl in the wrong place, her mother could with a look or a question.

"I'm fine."

"It's nice of you to drop by your father's church," Clare commented, crossing her legs with her pointed gold shoe directed to her. Before Raven could respond to her mother, her brother spoke up in a teasing tone.

"How's the work in the world?"

"Hectic."

"We need people like you to be the light in the world, Raven. Those families you work with need you," Esther said, smiling. Raven smiled at her younger sister gratefully, but she still felt apprehensive.

"Well, we have the Lord's work to do tonight," Clare reminded everyone, giving a pointed look to Raven. "It's the most important work to do. Why you don't take your place in the family is beyond me."

"Come on now, Clare. We are not going to talk about Raven's career choices now. God has a plan and a purpose for her." Philip spoke to his wife in his gentle voice. Raven's eyes thanked him, though her heart had dropped to her feet.

The door opened and Esther's husband Angelo peeked in.

"The choir is ready for you," he said. Angelo, a striking five feet, nine inches, was the music leader at Calvary Worship, a dynamic musician and dancer. Everybody stood up and Raven followed suit.

"We are going to have a prayer session together before the service," Tahlia said. "You should come."

"It's fine. I'll be in the service shortly. I have to go over my case notes before the service anyway."

"Fine," Clare said quickly.

"We'll see you at home for Sunday dinner?" Philip asked his daughter, looking right into her eyes. It was as if he could see through her. He knew she felt uncomfortable whenever she came to the church and her mother was there.

"Of course," Raven said.

Her family gave her hugs then left her alone in the office. The last one to close the door was PJ, and he winked at her. Raven sat in her father's chair and looked at the family portrait on his desk. The massive office with a lounging area and connecting kitchen and bathroom were all built for his convenience. Philip spent much time in the building and had been known to spend the night, too.

Raven glanced at her notes but couldn't concentrate. She decided to go to the service early. She walked to the door, and before she could walk out she couldn't help overhearing two voices speaking about her family. They were often the subject of gossip and conjecture. She listened, smiling, but her smile soon faded when she made out what they were saying about her.

"I saw the other Davies sister today."

"The pretty one? Tahlia?"

"Esther and Tahlia are both pretty. The dark ugly duckling, what's her name. She's the only one not part of the church."

"You mean Raven?"

"Yeah. That's her. She has an unusual name, too."

"She *is* different from all the rest. Maybe if she smiled or did something to her hair."

"Being the oldest and not married, too. Esther's been married for three years."

Raven didn't want to hear any more. She knew how to leave the building without leaving her father's office and entering the church again. With tears frozen in her eyes she made it out through the kitchen and walked to her car. She didn't cry. She had stopped crying when she turned sixteen.

CHAPTER 3

For as long as she could remember adults had gushed over Tahlia and Esther.

"Oh, what pretty brown eyes they have."

"That one is so dark."

"She will become prettier when she starts using makeup."

What was it about skin color that caused people to judge your heart, judge your worthiness? Lately it seemed it was acceptable for men to be dark skinned but not women.

When she was younger, the three sisters used to sing in the service on Sundays. Raven remembered that one day just before the main service she had taken the face powder from her mother's purse and applied it on her face. She had made it just in time to walk onto the stage and it seemed nobody noticed until people started snickering and pointing. Clare had stared at her from the front of the pews, her mouth wide open. Raven had sung her heart out but at the end of the song the other girls had turned to face her and noticed, their eyes wide with shock.

"Raven Clarissa Davies! What have you done to your face?" Esther had asked.

"Nothing," eleven-year-old Raven replied as they walked off the stage. Esther reached for her face and ran her finger down her cheek. Raven pushed her hand away.

"You put on makeup?"

"No. I didn't."

"Yes you did," Clare said from the door and walked towards the girls. "What is this? My Estee Lauder?"

"I . . ."

"Why did you do that? Why would you want to mess up your beautiful skin?" Clare asked, taking the powder from her purse. It was caramel in color to match her skin tone but on Raven it made her look like a ghost, barely covering the dark tones of her skin.

"I just wanted to look pretty, too," Raven said, wiping the tears on her face and covering her hands with the pale powder.

"Oh, my child, help me. Raven, you *are* pretty. Who said you had to wear this mess to be pretty?" Clare shouted, holding the powder up.

"Everybody says Tahlia and Esther are pretty, they have pretty eyes, but I have dark skin and dark eyes."

"Skin color doesn't make somebody pretty," Clare cried, looking from Raven's face to Esther and Tahlia. All her daughters had pretty, full, upturned lips and big eyes, but it was true that there the similarities ended. Raven had high cheekbones and a toned, athletic body, whereas Tahlia and Esther seemed to have inherited her curves and as little girls looked chubby with baby fat. Raven didn't have that. She was always thin as a reed. And of course they had different skin tones. Did that difference in shade have to make her miserable and feel worthless? She wanted to yell at all the people who made those meaningless statements, though she had grown up with that misguided idea, too.

The sadness in her daughter's eyes broke her heart.

"You can't change your skin color, Ray, just like I can't change mine. When you get older you can get face powders to match your skin, but not to change it, all right?"

Raven had nodded but hadn't felt any better. And her feelings had not changed. At some point in her darkest moments she wanted to find out how Michael Jackson had lightened his skin. She understood how he must have felt, hating the way he looked, wishing he was someone else.

Raven arrived at the Philips Center on Saturday. This was the first day Amari was coming to work with the kids. She had not told them he was coming. When he walked in she was working with a ten-year-old boy, Jalen, on multiplication. Jalen was so far behind she was using third-grade materials instead of fifth grade. That was great for her, anyway, because she sucked at math.

She knew when Amari walked in because there was a loud scream from the girls and gasps of excitement from the boys. Raven turned and looked towards the entrance. Amari walked in wearing jeans and a T-shirt, his wavy, short hair cut close to the scalp. No fuss. No earring. Just plain and simple but magnificently gorgeous.

"Amari Thomas!" Jalen called out. Raven sat back and let the excitement wash over the students. There were three volunteers, and Amari would now make a fourth.

"All right, boys and girls," Raven said, using her authoritative voice. "I'll give you some time to meet with Amari Thomas and ask some questions, and then he's going to want to work with some of you on math." Raven stopped talking and looked at each child in turn. "Now take your seats and let's go round and say your names."

Amari sat next to Raven, his tall frame towering over her. She felt very small and unsure next to him. They introduced themselves shyly, but the excitement was still in the air. Raven was sure the students who missed that morning would regret it when their friends told them that Amari Thomas tutored them in math. Amari talked to them about the importance of math and then the students asked him questions. After that it was work. She assigned him two tenth-graders who were failing in math.

While Raven sat with her student she watched Amari explain to the boys, and was amazed at his patience. She had to force herself to focus on Jalen, who wasn't getting the division.

"Come on, Jalen. What about this? If you had four oranges and you had to share with Amari Thomas, how much would you have and how much would you give him?"

"I'll give him all four," Jalen replied, smiling in Amari's direction. Raven rolled her eyes, frustrated.

"Raven, he's a big man. He's gotta eat about four or five oranges."

"What about if you had to share with me? What if you wanted me to have half of the oranges?"

"Then I'd give you . . . two."

"That's right, Jalen. What's the division sentence for that?"

"I don't know."

After an hour of academics the boys and girls prepared to have a practice session of basketball with Amari. Kendra went out to watch and make sure the students were cooperating, though Raven doubted Amari would have any problems with them. She walked into the office, but her mind was also outside with Amari Thomas.

She could understand why she was now growing preoccupied with him. He was not only gorgeous, but he genuinely cared for the kids. He could be doing anything he wanted on his day off, but here he was in their dingy building working with their difficult students and seeming to love every minute of it. Raven wished she could talk to him about it, find out what motivated him, but there was no way a man like that would ever want to spend time with a woman like her.

I'm not his type, and I have nothing to say that would interest him.

Raven was powering up the computer when she heard a knock on the door.

"Come in," she said and was surprised when Amari walked in.

"There you are. I need to buy one of the boys some shoes. He says he doesn't have any gym shoes. Can you show me the nearest place to get them?"

Raven stared at him for few seconds, struck by his eyes. They hypnotized her and she felt foolish realizing that he probably had that effect on every woman breathing. He probably knew it, too. Even in the loose jeans and T-shirt he was a handsome sight.

"Do you know where The Sports Place is?" Raven asked.

"No."

"Do you know where . . ."

"Just come with me and show me? I feel bad that he can't participate. Can't be too far, right?"

When he spoke Raven wasn't even thinking, but listened to how his voice seemed to be entering her very being as it caressed her senses. She really felt lighthearted and breathless and wished her body would stop reacting that way.

I must be losing my mind, she thought. *This is completely insane that he turns my knees to jelly and my mind to mush. Ridiculous!*

"No," she managed, then swallowed hard. She hadn't felt any feelings since her very short-lived relationship at the end of college with Kevin Stanly. In the short time they had been together she wasn't even sure he was the one but had felt the need to try and have a relationship. He was a mixture of Italian and German and also had a bit of Indian from his mother's side. The only guys that ever seemed remotely interested in her were all white guys. The connection died when he had a one-night stand after a football game. She had told him it was over, and in all her adult life she had not had a single love affair to speak of. At thirty she had given up on ever meeting the right guy and knew very little about men. She was so averse to bars and on-line dating she just decided that if there was a man out there for her, he would look for her, not the other way round. Her father liked to tell her that God would bring a man to her but she doubted it. Raven felt many men were not attracted to her type at all.

And what type is that, an inner voice taunted. She would not even answer that.

What she was feeling for Amari all of a sudden was new and frightening. She was desperately trying to come up with a plan to kill the emotions for good.

"Let's go get them," Amari said, and Raven couldn't think of any excuse not to leave with him for just a few minutes. She picked up her cap and he held the door for her. She held her breath as she walked past him.

Outside, the June sun was out in full force and a touch of humidity was in the air. Amari led the way silently to his car and opened the door for her. Raven sat in the car and was amazed at how clean it was. It looked brand new. She sat back and pulled the seat-belt and the moment he sat on the driver's seat she cursed herself for agreeing to go anywhere with him. She should've sent Kendra.

"Which way?"

"Turn left and then drive across two lights, I think," Raven said, glancing out the window. The music started, and Raven was surprised to hear old-school R&B. She was sure he was going to have the latest woman-hating CD calling all women whores and gold diggers. The music made her relax a little.

"Is the air a'right?" he asked.

"It's fine." Though the air-conditioning was full blast, she felt hot. She couldn't look at him.

"So when did you start working for the center?" he asked.

"A year ago. It's quite new."

"What's your other job?"

"Social work." Amari laughed and Raven looked at him, surprised.

"What's so funny?"

"You are."

"I haven't said anything funny," Raven said, looking at him and realizing his profile was just as good.

"No. For a moment there I thought I was conducting an interview." Amari glanced at her. Raven frowned.

"What?"

"Thing is, I kept asking you questions and you gave me one-word answers. That's an interview of some sort isn't it?"

Raven didn't know what to say to him. Instead she looked at the road and realized that they had passed the turn.

"Stop. I mean go back. I'm sorry. We missed the road," she apologized, craning her neck to read the street signs.

"That's okay. I'll turn right at the next street and make a U-turn."

When he was driving back she decided to ask him a question, too. Many questions came to her head but she tossed them all aside; "How long have you played basket-ball?" sounded too stupid. "Where is your family?" was even worse. "Do you go to church?" sounded ridiculous. "Are you married?" was laughable.

"You like old-school music?" Raven asked and wished she could hide under the seat. What a silly question. *Of course he likes it, fool, that's why he's listening to it.*

"Yeah, and you?"

"That and classical," she said.

"Really?"

"Well I was reading this book about health and stress that said some classical music relieves stress," Raven said.

"You stressed?"

"Turn here," Raven said quickly, then added, "Yeah, I get stressed. Maybe not as stressed as you get when you are about to shoot the winning three-pointer."

"You watch basketball?"

Raven shook her head. "No, sorry. I only catch glimpses when I visit my family. I may have seen you play, but I'm not sure."

Amari laughed. "I don't know how to feel about that. I think you are the first person I've met who hasn't seen me play. I'm hurt." Raven shrugged when she saw he was joking. He didn't care whether she saw him play or not.

"I'll definitely watch the next game you play just to see if you are as good as you say."

"I haven't said I'm good," Amari protested.

"No. If you say I'm the only person who hasn't seen you play then I'm sure you think you are that good."

"Does runner-up MVP count?"

"What?"

"I guess you didn't know that, either."

25

"One thing I know for sure, you are not shy about tooting your own horn."

"I'm just hurt that I had the biggest year of my entire life and you missed it."

"It can't matter that much." Raven had relaxed as they drove and didn't pay attention to where they were going. "Oh, you missed the turn again!"

"You are the worst navigator I've ever seen. I might as well have come by myself or asked a blind person to show me where to go." Amari laughed, making another U-turn. Raven laughed nervously. She looked at him and for the first time since she sat in his car their eyes met. Her heart began to hammer.

CHAPTER 4

Amari was an incredible man. He was respectful and generous. What confused her was that, even though he was all these things, she still felt nervous and sparkly around him. She was angry with herself for being attracted to a man that gorgeous and that desirable. There was no chance he would ever be interested in her or even find her attractive. But she remembered their last conversation, after the basketball game. She played that over and over again in her head.

"Hi," Amari had called and she looked up from her computer, his eyes causing little tremors to run up and down her spine.

"Hi. Game over already?" she asked, a little breathlessly. She bit her mouth to keep herself from blubbering like a fool.

"Yep. Great workout. You work too hard. You must come to a party on the eighteenth. It's at a buddy of mine's place."

She was surprised and didn't answer immediately so Amari added, "They are cool people."

Was he asking her out? Was he really? Her hopes were dashed when he said, "Kendra said she knows how to get there. You can come together."

Kendra. Of course. He was interested in Kendra. Who wouldn't be?

"I'll see if I can make it," she said, and he walked over and shook her hand.

"It's great working with you, Raven. Enjoy the rest of your weekend."

With those words he had left. Hours later at home, Raven sighed. She looked out her window, hoping the beautiful view would take her mind off of Amari.

She had bought the apartment when the owners of the building decided to turn the building into a condominium association. Raven had jumped at the chance. Even though buying a home had been the last thing on her mind, she didn't regret it. Her home was a cocoon from the world she worked in that revealed the dark side of human beings she couldn't believe existed.

Being a social worker had shown her how evil men and women could be to their children and, as much as it depressed her, she wanted to keep at it. To save one more child from abuse. To help women get out of domestic violence. To have a chance to tell a young girl that she was loved. That God loved her even though everybody else neglected her.

Raven picked up her cellphone and dialed her friend's number. She needed to talk to somebody about her crazy day. Candice was just the person.

"Hey!" Candice answered on the first ring. "Just hold on. This baby is gonna kill me. He's getting heavy."

Raven smiled, happy to speak to her friend of over twenty years. Candice was not just a beautiful person physically but she was crazy, fun and very caring. She'd always been kind to Raven. When they were young Candice had always stood up for her when people made fun of her.

While she held the phone, Raven sat back and looked at her surroundings, wondering what Amari would think of her rather sparse decorations and scolding herself for being an idiot and a fool all in the same breath.

The spacious room was decorated in the earth tones she liked. Her beige loveseat complemented the hand-painted wooden vases from a traveling market. She didn't have art pieces on the walls, but instead had designed dried sticks and placed them against the white paint in an artistic way. She had seen the idea in a home decorating magazine and tried it. The results were stark and interesting.

"I'm back, girl. How are you doing?" Candice came back on the phone.

"I'm fine, girl. How's the family?" Raven asked, lying on the couch with her feet on the table. They would be talking for a very long time.

"Charles Junior is doing fine. I swear he said 'mama' today."

"You are just imagining things. He's only eight months." Raven laughed. "He will say Aunty Raven first."

"I bet he would, with the way he smiles every time he sees you," Candice said.

"And Charles Senior?"

"Great. Final year of residency, thank God! Soon all the money should start rolling in. I really thought marrying a doctor would mean I wouldn't have to worry, but it takes so long to see the fruits of your labor."

"You mean *his* labor?"

"Girl, his, mine, where's the fruit? I want my fruit." Raven could imagine Candice throwing her arms up.

"Time has flown. So where's he planning to practice?"

"We chose Beaumont Hospital. He was also looking into Henry Ford, and another offer came from Atlanta, but I want to stay close to my family. With Charles so busy my mother is the only one who helps me with the baby."

Raven listened as Candice talked. It was hard not to feel a bit envious. Candice grew up with a silver spoon in her mouth. Her father owned several fast food restaurants while her mother ran a chain of hair salons. Their parents brought them together, actually. Back in the day when Philip began his church, Candice's parents, Ernest and Ruby Tramaine, had decided to join the church in its early stages. Candice's parents contributed a lot to the growth of Calvary Worship.

Raven liked Candice from the first time they met, and as they grew up all the great things seemed to happen to Candice. She met a wonderful man who loved her and married him soon after graduating from college with a theatrical degree. Their wedding was the most talked-about event of the year, and now she had a beautiful baby boy who was so adorable he should be on Sean John's modeling catalogue.

"You should let the girls go to school together," Candice's father had suggested. "I know a great school that used to be private but is now a charter school. It is run by one of the most incredible educators I've ever met. I can speak to the principal."

And so in third grade Raven was enrolled at the Achievement Academy. Their friendship grew even though the two girls were as different as night and day. Candice was tall and thin with long black hair always done in two pony tails and a curly fringe. She became very popular in fourth grade and Raven basked in her sunshine. She was still a great person, which is what amazed Raven and still amazed her to this day. Once in a while she could act like a spoilt child, but Raven knew Candice had a good heart.

"So what's been going on with you?" Candice asked.

"Do you watch basketball?"

"Of course. That's all Charles and I get to do together, especially with the Pistons doing so well. Why?"

"I met one of the players."

"Which one?"

"Amari."

"Amari Thomas? Are you serious? He's not only the most incredible player, he's so fiiiine. I don't know which is giving him more fame, his looks or his game. He just came from nowhere . . ."

"Okay, so you do know him."

"Of course. Where on earth did you meet him? Don't tell me he was one of your social work cases. That would be interesting."

"No. No. He came to the center to help with the academic program."

"You're kidding, right?" Raven moved the phone away to keep from ruining her eardrum from Candice's scream.

"No. I'm not sure what to do. He invited us to a get together with some of the team people, I think."

"What!" This time Raven jumped up and rubbed her ear.

"Girl, you're going to bust my eardrums. I think you already did." Raven laughed and then lay on her couch.

"What do you mean, you don't know what to do?"

"Should I go?"

"Of course, silly! We should decide what to wear. You need some new little hot dress. No, maybe some flirty pants and . . . oh, I know we need to go shopping. I know just the place at Somerset."

Raven listened while Candice worked herself into a frenzy.

"Hey," she finally cut in, "this is not a date or anything like that. He invited both me and Kendra."

"Kendra? What? Lose Kendra!"

"I can't 'lose' Kendra. She was invited, too, so before you start planning my outfits just know that I might not go and it's *not* a date."

"Why not? You had the chance to hang with Amari Thomas and you haven't got a date out of him?" Candice sighed heavily. "Oh, I wish I was single again."

"Listen, Candice. I doubt he's interested in me that way. I'm certainly not his type."

"What do you mean by that?"

"I just know the women these ball players hang with. They marry models and they sleep with many other gorgeous girls who are just waiting to take off their clothes."

"Does Amari strike you as that shallow? Like a cliché of a black man?"

"It's not about being shallow, but just most guys in general. Guys want something to make their friends envious."

"You *are* lovely, Raven," Candice said off handedly. "Just because you are dark, you write yourself off."

"Thanks, Candice, but you are the only one who thinks so," Raven said without any bitterness. She had accepted that she would never turn heads the way women like Candice and Kendra and even her sister Tahlia do.

"I just think you don't try. Don't get mad, but I would like to do a makeover on you one of these days."

"I don't have time for that, Candice. No matter what I do I'll never look like my mother or you. Sometimes when I talk to God I want to ask why women have to be judged so much by how we look. But it's not His fault."

"You talk to God? How?"

"Just speak like I'm talking to you. He's my friend. You know what I mean."

"I do know that God doesn't help those who don't help themselves. So you need to accentuate your God-given talents. You have that hot body, no fat . . ."

"Thanks, Candice. *You* only put on weight when you had the baby."

"And still trying to lose it. I love my son, but I'm ready to go under the knife!"

"Don't talk crazy. I better get going, Candy."

"All right, but we go shopping tomorrow. Okay?"

"Fine. Fine, but don't get too excited. I'm not spending money on clothes I might not even wear."

After she hung up Raven powered up her computer and, feeling guilty, connected to the internet and looked up Amari Thomas's website. After a few clicks his picture came on looking right at her. Her heart skipped a beat like he was right there in the room watching her. Without reading any more she shut down her web browser. She felt like a trespasser, looking up his life like a schoolgirl with a crush. That was stupid. She hated that she was becoming exactly like the girls in high school who kept posters of boy bands and movie stars as if they were angels or something. She would not read up his profile. At least not that night.

CHAPTER 5

"Why don't you come over to my place? Then we can both drive over to Owen's house," Kendra suggested over the phone.

"All right. I'll be there in a few," Raven said nervously. She looked in the mirror and wished she could stay home and read. The pants she wore skimmed over her slim body and the loose-fitting peasant top covered up her breasts. She didn't want to hope. She trusted God to send her the right man and doubted Amari was the one. He was just too good and hoping for anything at all with him was just a set-up for great disappointment.

She drove towards Kendra's house, getting more and more anxious by the minute. Amari had been away for two weeks instead of one week like he had told her so she hadn't seen him at all since the first day he came to the center. She was sure he wouldn't even remember her.

Raven arrived at Kendra's house, where she lived with her mother, two younger brothers and stepdad. The house was on a quiet, tree-lined street off Grand River. Raven parked in front of the Kendra's yellow Dodge Neon and got out of her Mini Cooper. Kendra walked out looking so lovely Raven felt dowdy and dull in comparison. Her stylish white capris hugged her body and the gold top complemented her gorgeous, flawless caramel skin. The skimpy gold stilettos added to her height and sophistication.

"Hey, Rave. Let's get out of here. I'm so glad to be leaving the house. Dumb and Dumber in there are driving me crazy." She gestured towards the house referring to her brothers, Terence and Trey.

"You look great," Raven said.

"Thanks. So do you," Kendra said off-handedly and pressed the button to open her car door.

"So follow me. I know where we're going."

"Fine," Raven assented. She had agreed to drive her own car in case she wanted to leave early. Who knew, she might feel so uncomfortable that she didn't want to be stuck in the middle of a party with no means to get home.

Though Raven drove fast it was hard to keep up with Kendra's reckless driving and dangerous maneuvers on Highway 696. She was surprised Kendra hadn't had an accident yet. After a few turns and twists, they arrived at the house. Kendra drove in and parked behind a huge Dodge Ram. Raven tried to squeeze behind her. When she got out she spotted Amari's car. She recognized his plates. Her heart started beating and she wondered how she would feel when she saw him if the sight of his car made her feel so unsettled.

"Come on, Raven. Let's hurry up before all the cute guys are taken," Kendra called out, adjusting her top so her cleavage showed to greater advantage.

"I'm not sure I want to go in," Raven said, staring at the brick mansion in front of her. She could hear music and saw smoke floating up into the air above the roof.

"Come on, girl. We've come this far. It won't be so bad. I'll stick with you," Kendra said. "I don't know anybody here, either."

Raven nodded then walked towards the house. She was dreading the moment of meeting everybody and very nervous about seeing Amari again.

Kendra rang the bell and looked at Raven, smiling Raven tried to smile back.

"Hello," a young woman said, opening the door.

"I'm Kendra, and this is Raven. We are friends of Amari Thomas," Kendra said confidently, walking into the air-conditioned foyer.

"Hi. Come in. Everybody's in the back."

"Thanks," Kendra said, and they walked towards the backyard. Raven could see about twenty people gathered around the pool and sitting in groups in the spacious back yard. Raven spotted Amari about the same time as Kendra did.

"There he is," Kendra said, and Raven almost faltered when he looked in their direction and grinned. He waved them over, holding a can in one hand. She couldn't see the other tall men next to him or the ladies in skimpy outfits lounging by the pool. All she could see was him, looking good even as he squinted in the sun.

"You made it," Amari said, and Kendra leaned in to give him a hug. Raven stood back, but he opened up his arms and nervously she leaned close to him and felt herself pressed against his hard chest engulfed by his maleness. She felt her breath catch in her throat, forgetting to breathe.

"What took you so long? I thought you would get here early," Amari added releasing Raven but keeping his arm around her.

"Hey, everybody, this is Raven. The lady who got me hooked up with the center."

"Nice to meet you, I'm Mike," a tall, thin man said. Raven had to look right into the sky to see his face. He must be a teammate, she thought.

"This here's Kendra. She also works at the center," Amari added.

Everybody around began to shake their hands and introduce themselves.

"Raven Davis. I go to your father's church," a young woman said.

"Oh, yeah. Raven, this is Ashley. She works in our offices and she told me about the Philips Center."

"Hi, Ashley," Raven said and turned to the lovely woman. It seems everybody was gorgeous at this party.

"I love your father's church. Your father is such an anointed man, and I hang on his every word. He really helped me turn my life around," Ashley said.

"He's great," Raven agreed.

"Come with me. I came with my brother. He also goes to Calvary Worship. He would be happy to meet you." Ashley took Raven by the arm. Raven tried to tell Kendra she was leaving but she looked busy saying something into Amari's ear. Amari had to bend down in order to hear what the sexy Kendra was saying. Amari had clearly found his match.

Raven met Ashley's brother Andrew.

"You are so lucky to have a father like that. You must be so spiritually strong having him minister to you any-time you have a problem," Andrew said.

"Well. I don't spend that much time with him. I don't live at home anymore," Raven said.

"Oh. But I'm sure you call him all the time," Ashley said.

"I speak to him often," Raven said, then braced her-self for the next question.

"How come we never see you? I see your sisters a lot," Ashley asked with what seemed like genuine interest. Raven had to answer that question at least once every week. Why wasn't she involved in her father's church? Why didn't she look like her sisters and stunning mother?

"I have another career," Raven responded, trying to keep her irritation at bay. "I don't think we are *all* called to the ministry just because we are in the same family."

"You're right," Ashley agreed. "I didn't mean to make you uncomfortable. I was just curious."

"It's okay. So what ministries are you involved in?" Raven decided to do the asking so she didn't have to explain her peculiar role in her family. They talked, and after a while they all went to get some food and went back to sit under a white umbrella.

"So you met Amari at the center?"

"Yeah. He wants to get involved in our program," Raven said, taking a bite of ribs. Her plate was filled with corn, ribs, potato salad and raw carrots.

"He's a great guy," Ashley practically sighed. "So down-to-earth and genuine. He should have a big head with all his success, but that's not his style." Raven nodded, taking a bite of corn. She looked in the distance where Amari sat with Kendra and another group of people talking. She felt a stab of jealousy but tried to cover it up by chewing the tasty corn.

"I'm surprised he's not married yet," Ashley continued, holding her biscuit delicately so she wouldn't ruin her long designer nails. "He's what I call a renaissance man. You can't put him in a box. He plays sports for a living but there is more to him than that. He appreciates art, and kind of does his own thing. He's not like anybody I've ever met."

"Isn't he dating someone?" Raven asked. She wanted to learn more about him, but she didn't want to appear too inquisitive.

"They broke up. She wasn't his type anyway, I thought. He has strong morals, and I think Monique had none. Oh, we were all so happy when they broke up."

"So does he have these get-togethers often?" Raven decided to change the subject.

"Oh yeah. These guys are all from out of town. Like Owens used to play for Duke, but he grew up in Texas," Ashley said. "These get-togethers help them keep a sense of family. The food is always good, and as soon as it's getting dark the music and drinking is good, too."

More people arrived as the sun set and by about 10 p.m. the party was in full swing. She saw Kendra on the dance floor as the DJ began playing a rap song she didn't recognize. Raven had enjoyed her evening talking to Ashley, but, although she was introduced to more people, she never saw Amari again. After watching the dancing she realized it was getting late. She had to get up early for church, so she went to look for Kendra to tell her she was leaving.

She looked in the dimly lit house where a few people lounged around the furniture, but Kendra wasn't there. She stepped outside again, fighting the crowd to get across the backyard. She rounded the corner and saw that Kendra and Amari were very alone. They sat on chairs facing each other. Not wanting to disturb what looked like an intimate conversation, she walked away and decided she would just have to leave and call Kendra later. The two of them seemed to have hit it off just as she had expected.

She ran into Ashley on her way into the house.

"Are you leaving already?"

"Yeah. I have to get up early tomorrow," Raven said.

"Good night, then," Ashley said and gave her a hug. "It was so nice to meet you. I would like to get the publicity guys to do something with what Amari is doing. That needs exposure."

"Sounds good. Take care," Raven said and walked through the house and out the front door. It was quite a walk, and when she got to her car her heart sank.

"Oh, man!" she muttered, putting her hand on her waist. Someone had blocked her way out. There was no way she could squeeze out, and she knew that it would take forever to find out whose car it was. She turned around just as the door opened and Amari walked out. He seemed to be looking for someone.

"Raven. You leaving already?" he called. The joy that filled her whole being took her by surprise. Had he been looking for her?

"Yeah. I have to get up early tomorrow," Raven said when Amari got close to her.

"Sorry I didn't get to talk to you much. You have a good time?"

"Yeah. It was a nice party." She turned and pointed to her car. "But now I'm stuck."

Amari laughed. "There. Now you have to stay for at least one dance with me."

"Dance? I can't dance."

"If you can walk you can dance. There's no right or wrong way to dance."

"There might be a few exceptions," Raven said, smiling, enjoying his presence, the warmth emanating from his body.

"Is it too immoral for you?"

"What do you mean?" She didn't know if he was making fun of her or really meant it.

"I know it was getting a bit rowdy. The dancing wasn't your usual Sunday church dancing and praising?"

"This is not church. I can handle it."

Amari leaned against the car. He looked comfortable. "Is this little toy yours?"

Raven laughed. "Yeah, and it's not a toy. I call it Old Baby."

"You named your car. What else is next?"

"My kids," she blurted out, and wished she could take back the words.

"Oh. The preacher's daughter's already thinking babies."

She shook her head, berating herself, then decided to ask. "How did you know I was out here, anyway?"

"I saw you when I was talking to Kendra, and Ashley told me you had left." Raven nodded understanding. She wished she knew what he was talking to Kendra about.

"I'll definitely be at the center next weekend. I still want to sit and discuss with you what role I can take. I want to do more than just help on weekends. I want to play a bigger role."

"I can arrange a meeting with my father," Raven suggested.

"Before we do that let's talk about what your needs are. Then we can have a plan," Amari continued.

"Why are you so eager to help?" Raven asked suddenly.

"It's a crazy story," Amari said.

"Oh. Is it a private reason?"

"No. I made a pact with God," Amari began. Raven raised her eyebrows, and in the outdoors lighting she could see his sheepish expression.

"When I was young I wanted to play for the NBA so bad and many people discouraged me."

"Was that your only dream growing up?" Raven asked.

"You won't believe my other dream."

"What is it?"

"You won't laugh?"

"It can't be worse than mine, so tell me."

"I wanted to be an actor." Raven bit her lip to prevent the laughter.

"I even acted in high school plays. I thought I could be the next Denzel Washington. I even wanted to try comedy like Will Smith."

"I wasn't expecting that," Raven said.

"But I also wanted to play basketball. Like an acting basketball player." Now Amari stood straight, pretending he was holding the ball. "You know after shooting around I would go and practice my lines for the play. But anyway, I was told that it was tough to make it in the acting world. I can't remember exactly, but they said that the chances for making it in Hollywood were smaller than winning the lottery."

"Wow. That bad, huh?"

"So my next plan was the NBA, and I worked hard. I had made a pact with God that if he helped me make it I would do something great with a third of my salary for other less fortunate people. I wanted a project that was really doing something for kids. Like your program. God held up his end of the deal, and now it's my turn to pay Him back by showing a little bit of love to His children."

"That's wonderful, Amari," Raven said softly.

"Thanks. I know I can never repay God for His faithfulness in my life, but I'm going to try." Raven smiled, realizing in that moment that it was so easy to fall in love with this man. His passion for what he believed in was so enthralling. She could easily be swept away by him, but he was just nice to everybody.

"God knows your heart," Raven said. "Even if you don't accomplish everything exactly, He knows you are trying."

"That's good to hear. Now how about you? What was your dream?" Raven smiled shyly. He seemed genuinely interested as he folded his arms and looked at her. Raven looked down. Standing this close to him was disconcerting.

"You promise you won't laugh?" she echoed what he said earlier.

"I promise." Amari laughed.

"At first I wanted to skate. I used to love watching those couples on ice. I would dream of flying high in the air and landing perfectly on one leg, floating on the ice."

"That's not a bad dream. What happened?"

"I don't like the cold." Amari laughed again, and Raven shook her head.

"You promised not to laugh," she said.

"Well, you don't see too many black people playing at the Winter Olympics."

"Yeah, is that why you didn't make the Red Wings?"

"I don't know if I could ever play a sport where I'm cold and lose my teeth at the same time."

They both laughed. They talked about a lot of things that evening standing out in the driveway, not feeling the slightest bit uncomfortable. It was almost midnight when the driver of the truck blocking her arrived.

"Oh, sorry. I've blocked you in," the man said.

"It's fine," both of them said at once, then stared at each other and laughed.

"It looks like you didn't mind," the man opened his car door and moved his truck. When he left, Raven looked at Amari, reluctant to leave but realizing she didn't have a reason to stay.

"I better go. Thank you for keeping me company," she said putting her key in the door.

"I take it your car doesn't have an alarm," he said.

"I doubt anybody would want to steal it."

"You may be right about that," Amari said and Raven reached impulsively and punched him on the arm. Amari jumped back, laughing.

"She's very sensitive," she said, opening the door. Was he expecting a hug goodbye? Raven didn't know so she didn't turn back but settled herself behind the wheel.

"I don't know how you drive it. I would be terrified to drive near a huge truck in that toy car," Amari insisted, holding her door.

"You get used to it. Hey, at least I can fit in the tiniest parking," Raven said.

"Good point." Amari was still holding her door and Raven didn't want to close it. Oh, she didn't want to leave at all. She could have talked to him until the sun came up.

"Thank you for the invitation," she said instead.

"Anytime. Next time I'll have something at my place. Something smaller and more intimate," Amari said and watched her reaction. Her eyes widened.

"I hope you can come," he continued.

"We'll see," Raven said instead, putting her key in the ignition. Amari closed her door and watched her struggle to start the car.

"Does it work?" he asked.

"Give it time," Raven said, and after the second try the engine came alive. Amari shook his head.

'You see? It's so small I don't struggle getting out of spaces," Raven said.

"You can defend the Old Baby all you want, but I'm not convinced it's even a car," Amari teased.

She waved at him and drove out of the driveway. The strangest thing happened. He was still standing watching her car as she turned into the street. The feeling she had was enough to make her heart explode.

"Oh, God, I think I'm in love," she said out loud in her car.

And I'll die if he doesn't love me, too, her inner voice screamed.

CHAPTER 6

"Is Amari coming in today?" Kendra asked, holding the photocopies. They were both preparing the room for the tutoring sessions, setting up tables and chairs. Raven paused from moving a desk and looked at Kendra. She usually didn't work on Saturdays, but since Amari started coming, then Kendra volunteered to tutor the kids on that day as well.

"I think so. I have a meeting with him after today's session. Why?"

"I don't know. The last time I spoke to him he said he might not come in," Kendra said, admiring her nails. Raven looked at her sharply. She had spoken to him?

"He called you?"

"Yeah. After the party. We had a long talk that evening and then : . . well, I don't know if I should tell you."

Raven felt her heart plummet to her feet. She remembered the long talk she had with Amari. It was just a talk. He didn't ask for her number, so it didn't mean anything. He clearly had Kendra's number.

"What?" Raven asked, feigning interest. She really didn't want to know what Kendra and Amari had been up to.

"Well, he kissed me. I think you came to look for me just when he had finished."

"Oh," Raven managed to say.

"Yeah. He's such a good kisser," Kendra said dreamily, her hands on her ample bosom. Raven couldn't have faked a smile to save her life. She didn't know why she'd hoped he liked her a little, just a tiny bit, but now all her hopes were gone. They would make a nice couple. Kendra was every man's dream. It was as it should be. So why did it feel like her heart was being crushed by a huge truck?

"That's nice," she said finally, then turned and left the room. She didn't see Kendra's smile. Kendra had set her eyes on Amari the moment he walked into the center. She wasn't too worried about Raven as competition. Kendra knew she was pretty. She always looked good, and her caramel skin was flawless. Raven was no competition.

❧❦

"Count backwards to two and tell me how many fingers you are holding up," Raven coached Jalen. This week he forgot how to subtract. Raven continued to coach the boy, but froze when she heard Amari's voice.

"Here, try it like this. Say the number in your head and count backwards. You can count backwards, right?" Raven looked up and saw Amari. She hadn't seen him come in, and his voice disturbed her concentration and sent her heart racing.

"It's okay, I got it," she told Amari, holding her hand up. She placed wooden blocks on the table in front of Jalen.

"Just trying to help," he said with a smile.

"Thank you, but why don't you go and work with those students over there? Kendra could use your help."

Amari raised his eyebrows at her unfriendly expression. He left and walked towards Kendra. She stood up and hugged him. Raven watched, bitterness filling her heart and spreading to her mouth. She ignored Amari the whole morning and still felt like an idiot.

He's here to help the center, she told herself. *Stop thinking about yourself and focus on the kids. They need him. They love him. In fact, just grow up!*

By 3 p.m. most of the students had been picked up. She had forgotten that she had agreed to meet with Amari until he walked into the office.

"What can I do for you?" she asked after a quick glance at his face. "You are free to go home now."

"We have a meeting, remember? We were going to come up with a plan . . ."

"Oh, damn. I mean, darn," Raven said, totally flustered.

"The preacher's daughter curses." Amari walked in, but before he sat down Kendra came by the door.

"So I'll call you Monday," Kendra said to Amari. Raven watched as he turned to face the beauty.

"Cool. Enjoy your weekend," he said and turned back to Raven. Raven waved at Kendra, who waved back, but didn't smile. A few seconds after Kendra left, Raven heard a sound from outside.

"Was that thunder?" she asked, surprised.

"Yeah. I could see the clouds forming when we were finishing basketball. We should hurry. Supposed to hail, too."

"Okay," Raven sighed.

"So what do you think I should focus on?" Amari asked, and Raven shook her head to shake off the effect of his presence on her thoughts. She imagined him giving Kendra delicious kisses, and that strengthened her resolve to remain unmoved by the man.

"What you are doing is great. Your participation in the program has already increased enrollment and volunteers," Raven said, placing her hands on the desk and shrugging. "Ashley suggests that we do a press release on your role here. What do you think about that?"

"Not sure I want that. I'm not doing this for publicity."

"I know, but some good press would help us raise funds for the kids and the center."

"Right. That might work. It might bring a lot of kids from the street to come here instead."

"It's amazing how many kids finish school at 3 p.m. and go home with nothing to do and no one to watch them. That's when they end up getting into trouble. If we make this an exciting place it could be like a private club for inner city kids. We could have dance, music, painting classes . . ."

"You should see how your face lights up when you talk about this," Amari interrupted her, and Raven widened her eyes surprised. She covered her face with her hands. Amari reached across the desk and pulled her hands away from her face. She was so surprised she couldn't breathe for a second. She looked at her hands in his large, beautiful ones.

"No. Let me see. You look amazing when you are this excited," Amari repeated, and she looked at him to see he was serious. "I think you are amazing."

"Well. I'd forgotten about the meeting. I'll have to go home. I'm meeting with my father this evening and a family friend will be there," she said, pulling her hands back and standing up. She made a point of tidying up her desk and then picked up her bag. At that moment she heard another loud clap of thunder, which made her jump. Her nerves were already a mess, and the weather wasn't helping.

"It's just thunder," Amari said. She walked around the desk and then right past him.

"I need to go. We can talk about this again next time," Raven said.

"How about tomorrow? We can go for coffee or a drink . . ."

"No. I mean, I can't. I have church tomorrow." Now Amari looked distressed as he saw how flustered she was. Was there something about him that she didn't like?

"You have church all day?" he demanded, totally surprised.

"Not all day," she said and left the office. She stood looking at the pouring rain outside. Their two cars were parked in the gravel lot being assaulted by heavy rain and hail. It looked so dark outside that it was hard to believe it was only 4 p.m.

"Why don't you wait until the rain lets up. It won't take that long for the storm to pass," Amari coaxed, watching her hold the door that led outside. Her next words caused him to raise his eyebrows questioningly.

"I better run." Raven opened the door and ran out into the rain. She was looking completely drenched after a few seconds. Amari would have laughed if he wasn't so shocked. She was practically running away from him and leaving him in the center alone. *Who was going to lock up? Was she crazy? Surely she was going to come back.*

He watched her get into the car and insert the key to start the engine as lightning brightened up the doorway and a loud, deafening peal of thunder followed. In the lot, the "Old Baby" just coughed and spluttered, and the engine refused to come alive. Was she really going to drive away? He could hear the car make a scratching sound like a dying elephant and after a while he realized that she had given up. Her car had finally died. About time, too, Amari thought smugly. That serves her right for running out on him as if he was about to assault her or something.

CHAPTER 7

After a minute Amari grasped that Raven was just going to sit in that car and leave him standing in the center like an idiot. He ran outside and knocked on the half-open window. Rain was falling into the car and she didn't seem to notice.

"Come inside, Raven," he commanded, his deep voice reaching her frozen, wet stupor.

"It won't start," she complained, pulling the key out of the ignition.

"So I see. Come inside and we'll figure out what to do." Raven got out quickly before he got soaked through, too. She eyed the hood of his sweater that covered his head with envy.

She got out and they both jogged back to the center. She was breathing hard as they stood by the door watching the rain, hail and wind do its worst. He watched her as the water poured down her face and he couldn't stop his eyes from traveling down her white shirt that was plastered to her skin, revealing pert breasts that stood to attention. He coughed and looked back outside. Raven looked at him just as he turned away and folded her arms in front of her chest. He was wet, too. She wished Kendra hadn't told her about their kiss. It made her dislike him somehow. Did he just go around kissing one woman and then holding the hands of another, she wondered.

She stood shivering next to him, her eyes on the pounding rain outside.

"Do you want to dry off?" he asked.

She glanced at him then shrugged. "I don't think we have towels." She folded her arms in front of her chest. She had seen him looking and it made her uncomfortable. He affected her so much. She could now understand how desire could make people act irrationally. He walked into the bathroom and came back with a wad of paper towel.

"Here," he said as he handed them to her.

"Thanks," she muttered and wiped her arms and dabbed at her face.

Amari wiped himself. She watched him from the corner of her eye.

"That was stupid. Why did you run outside into the rain like that?"

"I told you I was late to go to my parents' house. My dad wanted to discuss something with me, and I have to meet a doctor who works at the church clinic in Kenya."

"So who was going to lock up?"

"I forgot. I have to lock up," she responded without looking at him, so intent was she on drying off and trying to stop her shirt from sticking to her skin.

"Okay."

"I'm sorry," she said at last. "You must think I'm crazy."

"A little," Amari said. She punched him again and he laughed. "I've never had a woman run away from me before."

"I don't usually run away from people," she said, still looking outside.

"Let me wipe your back," Amari said, touching her back. She jumped like she had been burned.

"It's okay. I got it," she snapped and reached for her back, dabbing ineffectually at it.

"Here. I won't bite," he insisted, then turned her around. She stood as still as a tree as he dabbed at her back and the paper towel absorbed the moisture on her shirt and skin. After a few seconds Raven closed her eyes. She was intensely aware of the feel of his warm touch. One of his hands held her arm while the other wiped her back. She didn't know when he had dropped the paper towel, but now she felt his hand going to her waist and turning her around. She now stood facing him. She opened her eyes. He looked at her, an intense look entering his eyes. Was he going to kiss her?

"It's stopped raining," he said with his face close to hers. She nodded, looking at him. For a while she couldn't find her voice.

"Oh. You're right. I-I should try my car again. It doesn't like rain." She took a step from him and cleared her throat.

"I don't think your car's going to start. I'll take you home," Amari offered, smiling lazily.

"I'll try it again," Raven insisted, stepping out on the wet pavement. She locked the door while Amari stood by, and then walked to Old Baby while he went to his car. She turned the key in the ignition without much hope and the engine didn't even make a sound. She got out of the car and awkwardly walked over to Amari's SUV. He opened the door for her and she got in. She felt as if she was entering the lion's den.

Amari started the engine. His practically purred to life, somehow mocking her now-dead little car, and she shook her head. ·

"I'm sorry about your seats," she said.

"No big deal. I'm also wet," Amari said. "So, which way?"

"Do you know how to get to Jefferson?" she asked.

"Yeah."

"I live on River View," Raven said. "Just off Jefferson."

"Cool. Shouldn't be too hard to find," Amari said, joining the Saturday traffic. Raven was uncomfortable for more than one reason. First, she was damp and cold. Second, Amari was gorgeous. And third, he kissed Kendra.

They got to her apartment quickly, and when the gates opened she directed Amari to the underground parking.

"Thank you," Raven said.

"I need to dry off. Really long drive." Amari raised his eyebrows questioningly, giving her a look she felt clear to her toes. She looked at him, trying to decide what she should do. He had given her a ride. The least she could do was let him get dry and dry his clothes for him. Still she hesitated. Being alone with him in the car was stressful enough. Having him in her apartment would double her anxiety. The way he had touched her at the center and the way he seemed to be able to melt her heart with just one smile made him dangerous.

"Come in. I'm on the twentieth floor," Raven said as she got out of the car. In the elevator they stood facing each other.

"You like living here?" Amari asked. Raven nodded trying to avoid looking into his eyes. They were so intense they made her skin hot. The elevator seemed slower than usual, and it seemed forever before it finally opened on her floor. She opened the door, trying to remember if her place was presentable or not. She walked in and threw her keys on the table and immediately removed her wet sandals.

"Not bad," Amari said, walking to the window to check out the view.

"The bathroom is over there. I don't think I have anything that could fit you," Raven said, walking into her bedroom. She looked in her closet while removing her wet top and pants. As she stripped she felt completely vulnerable. Amari Thomas was right in her apartment while she stood naked in her bedroom. Had the world gone crazy?

She quickly put on a robe as if he could see through walls. There was a T-shirt from Calvary her father had given to her. It was XL, and she hoped it would fit him. She looked in the mirror and hated how her hair had gone all frizzy and curled.

"So much for looking good in the rain," Raven muttered and at the same time jumped when she heard a loud crash in the living room. She opened the door and ran in to find Amari looking guilty standing by her linen closet with all her artifacts from Africa on the floor.

"Oops." Amari looked at her, guilt all over his face. "What's all this?"

"That's my stuff," she said walking towards him. He stood back and picked up a wooden carving of a giraffe.

"Where from?"

"Africa. Kenya," she said.

"You've been to Kenya?"

"Yes." She picked up more artifacts and tried to jam them back in the closet. Now he'd think she was a slob. She'd planned to decorate her apartment in an African theme, but she just hadn't had the time. These were all her favorite things that she kept in the closet waiting for inspiration.

"I've never been to Africa," Amari said.

"You should go," she said holding a zebra candle holder. "I got this on the island of Mombasa."

"Who did you go with?"

"Myself," she said, smiling at Amari's surprise.

"Raven. You went to Africa on your own?"

"Yeah. Nobody else wanted to go. My friends were worried about being in a strange country."

"Weren't you?"

"A little. My father knew some people there who opened a clinic and they put me up in Nairobi, but I traveled to Mombasa alone."

"The lone soldier. You didn't have a boyfriend to go with you?" Her expression changed at that question.

"Don't have a boyfriend," she said, moving away from him.

"Is that mine?" Amari asked, pointing at the T-shirt she was holding.

She tossed it to him and stood rooted while he took off the T-shirt he was wearing. When Amari smiled she turned away and walked to the kitchen.

"Tea?" she asked busily, filling the kettle with water. She managed to catch a glimpse of his chest and hard stomach from the corner of her eye. Now every time she closed her eyes she would see him half naked in her living room, she thought gloomily.

"Sure." He walked towards her and sat by the kitchen counter, looking out the windows.

"What a view," he said, looking at the waves of rain outside. The storm had finally passed and all that remained was a light drizzle.

"Yeah. I never get tired of it." He looked at her then put his wet T-shirt on the counter. Raven picked it up.

"I should put this in the dryer."

"Never mind. This one fits fine," he said, looking at the slightly snug one he wore. This close she could see his muscled arms. It was still hard to believe that he was really in her apartment, sitting on her kitchen counter.

She poured hot water over teabags in two mugs and handed him one. She watched him put his big hands around his mug and took a sip of the tea. She nearly burnt her tongue.

"So tell me about Kenya," Amari said.

"It's gorgeous. I loved the people, the game parks, the music . . . Nairobi reminded me a little of New York. A rustic version with crowds, and cars honking. It felt good being there. I can't really put it into words."

Amari liked the way she was relaxing. She had been tense with him. He still couldn't understand why, but she seemed jumpy around him before, as if she thought his intentions weren't noble. He had to admit there was something totally primal in him that drew him to her. He was fascinated by how her upper lip made her look sulky, but when she smiled her eyes brightened and her white teeth glistened brighter than the sun.

"And where's Mombasa?"

"Mombasa is an island where I took the ferry and drove about an hour to the beach. There were camels on the beach, and I took scuba diving lessons. I met people from all over the world on those beaches, from Germany, Switzerland, Australia, you name it. A lot of people on their honeymoons, too."

"That where you want to go for yours?" Amari asked, and he could have kicked himself at the look that entered her eyes. The relaxed girl was gone, replaced by the wary woman.

"Haven't thought of that," Raven said and looked at her watch. "I really must get going. I need to shower and go to my parents."

"And your parents will what? Scold you if you are late?"

"It's not that. Dr. Harding will be there, and Daddy really wants me to meet him . . ."

"Is he matchmaking?"

"No!" Raven cried, surprised. "He's a wonderful man who works at the Calvary Church clinic in Kenya in Mombi Village. My dad is trying to build a center with a school, hospital, and library, and, well, Doctor Harding went there and has given his life to seeing my father's vision through."

"Sounds like an excellent man," Amari commented and sipped the tea. Raven could tell he didn't like it as he reached for the sugar bowl.

"He's amazing," Raven smiled, and then looked up at Amari and caught her breath. Amari was the incredible one. His eyes were intent on her, seeming to watch every move she made. She walked around the counter and Amari stood up and met her right at the kitchen exit. She gasped, stopping right in front of him. He put his hands on her shoulders.

"Thanks for the shirt," he said. She shrugged, swallowing hard. He knew he made her nervous. She acted like she had never been touched by a man. Could that be true? He was really curious as he touched her cheek.

"What—are you doing?" she asked.

"Can I thank you properly?" Amari said.

"What?" She took a step back. "Were you thanking Kendra when you kissed her?"

Amari laughed. She stared at him, bewildered.

"I've never kissed Kendra. That what she told you?"

Raven shrugged.

"That's a lie. The only woman I wanted to kiss was you," he said. His words took her breath away as she stood rooted to the spot.

"Why does that shock you?" He took a step closer and this time she had nowhere to go. Her back was against the fridge and Amari advanced, making her feel weak even though he hadn't touched her. She looked at him, breathing hard as he leaned closer, unmistakable desire in his eyes. He didn't do anything until he saw her eyes close, and then he leaned in and tasted the soft lips that he couldn't stop thinking about since the rain soaked them and made them wet and inviting. He coaxed her lips open with his tongue, still in control, but when she whimpered his desire took over and he pulled her close, molding her body to him. She clung to him, putting her arms around his neck like someone drowning and holding on for dear life.

The phone ringing seemed to come from a million miles away, and though their lips broke apart he started planting kisses on her neck.

"I must get that," she whispered, putting her hands on his chest.

"Let the machine take a message," Amari groaned. What was he planning to do? Surely he didn't think she was just going to sleep with him just because his kiss made her lose her mind.

She pushed harder and Amari stepped back, hands held up as her phone shrilled again. She walked around him and, in a daze, picked it up.

"Hello," Raven said, and coughed to clear her throat. She sounded like someone who was coming from a deep sleep.

"Raven. Where are you? We were expecting you here an hour ago," Clare complained.

"Oh, Mom, I'm on my way," Raven said.

"You are still at home. We'll have to start dinner without you. Raven, you can be so inconsiderate. Your cellphone is off and your father was getting worried."

"Sorry, Mom. I'll be there in a few," Raven apologized and hung up. She looked in Amari's direction but couldn't bring herself to look at him.

"Do you need a ride?" he asked.

"Are you sure?"

"I can take you. Who'll bring you back?"

"So many people, my sister or brother," Raven said biting her lip. "I'm gonna jump in the shower, can you wait?"

"Don't do this to me."

"What?"

"Shower while I'm here. Just thinking about you in there . . ." Raven shook her head to clear it. She was still in a daze. She glanced at him quickly and was amazed at how her heart quickened, thinking about where his imagination was taking him.

"I'll hurry," she said. He walked towards her again and kissed her without any warning this time. She clung to him mindlessly. He was so big and it felt so good holding him, holding her hands on his back. And his hands on her face, pure bliss.

"I better go," she muttered, her lips on his neck. "This is not good."

"It's so good," he said.

"No. I shouldn't do this. My mom will kill me, and it's wrong," Raven said as he took her lips again, making her body burn.

"Nothing wrong," Amari echoed bringing her closer.

"Amari," she said and he looked at her. She had never really said his name before, and with her sweet soft voice it sounded so excitable. "I must go." He knew he had to let her go. She thrilled him. She wanted him to let her go because she couldn't do it herself. With the willpower of a lion he stepped back and watched her go in her bedroom. It took a lot from him not to follow her and have her melt in his arms again, but instead he went to her book shelf and started looking around while he imagined her naked in the shower with steam and bubbles all around her. What *he* needed right now was a nice *cold* shower.

CHAPTER 8

"Where have you been?" Clare yelled as soon as Raven walked in. This was one of the family's twice-monthly dinners, and Raven was two hours late and they had an important guest in the house. The guilt was all over her face as she sat at the dining table that had food ranging from macaroni and cheese, Cornish hens, greens, her mother's delicious sweet potatoes and potato salad. Everybody was almost done eating and Raven waved at Tahlia, Esther and PJ. She hugged her father then took her place next to him.

"I'm sorry. My car died," Raven said.

"Old Baby finally threw in the towel?" PJ asked.

"Yes. A friend gave me a ride here," Raven nodded, looking sheepish.

"Oh. I always worried about you driving that car. I hope now you'll let me help you buy a new one."

"Dad, I can afford one. If I can't get it fixed I'll buy something else."

"Which friend brought you?" Clare asked.

"Amari," Raven said, then cleared her throat.

"Amari Thomas. You mean A-T?" PJ asked, excitement and disbelief in his voice. Raven looked at her brother, irritated, her eyes telling him to shut up. Now the whole family looked at her with interest and forgot all about the delicious dinner. Since Raven was no longer working in the church, her parents were adamant that she attend the family dinners. However she hated being on the spot like this. She usually had nothing interesting to share with them.

"Who is he? Is he a singer?" Clare asked, looking around the table at each of her children's faces. "The name sounds familiar."

"Mom, he's gorgeous," Tahlia said. "He's so good at basketball, too."

"Averaged about 25 points a game last season and is also a good defensive player," PJ said. "He's now perfected 'the Lethal Pass' that he tosses behind his back."

"What's he doing with you?"

"He helps at the center, Clare," Philip Senior said, and Raven looked at her dad gratefully.

"You must be careful. Those kinds of men wouldn't be interested in girls like you except for one thing," Clare said, looking pointedly in Raven's direction. Clare saw Raven flush and her eyes widened. Raven could tell from her mother's expression she'd soon have to endure a mother-daughter talk.

Raven was embarrassed as she remembered what had taken place in her apartment, what might have happened if the phone hadn't interrupted the heated kiss and Amari had not stepped away from her. She was totally powerless, and now she felt humiliated. Her mother was right. He probably just wanted to use her. An easy, inexperienced woman to seduce and toss to the side.

"We just work together. He was at the center when my car broke down," Raven said.

"Oh, lucky you," Tahlia said, grinning.

"Tahlia. There's nothing lucky about being stuck with a man who she doesn't know that well," Clare cautioned, then looked at Raven's plate and added, "You might as well warm up your food. It's already cold. We're about to have dessert."

When Raven went to the kitchen to microwave her food she was relieved to hear the conversation return to events at the church. She nearly jumped when Tahlia tapped her on the shoulder.

"Amari, huh?" she said, putting her plate in the sink. Raven shook her head. Her little sister was eagerly looking in her face.

Raven couldn't believe the tingle that went up and down her spine at the mention of his name, but she shrugged. "Tahlia, he's just helping the kids."

"If he brought you why didn't he come in?" she asked. Raven remembered the ride in his car and the longing she had never in her life felt or thought she was capable of feeling. Yes, she desired him. The way he put his hand on the small of her back when she got in the elevator and told her she smelled lovely. She flushed again, remembering the unmistakable look that entered his eyes.

"Oh, my goodness, something's going on," Tahlia said.

"No." Raven shook her head and took her plate out of the microwave. "Don't start or you'll have Mom all over me about this."

"Okay, you can tell me. Is he as nice as people say?" Tahlia asked, leaning in.

"I don't know what people say, but he's so good-looking in real life. He takes my breath away," Raven confessed, and they both giggled.

"What are you talking about?" Esther walked in, holding two plates up like a waiter. PJ was right behind her with his plate and some glasses.

"Work," Raven said quickly. "I had a tough case this week."

"Oh," PJ said. "I thought you were talking about Amari Thomas. If he's at the center I'll have to visit. I admire the guy."

"Oh," Raven said. "Because he averages 20 points per game?"

"That too. He never loses his cool." PJ went on to describe more of his moves on the basketball court and some famous shot he made to win the Eastern conference. As they were about to have dessert the doorbell rang.

"That must be Josh," Clare said loudly. "Better get it."

Her husband walked to the door and opened it.

"Josh!" Philip said and gave the young man a hug. "We thought you weren't going to make it."

Raven walked into the living room just as Josh and Philip walked in. Raven had heard so much about Josh she wasn't sure she had expected to see such a young and handsome man. When her parents talked about him in her mind she had pictured someone much older.

Philip introduced his daughters. "These are my girls, Raven, Tahlia and Esther," Philip said.

"It's wonderful to meet you," Josh said.

"How's Kenya?" Clare asked.

"Great!"

"You're still there?" Esther said. "Are you now becoming an African?"

"Almost. I can speak fluent Swahili now."

"That's incredible," Clare said. "Come in. Would you like some dinner?"

"I'm fine, but that looks good," Josh said and pointed to Philip's plate. It was filled with peach cobbler and whipped cream.

Over desert Josh told them that he had come back home to check on some of his investments and also see his parents. Raven listened to him intently, excited to hear about all that he was doing for the people in remote villages in Kenya. He was the only doctor for miles and sometimes served as a pastor.

"Raven, your dad told me about what you are doing at the center," Josh said.

"Oh. It's just starting," Raven said.

"She's even recruited a professional basketball player to help there," Philip added.

"Who?" Josh asked, turning to Raven.

"Amari Thomas," she responded and she pictured him kissing her in her apartment and almost swooned. She had to get herself together or they would all see through her silliness. It was just a kiss. An incredible, knee-melting kiss. A kiss that must never, ever happen again.

"Why don't you spend the night?" Philip Senior asked when his older daughters were gathering their purses to leave.

"Next time, Daddy," Esther said, hugging her father and then her mom, Josh, Tahlia and Phil. "Besides, I didn't come prepared to sleep here, and I'm going to drop Raven at her apartment."

"Take my car," her father said, his arm around Raven's shoulder. "I still don't like you living in that building all alone."

"It's safe, Daddy," she said and hugged him. The hugs continued as she embraced the whole family. "I'll see you tomorrow."

As soon as Raven buckled her seat belt Esther turned to her, soft brown eyes inquisitive. "What is going on with you and Amari?"

"Oh, not you, too," Raven whined, looking out the window at the dark evening. Now that the afternoon rain was gone the night sky was filled with stars and clean, dewy air.

"When you walked in at dinner there was a sparkle in your eyes. Is it because of him? Did he do something to you?"

"What do you mean?"

"He's a professional athlete and I don't know much about him, but from what I hear these guys sleep around a lot."

"Don't all guys?"

71

"Yeah, but these guys are chased by women so for them it means nothing to take your innocence away."

"Nothing happened. He just kissed me," Raven confessed, looking at her sister. Esther jerked the car forward.

"That's all. What does he want? Are you dating?"

"No. He just kissed me and I was a total fool. I completely lost my mind."

"Well, he is fine," Esther said, getting onto the highway. She was driving well out of her way. Her new home was in Farmington Hills, right by a golf course, but Raven knew that Esther didn't mind a long drive if it included a juicy story.

"I don't know, Esther. I've never felt like that before."

"It's lust," Esther said, shaking her head. "Or infatuation."

"I guess so. I never thought I would be lustful."

"Well, don't give in to temptation. Don't sleep with him, Rave," Esther begged, her eyes on the road.

"I won't. I wouldn't," Raven said with very little conviction.

"It's nice to wait," Esther advised, smiling.

"Did you and Angelo wait until you got married?"
Esther nodded.

"You never did anything?" Raven asked and Esther sighed.

"No. That's why we got married quickly. It says in the Bible to do that."

"Yes I know . . . In Corinthians, right," Raven said and echoed Esther as she quoted the verse, "But if they cannot control themselves, they should marry, for it is better to marry than to burn with passion."

"Did you burn for Angelo?"

"Yes. But it was nice to wait, too. Made it more special."

"Was it your, you know, first time?" Raven asked. Esther nodded as they entered Raven's apartment complex.

"And him?"

"Oh, you know Angelo's testimony. He was bad! He was a womanizer who actually took advantage of women in the church," Esther said.

"Oh. I don't remember. He always seemed like an angel."

"You can't judge a book by its cover, that's for sure."

"Oh, he was that bad?"

"Raven, Angelo confessed everything when he got born again. He told me how his old desires were completely gone and he just wanted to please God. God gave him a new heart."

"That's beautiful, Essie." Raven smiled. "I'm glad you got a man with a new heart. So what is it like?"

"What?"

"Being intimate. Do you like it?"

Esther laughed, seemingly embarrassed. "It's wonderful. When you are about to get married we'll have this talk. I hope you remember what I said about waiting."

"Oh, Essie, you are getting way ahead of yourself. I don't think I have to worry about that. Amari and I just work together once every couple of weeks and the kiss was just a one-time thing. Don't worry."

CHAPTER 9

When Raven got home her mind was on Amari. She wanted to talk to him, and though he had left his number she resisted calling. That would make her desperate and crazy all at once. Raven was woken up by the phone ringing at seven in the morning. She still had two more hours before she would get ready for church. She picked up the phone beside her bed.

"Hello," she said, wondering who would be calling so early.

"It's Amari."

She was instantly awake. Amari. How did he get her number?

"Hi." She sat up, letting her sheets fall off her body. She looked at her dresser where she had put his T-shirt when she found it in the kitchen. She no longer looked at her kitchen in the same way. It brought back memories of the kiss, and her living room brought back memories of Amari's chest and bare arms.

"Did I wake you?" he asked.

"Yes. No. I was lying in bed," Raven stammered, bringing her knees up to her chest.

"How are you getting around with no car?"

"Just staying at home."

"A girl has to eat. Are you free for dinner tonight?" Amari asked. Raven widened her eyes in surprise. He was calling her for a date.

"Dinner?"

"Yes. Can you come?"

"Sure. I mean it will have to be early, but okay."

"I'll pick you up at six?"

"Six," she said, and when she put the phone down she stood on her bed and shrieked so loud she shocked herself and fell on the bed laughing. In her excitement she quickly dialed Candice's number.

"Who's this?" a sleepy Candice asked.

"Oh Candy—sorry. It's so early. I'll call you later," Raven apologized.

"No. Tell me why you called," Candice insisted, her voice still husky from sleep.

"Amari asked me to dinner. I don't know what to wear. I'm so nervous." The shriek on the other side caused Raven to move the phone away from her ear.

"Oh, my goodness. You'll have to miss church. I can call my hair stylist. This is an emergency. He can do your hair and nails."

"No, no. My hair's fine. I had it done last weekend," Raven said.

"All right. Let's meet later after church. I can give you some tips."

Raven laughed and said good bye.

Amari. She was going on a date with Amari.

She walked to her dresser and picked up his shirt, bringing to her face. It smelt of rain and soap and him.

She hugged it close to her and fell on the bed, the shock of his call and voice still making her skin tingle.

Amari was amazed at how happy he was to see her. When he dropped her off at her parents' mansion he wasn't ready to let her go, and now seeing her again confirmed the emotions she had evoked in him. There was something incredibly warm about her, something soft and irresistible. She was different from any woman he had ever dated. She was so different, in fact, she could have been from another planet.

"Hi," she said, and he could tell she was shy and uncertain, something he did not see in most women he met. That thrilled him and evoked feelings of protectiveness and tenderness towards her. He liked what she wore, an embroidered tunic and white pants that wrapped around her slim legs and rounded butt. To him she looked fresh and sweet.

"These are for you." He handed her fresh flowers that he hid behind his back.

"Wow," she said, taking the beautifully arranged flowers. She kept her eyes on the bouquet when she spoke. "That's very kind."

"You like them?" Amari asked.

"Love them, thank you," she said and walked into the kitchen. "Would you like something to drink?"

"No thanks. We can go for dinner if you are ready," he said.

At dinner he got to know her better, and he liked her more as they talked. They laughed so hard as he told her stories of his life growing up in Detroit, with his cousins and uncles.

"What about your father?" she asked.

"Not in the picture," Amari said, and Raven nodded understandingly. "I think you are very lucky with your stable home family, your dad being the anchor for the family. That's very rare."

"I know. I should be grateful."

"Yes, you should be. But you are not?"

"I love my family, but I just don't seem to fit in," Raven said. He looked at her, surprised.

"Just you?"

"Just me. Maybe it's because I am not actively involved in the ministry. I don't know, but I just haven't found my place. It's silly I know."

"You want to be involved with your father's church?"

"No, not really. I chose social work, and I love helping out at the center. Maybe I'm still searching for my place. Do you think you have yours figured out yet?"

"Getting there. I know I can't play ball forever. There'll come a time when I'll have to do something else."

"What do you think that'll be? Acting?"

"You remember what I told you? Hey, I'll try just about anything."

They looked at each other across the table.

"So what about you? I'm curious, when did you become a Christian, or were you born one?"

"Well, I grew up in a Christian family. Dad became a pastor at a very early age. It's always been a way of life."

"My ma, too."

"What about you?"

Amari leaned back in his comfortable chair. "When I was born again? It's a long story."

"I'd like to hear it."

"I ignored God for most of my teenage years and early twenties, you know, when you know but just don't want to." Raven nodded and Amari continued, "I think for me it was a combination of things. When I played ball overseas it was lonely. I would hang with the guys even though I didn't really like what they were doing, you know."

He paused. He could see Raven was leaning forward as if she were hanging on his every word.

"There was one guy on the team. He was just different. I noticed he didn't hang with us. He was quietly encouraging, not saying much, and one day I noticed that when conversations became inappropriate or a bit too colorful he would just excuse himself. At dinner once, he prayed over his meal and the other guys just looked at him like he was crazy. He was a young guy then, about twenty-one, but he seemed to have the confidence of a much older man. So one day when we were working out I decided to ask him what religion he was.

"Well, this young man, Idris Cole, started sharing about his life, about how God had delivered him from the strife in his country and through many miracles led him to play basketball for this French team, but still he knew that he hadn't reached his destiny. He talked about Jesus as if they were friends. From then on I would hang out with him, and I started attending a small church close by with him. The congregation was mostly Africans, and these people were on fire for God. I gave my life to Jesus a few months later."

"Wow. That's incredible," Raven said, touched. "Where's Idris now?"

"He's coaching now, and also a youth pastor of sorts. I kept in touch with him, but when I came to the NBA it was a little different. I wasn't living my life the way I wanted to. I still struggle, but what keeps me strong sometimes is when I remember how watching Idris's life convinced me to follow Christ. That's how I want to be, not someone who just speaks about Jesus, but someone who actually tries to live like him."

"I think you do."

"No. I'm far from it. But I think I'm on the right road."

The evening was as smooth as the wine they drank with their seafood dinner and piano music playing softly in the background. Amari felt like he had known her forever. They were comfortable. She was easy to talk to. As they drove back to her apartment she sat with her head back. She seemed sleepy and relaxed. He walked her to her door, but he didn't want to leave. Being with her was just too good.

"Thanks for the dinner, Amari," she said. Her soft, full lips were inviting.

"It was good. I liked spending time with you," he said. She bit her lower lip, her hand twisting her purse straps.

"Me, too," she admitted. "Good night." Amari laughed at how quickly the words "good night" came out.

"Are you sending me away?" he asked.

"You can come in, but . . . ," she began.

"But nothing should happen?" She nodded.

"Like what?" he asked, following behind her. When he closed the door he could see the wariness in her eyes.

"Like this," he said and pulled her into his arms. She squealed as he planted kisses on her mouth.

" 'Mari," she whispered, and he moved back. He looked in her eyes. Longing filled their depths.

"I know. I'll leave soon and I'll be good. Let's just sit for a while. Talk."

She looked at him hesitantly and then walked over to the love seat. He sat down and pulled her down next to him.

"This is nice," he said close to her ear. "What do you think?" He could feel her relax a little as she leaned back against him. His arms were around her, enfolding her to him.

"It's good," she said.

"Now I only wish you had a TV," he said, staring at her unusual artwork.

"I've a CD player," she said.

"Great." He got up and walked to the stereo on the bookshelf that took over one whole side of the wall. He pulled up one book and showed her the spine. It read *Being Single and Loving It.*

Raven gave an embarrassed smile when he held it towards her. She wished she had thrown the book away. "That's from my sister, Esther. I haven't read it yet," Raven confessed. "Don't look at my books."

"Might learn something about you?" he teased.

He looked through the music, which ranged from Yolanda Adams, Cece Winans and Alicia Keys. He selected a Percy Sledge CD. "Some great old love songs," he said and put it in the CD player. His phone rang.

"I'll be right back. Get that," she said. As Raven walked into her bedroom, she immediately pulled off her three-inch heels and rubbed her feet.

"I don't know how some women wear these every day," she muttered. "But for Amari it's worth it."

She smiled nervously, imagining him making himself comfortable in her living room, filling the room with his aura. She opened the door and heard the tail end of his conversation on the phone.

"I'm in the house, man. I don't know what you were saying that she would never let me that close. You lose the bet so pay up, Cortez."

As Amari threw his head back and laughed Raven closed the door and sat on her bed. Anger replaced the warm feelings she'd had a few minutes earlier. Was he using her to win some bet with his buddies? Who did he think she was? It took her a few seconds to decide what to do. She slipped on her fluffy slippers and walked into her living room.

"Later, man," Amari said and looked at her as she stood by the couch. He looked very relaxed and the music from the CD player just added to the intimate atmosphere.

"Hey. Cute slippers," Amari said, looking at her feet.

"Thanks. I'm gonna go to bed, Amari. I'm really tired."

"Already? Thought we would hang out or . . ."

"I said I'm tired and I would rather you go," Raven said, folding her hands across her chest. She had wanted to remain calm, but her short fuse had already burst. Amari sat up, a look of surprise on his face.

There go your sordid plans, Raven thought happily. Hell would freeze over before she let him in her apartment again.

"You're joking, right?"

"No," she said, then, as she moved over to the CD player, she muttered, "You're the joke."

"What did you say?" he asked standing close to her as she pulled out the CD and made a point of putting it back in its case. But before she placed it on the shelf, he grabbed it from her.

"What's this? All of a sudden you just turned cold?"

"Nothing," Raven said and tried to grab the CD. He held it out of her reach and she widened her eyes at him, her annoyance rising higher.

"I can see you're upset," he insisted.

"I think this evening is over, so just be a gentleman and leave."

"Be a lady and tell me what's going on," Amari threw back, baffled but obviously not willing to put his tail between his legs and walk out.

"I just think you should leave," Raven shouted and moved towards the door.

"Tell me why?" Amari stood where he was looking at her. She glared back at him chin held up, lips pursed.

"I heard you talk to your friend Cortez just now about some bet." Raven stopped when she saw him laughing. Her anger increased, causing her skin to burn.

"That?"

"Yeah. I heard you, and I don't appreciate being a part of some childish game you and your friends play. I don't care who you are, I hate having my time wasted. So you won your bet, now leave!"

She opened the door and Amari walked to it and pushed it closed. He kept his hand on the door and regarded her. She could only stand and look at him in amazement. Was he this obstinate? Did he think he just had to look at her and she would forgive and forget?

"We were just playing. That's guys' talk. I really like you," Amari said. The pain in her chest eased a little.

"I don't trust you. All the time tonight I wondered why you were with me, and now I know."

"I wish you hadn't heard that. We just joke like that. I don't want to tell my boys how much I'm really into you yet. It's how boys talk."

"It's disrespectful," Raven said, her tone softening. Still, she wondered, why didn't he want to tell the boys? Was he ashamed of her?

"Sorry," he said, touching her cheek. "I think you are amazing. I do respect you."

She looked into his eyes and saw the sincerity in them. Was he for real? He could make her so angry one minute and the next she melted at his touch. When his eyes were on her, deep, dark, sensitive . . . she couldn't think of much else.

"Am I forgiven?" He put both his hands on his heart. She shook her head, still reeling from the feelings of betrayal she had just felt. "I don't want everybody knowing my business."

"So you tell them you are having a fling with me?"

"No. I don't want anybody to know how serious I am about you."

She couldn't deny the warmth in his eyes, but she still didn't want to forgive him.

"I like your style, your strong sense of right and wrong, your purity. That's rare and I really dig it." The blood rushed to her face, turning her eyes bright with embarrassment. He was saying something special.

"Now you know how I really feel. Are you still mad?"

"A little. I mean, no," Raven said. He smiled, but when he tried to reach for her she moved back, shaking her head. "Good night, Amari."

"You really mean it this time?"

"I do."

They looked at each other for a while. He stood there, and she felt her heart start to thud. Still he leaned close to her and kissed her, a confident kiss that left her forgetting she had told him to leave until he released her, checked his pockets for his keys and left. As soon as he was gone she wished she could call him back. She missed him already.

CHAPTER 10

After their first date, they were inseparable. Amari told her that he didn't want to play games. He claimed he could sense that they were right for each other. In an awkward discussion they both agreed that they were dating. Raven was surprised when Amari showed that he was eager to meet her parents, only two months after they became "official." They decided to visit her parents' home the first Sunday in October when Amari didn't have work.

That Sunday came quicker than Raven wanted. She was really nervous about taking Amari to meet her family. There would be questions, and she would be in the spotlight. They would all be wondering how Raven managed to be dating a guy as incredible as Amari. They would love him just as much as she did, but they would wonder, just as she wondered. What does he see in me?

They arrived at 2400 Mill Lane just before four. Dinner was starting later, but her mother wanted her and Amari to get there early before her brother and sisters arrived.

"You grew up in this house?" Amari asked, looking at Raven.

"Just for a few years. They bought this when I was in high school."

"It's tight," Amari commented, parking the car in the circle drive way where he had dropped her off the night her little Mini died. That car was probably on its way to a junk yard. To fix it cost more than buying another used car, so Raven had given in to her father and now Amari's desires and leased a brand new car.

"Wait till you get inside," Raven said as they walked to the door and rang the doorbell.

Philip opened the door.

"Daddy," Raven said and hugged her father tightly. She stepped aside and let Amari in.

"Good evening, sir." Amari cleared his throat. She had never seen him so nervous before. She watched the two men who, in that moment, meant the most to her meet. They seemed to like each other at first sight.

"Come in, come in," Philip said guiding them inside. Raven caught her father's eye and he smiled at her. She felt better now that the initial meeting was over. They walked into the living room and Clare stood up to greet Amari. She watched Amari's eyes admire her lovely mother. Everybody did, and at first glance her beauty could cause electrical storms.

"Mom, this is Amari," Raven said, watching her mother's expression. She seemed to approve. The wide, welcoming smile and glee in her eyes left no doubt that Amari was already a hit. She knew that Amari exuded warmth, confidence and gentleness despite his strong build. His amazing eyes showed the honesty and integrity within. You just couldn't miss it, and Raven knew her mother recognized it. Clare always made her decisions about people immediately.

"Nice to meet you," Amari said politely. Raven wanted to giggle with tension, nervousness and excitement all in one. Instead she walked over and kissed her mother on the cheek.

"Please have a seat, Amari," Clare said, indicating the white love seat. Amari sat down comfortably, long legs stretched out in front of him. Raven looked at her parents' tastefully decorated house, trying to gauge what Amari would think. Was it over the top? Her mom was obsessed with creams and whites, but the walls were a pale, bluish green color that complimented the furniture. It was a clean and pristine environment. Even when they had lived in the smaller house in which Raven had grown up, Clare was tyrannical about keeping a clean house.

There was a moment of uncomfortable silence, Raven couldn't think of how to fill it. She was relieved when her father broke the silence.

"Is the team ready for the season?" Philip Senior asked. Of course basketball. What else could they talk about?

"Getting there. Just have a few injuries."

"You have a good team, no stars, but players willing to work together. I'm sure Jackson will be able to play soon," Philip said.

"Amari would you like something to drink before you go into a full sports report?" Clare asked.

"Sure. Water's fine, thank you," Amari said.

"Ray, come and help me get the drinks," Clare ordered. Raven got up and left Philip and Amari talking about basketball again and reliving the championship of the year before.

"He seems like a nice man," Clare commented, gesturing towards the formal living room where Amari and Philip's voices could be heard.

"He's wonderful," Raven said. "You like him?"

"Well, I'll only be glad if the relationship lasts more than a year. I mean, you have only known each other for a very short time." Clare looked at Raven, the green flecks in her light brown eyes sparkling.

"It's been three months. It's going really well but we are not rushing it or anything."

"That's how it should be." Clare looked into Raven's eyes and put her hand on her daughter's cheek.

"You are not such a bad-looking girl. I can see what he sees in you, Raven. You have the eyes and heart of an angel. You are innocent, so I hope he doesn't take advantage of you." Clare turned and picked up the tray with the drinks. Raven was left alone in the modern kitchen filled with delicious smells.

Clare's words echoed in her ears, but Raven wasn't going to let them enter her spirit and steal the joy from this day. Amari thought she was beautiful and he wasn't going to take advantage of her. Raven shrugged and followed behind her mother's expensive perfume, not sure if their conversation had been complimentary or not.

A couple of hours later the whole family sat down to dinner. Esther arrived with Angelo and Tahlia, and PJ arrived a few minutes later. Amari was the main attraction. PJ and Angelo, both avid basketball fans, totally dominated the conversation. For a few seconds Amari had a moment to breathe when church business came up. The older people in the church were complaining about the type of music Angelo selected for Praise and Worship and wanted more of the old hymns sung. Raven turned to glance at Amari and the look on his face took her breath away. His eyes made her feel powerful emotions, and he only broke away when Clare asked him about his family.

"It's just me and my mother," Amari said. "It's good to see a family like yours that gets along."

"Not all the time," Tahlia said. "PJ here can drive us crazy sometimes with sports talk."

Raven looked at Amari as he laughed at Tahlia's comment. Tahlia was beautiful, soft and sweet. Raven wondered if Amari was comparing her to her gorgeous sisters.

Everybody laughed and talked so naturally. It was a great evening. Still Raven waited for something bad to happen. She couldn't be that blessed!

❧

After dinner Amari and Raven left first. Amari had to get to bed early as he had early morning practice and then a flight to Arizona.

"That was great!" Amari announced as soon as they settled in the car.

"You had fun?"

"Your family's great. Did your mom cook all that food?"

"Yep."

"Wow. You cook like that?"

Here we go, Raven thought. Compare, compare.

"I try. You can't live with Clare Davies and not have some of her culinary talents rub off."

Amari whistled. "She didn't even look like she had cooked that big a meal."

"She can give Superwoman a run for her money."

Amari reached for her hand and she looked at him, surprised. "You are like her. Strong, independent. It's great to meet your mom. I can see how you'll look when you have four grown children."

Raven smiled. "I don't know about that."

"Your dad is easygoing, too."

"Oh, he's the best," Raven gushed. "I'm a lot closer to him."

"I could tell. You are Daddy's little girl."

"I guess I am."

"So why don't you work in the church with him?"

Raven sighed, looking at his hand in hers. "I'm too busy."

"That's okay. You do so much at the center. And I wouldn't have met you if you hadn't been there, right?"

"Exactly."

Amari could sense she wanted to say more, but he waited patiently, keeping his eyes on the road. He let go of her hand to guide the car towards the entrance to her apartment.

"Besides," she added, "it's hard."

When she said this they were walking into the elevator. Amari took her hand, and she loved it when he squeezed her hand reassuringly.

"What is it? What's wrong?" Amari turned to her in the elevator and pulled her close. She leaned into him.

"We can talk when we get inside."

Once in her apartment they walked and sat close on the couch. Amari looked at her curiously, wondering what she was thinking. "So what's going on?"

"It's kind of complicated with my family."

"It is? Did something happen?"

"Nothing ever really happened."

"But something is bothering you?"

"Not so much bothering me. I love my family. I love the church my parents built. It's just that I don't feel like I have much to offer there."

"What? That can't be true." He took her hands, entwining them with his. She felt lightheaded when he touched her. His gentleness always surprised her and made her feel protected. Such a strong man, but always tender. "Do you feel like you don't really fit in?"

"It's weird, right? I mean I'm the oldest child, but I can't find my place in my father's church."

"It's okay. I don't think just because your father is the pastor that you also have to work in the church. God can use you anywhere you are."

"I know. I know. But I have to be honest. Deep down, I don't think I'm skipping church for the right reason. I should be there. I wanted to be there."

"Then what?" Amari had a puzzled look on his face. This was hard for her to tell him, but at the same time she knew that if she told him this one thing then he would really understand her. She had never confessed the feelings she had to anyone. Not her father. Not her sisters or brother, and not even her best friend, Candice. She even avoided praying to God about it because she knew what He would say.

"The people at church kept comparing us," she began after taking a deep shuddering breath.

"Comparing you to what?"

"To my sisters, my mom."

"In church?"

"Yep. I tried not to show that it bothered me, but after hearing some of the people say 'Why is she so dark? She's not as pr—' "

Before she could finish Amari moved to her and kissed her. The kiss took her by surprise.

"Don't say it. Don't let people's words affect your destiny."

When he kissed her like that she couldn't think straight, but she had to get some things off her chest. "I wonder what you see in me. If you really want to be with me."

"Why? I see my future with you. I see this amazing, gorgeous chocolate princess."

He kissed her again lightly, softly.

Me? Chocolate princess? Does he mean that?

"Now I'm beginning to feel better," she said.

"Never doubt that." He moved away from her a little. "Being close to you makes me want you but I intend to keep our promise. Which means I better go now, Ray."

"I know."

"I want to say this." Amari sat down again and brought her close. "I've dated the perfect tens, as the guys call them. And sometimes if you look deep inside, and sometimes not even that deep, you can tell that it's not working. So all the guys look at you and applaud you and all. But in the end you have to spend each day with her. Get to know her, but you find nothing of substance."

Raven nodded but didn't know how to feel about what Amari was saying. Who were all these perfect tens, she wondered.

"I like being with you, Ray. I like everything about you."

"I like being with you, too," she responded, still reeling from his words. He kissed her.

"Well, I better go or else."

Amari walked out the door after a few minutes. Raven sat there for a while wondering if he understood. She listened to the silence, thinking of the evening. The dinner, her family accepting Amari into their hearts. She had felt good about the evening, but now his words about perfect tens made her uneasy. She still sat on her couch, puzzling over his statement, when the she heard a knock on the door. Did Amari forget something? She looked through the peep hole and there he stood. She flung the door open.

" 'Mari."

He pulled her in his arms and Raven melted against him. She didn't know why he had come back.

"I love you," he said simply. "I got to the car but didn't want to leave without telling you."

"I love you, too."

After a quick kiss, Amari left again. Raven leaned against the door her fingers on her lips. She floated to her couch and lay down staring at the ceiling, smiling and giggling. Who cares about the perfect tens? Amari loves me!

CHAPTER 11

"So you and Amari are really serious?" Candice asked Raven as they sat for lunch in their favorite restaurant, Sweet Mamma Georgina, a few weeks before Thanksgiving.

She was learning several things about having a boyfriend, and not just any boyfriend but Amari "Too-Good-Looking" Thomas! One, she grinned all the time. Two, she felt sparkly and interesting and attractive. Three, she still couldn't believe it, and four she had bruises from pinching herself so she could see if she was dreaming. It was so unbelievable, and yet she loved him and he loved her back! How amazing was all that!

"I think so. Yep." Raven smiled.

Candice met Raven's eyes then forced a smile. "So is he the one? You've been keeping him to yourself. I haven't even met him."

"Sorry, Candice. I guess I'm still getting used to being with someone," Raven apologized.

"So, have you . . . you know?"

"No. We haven't slept together or been close," Raven said, looking into Candice's questioning eyes and trying to hide her embarrassment.

"Wow! A guy willing to just hold your hand, huh?"

"Not really his choice. It's my decision, my body, and he's patient enough. He's saved and wants to do the right thing, too. Besides we hardly see each other since the season started, but when he's home we are together most of the time, just getting to know each other."

"He met your family?"

"Two months ago. I told you about it, remember?" Raven said, but she could see Candice seemed distracted so she decided to change the subject. "How's Charles?"

"Fine. Working too much, as usual," Candice complained, looking at the menu.

"You don't seem very happy."

"We are not all getting everything we want in life like you, Raven," Candice said, a bitterness in her voice that Raven had never heard. Raven opened her mouth to speak but was too stunned to say anything for a while.

"Candice, is something wrong? I've never seen you like this."

"I want to kill someone, that's all," Candice said, closing the menu. "Where the hell is that damn waiter? I tell you just because we are black nobody's gonna serve us. They are all over those white patrons. Look at them." Raven looked at a young blonde waitress leaning over an elderly white couple.

"Weren't they here before us?" Raven asked.

"No. We were here first," Candice said. Raven shrugged and decided to change the subject quickly. Candice was always on the lookout for unfair treatment and racism, but today she seemed more intense.

"Oh, here comes our waitress," Raven said quickly.

"My name is Jenny and I will be your server. What will you drink today?"

"Since you took so long I think I'm going to order my drinks and lunch now. I'll have a gin and tonic and the salmon." Jenny wrote down the order, the smile quickly gone from her face.

"I'll have the same," Raven said, "but change my drink to iced tea, please."

After she was gone Candice glared at Raven. "Why are you being nice to her?"

"I just don't want my food spat on. Haven't you heard that if you are rude to waitresses they might even wipe the floor with your food and put snot on it?"

"Yuck! If she does that then I'll just go and smack her back to wherever she came from," Candice growled.

"Okay. I can see you are mad. I've never seen you like this. What's going on?"

"I think Charles is having an affair," Candice offered suddenly, her eyes cold and angry.

"No way. He's just working late, that's all."

"I can sense it. I saw some white woman's blonde hair on his shirt," she said.

"So? He has white patients, right?"

"I can sense these things, Raven. When I find out I'm off to jail."

Raven frowned, watching Candice work herself into a frenzy. "Don't be dramatic. That's not possible. Stop saying that, it's not true. Charles loves you and you know it."

"Raven, you know very little about men. I might as well tell you now. Most men cheat." Raven didn't say anything. She looked at Candice in shock as her friend continued to speak.

"Trust me, I know. There are too many women and so few good men, and the few good black men are becoming gay or marrying other races. Any race but their own."

"You can't paint all men with the same brush and anyway you are not even sure about Charles. Did you see him with somebody else?"

"If I had they would both be in a morgue right now, but I'll find out."

Raven didn't know what to say. She had never seen this side of Candice. Candice's life was as perfect as the roses that grew in her garden in summer. Charles loved her; she remembered his tears at their wedding as he promised to love her and be faithful to her, almost choking on the words. Had he choked because he was emotional or because he knew he couldn't be faithful, Raven now wondered.

Raven thought about Candice's situation all the way home. The whole lunch had been terrible as Candice went on and on about her suspicions. She had always been paranoid about racism, but now she seemed to notice it everywhere. Raven wanted to help, but Candice was right. She had very little experience with men and didn't know what she would do if that happened to her.

Raven drove Candice home after their lunch.

"I'll just come in and see the baby. Just for a second. Have to rush."

"You always have to rush."

"I heard it might snow," Raven reminded her. Candice was still in her foul mood.

Charles was home watching a sports channel, relaxed after a busy week.

"Where's Junior?" Candice asked as soon as she spotted her husband on the couch. There was a bottle of beer on the table that Candice picked up and took to the kitchen.

"Hi, Ray. How's your new man? Mr. Thomas?" Charles said to Raven.

"My only man," Raven replied, glancing around the well-furnished house.

"He's my favorite Piston. Got his jersey, too."

"I'll tell him."

"Charles. Where's the baby?" Candice repeated, irritation in her eyes.

"He's taking a nap," Charles responded.

"What? It's almost 4 p.m. and he's still sleeping? What did I say? You only have to stay home with him once in a while and you can't do something as easy as look after your own child and keep him on a schedule? What kind of doctor are you that you can't do the simplest thing . . ."

Raven caught Charles's uncomfortable look and felt bad for him. Candice was always yelling at him about the baby, about doing things around the house, about how he couldn't do anything right if he tried. She rarely wanted to spend time with both of them at the same time because they argued, or more precisely Candice complained about everything Charles did. Was marriage always like this?

"I better go, Candy." Raven walked towards the door.

"You see what I have to deal with, Raven? Look at Junior's food . . . it doesn't even look finished still on the high chair, and look at that cabinet, he's supposed to have put it together. I swear if I don't do it myself nothing gets done around here."

The baby woke up from the ruckus and Raven managed to give the adorable little boy a kiss before rushing out of the house, avoiding meeting Charles's humiliated eyes. She did not want to be part of this domestic bliss.

❧

Raven had been forced to listen to Candice rant and rave, and as she drove home she prayed silently that she would not be a shrewish wife like that. But as she gave the matter more thought, she came to the conclusion that most men had to put up with women running the show. Her mother definitely ran their home and even Pastor Philip Davies of Calvary Worship had to toe the line just to avoid disappointing his perfectionist wife. What a mess.

❧

Christmas morning was at Clare and Philip's house. Raven arrived at 9 a.m. sharp with her bag of gifts. She had worn herself out trying to get the best gifts for her family. Her sisters were easy; they pretty much hinted or sent catalogues with items circled. Clare liked to be surprised, hence the stress. Philip and PJ got almost the same things from everybody. This year, though, she tried to get them unique stuff. She bought her father the Bible on DVD. He wasn't into technology, but she would get him started. PJ was into gadgets, so she purchased a navigational system for him. It cost the most, but he was worth it.

The Pistons were playing Christmas Day and New Year's Eve. Raven was already getting a taste of what life with Amari would be like. She would see him after Christmas.

"Where is Amari this week?" Tahlia asked, taking a sip of her cup of coffee.

"San Antonio," Raven said. "I'll see him tomorrow evening. He'll fly to see his mother first then he'll be here later."

"Have you met his mother?"

"No. I've seen pictures. She's a very tall, lovely lady who loves her baby boy."

"Uh-oh. I have heard about mothers with only one child. The only baby boy. It should be interesting," Tahlia giggled. "We all know how Mom is with PJ."

"I look forward to meeting her. She raised Amari very well," Raven said, trying to be positive.

Christmas with her family was lovely even though she couldn't stop thinking about her first Christmas with Amari. The night after Christmas, Raven waited for Amari in her apartment. For the first time she had a Christmas tree right by the window and she placed Amari's presents under the tree. She put on a Brian McKnight Christmas CD while she lighted the candles she had placed all over the room. The room glowed with warmth and intimacy even though outside it was cold and snowy.

A thought crossed her mind. Maybe she should just give in and sleep with him; but just as quickly as it came she squashed it and turned off the oven, wishing she could turn off her desires just as easily. The past few months they had become comfortable with the knowledge that they wouldn't do anything until their wedding night. Amari never put pressure on her and slept on the couch when he spent the night. Besides she would be too nervous to do anything. She had made a promise. Her father had bought them all promise rings when they were teenagers. They promised to wait for marriage even though all around them girls were giving it up in their boyfriend's bedrooms and classrooms all over the high school. She didn't want to give herself any credit. She didn't exactly have guys fighting to talk to her.

It was hard to remain chaste when she was with Amari. He evoked the most incredible sensations, feelings of love and need that almost swept her away and made her forget the promise she made to God and herself.

She was standing in the middle of the kitchen when she heard the doorbell. She looked at the clock. It was almost 10 p.m. and Amari had used his pass to get in.

"Hey you," Amari said when she opened the door and threw herself into his arms.

"Hey," she said, her arms tight around him, her breath catching in her throat at the feel of him underneath the coat and sweater. Reluctantly she let him go and brought him further into the room.

"This place looks great," Amari said, only now noticing the candles.

"You like? Merry Christmas," she said.

"Merry Christmas to you," Amari said and gave her a long, sensual kiss. With him looking this good and tasting this great it was not going to be easy to resist him. The need to be that close to him made her weak. Amari thankfully actually let her go and stepped away from her.

"I have something for your tree," he said and pulled a big bag full of wrapped gifts from the hallway then closed the door.

"Wow. When did you have time to go shopping?" she asked, her smile filled with amazement.

"In between things." He walked over to the tree and took out about ten boxes and put them under the tree. He stopped and looked at her standing close by, watching him. She wore a cream wrap dress that showed her beautiful body to perfection. Her eyes drew him in with their warmth, kindness and sweetness.

"You had a great game," she said. "I watched with everybody."

"I wanted you to come," Amari said, taking her hand.

"You know my mother would never let me live if I missed our Christmas. Even Esther and Angelo have to come every Christmas, as if he has no family."

"It's like that, huh?" He brought her into his arms again and she sighed, forgetting what they were talking about as his mouth claimed hers.

"Want to open your presents?" he said in her ear, breathing against her neck.

"Mmmh," she mumbled. Her brain had turned to mush.

"Let's open your presents," he said again. Raven had to blink rapidly so she could focus.

"That's a lot of presents. Aren't you tired? You just flew in."

"I am, but I want to see if you like what I got you," Amari insisted.

"Are you opening yours?" Raven walked to the tree.

"You first. Start with the biggest and work your way down," Amari said.

"Okay." Raven smiled at him suspiciously. "You didn't get me something crazy, did you?"

"No. I wouldn't do that to you." Amari sat back, took off his coat and placed it on the armrest. Sitting on the couch, he watched her bend towards the Christmas tree.

She took the big box wrapped in gold and tied with green ribbon and walked back to sit next him.

"Is it fragile?" she asked, sitting the box on her lap. It felt very light like it contained clouds.

"Open it," Amari said his deep voice caressing her senses.

She took her time taking off the wrapper while Amari looked on. When the wrapping was off, Raven opened the lid to the box. Her smile froze when she looked inside. There was a small box with an unmistakable shape. Her heart started racing as she picked it up. Could it be? Was it? She held it in her trembling hands, her eyes filling with tears. She glanced at him and the emotion on his face was too much to take so she looked at the box in her hands.

"Open it," Amari whispered. Slowly biting her bottom lip, she did. The sight of the beautiful diamond ring had her mouth wide open.

"Raven," Amari said. She looked at him, about to hyperventilate. This had to be a dream. Amari got off the chair and she watched him in slow motion.

"I love you, Raven. I couldn't wait another minute to ask this. Will you marry me?"

She was sobbing now as she muttered, "Oh, my God."

"Ray?"

"Oh, Amari, yes. I love you!" she cried as he took the ring from the box for her. He took her shaking hands and, with tears in his eyes, placed the ring on her finger. Gently he kissed the hand where her ring was and she knew she would never forget that moment. Like a dream he kissed her and she knew this kiss was different. Though it was soft it held a promise of more powerful pleasures. Pleasures her body suddenly yearned for. She deepened the kiss and her left hand reached of its own accord to his chest and ran her fingers up to his neck, loving the feel of his skin.

"Hey, hey. I am not made of steel," Amari said huskily, taking hold of her hand. "I want you."

"Me, too," Raven said, their foreheads touching.

"Are you sure?" She nodded and kissed him again. Amari didn't need any more encouragement as his hands traveled to her neck and brought her closer to him. He lifted her easily and sat her on his lap without letting go of her mouth. The shrill sound of the phone broke them apart.

"Who's calling?" Amari asked. Raven focused as the ringing continued.

"I'll listen to the voicemail," Raven said huskily.

"Raven! Raven! Pick up! It's Mom," the voice said.

The urgency in Clare's voice made Raven jump out of the seat and rush to the phone.

"Hello, what's wrong?"

"Oh, it's Tahlia. She was in an accident. She's been taken to the Henry Ford."

"Oh, my God, is she okay?" Raven said, feeling faint. Amari ran to her and put an arm around her.

"We're on our way there. Come as quickly as you can." Raven put the phone down and turned to Amari.

"It's my sister," she sobbed. "She-she was in a car accident."

CHAPTER 12

It was only after the doctors had told Raven's family that Tahlia would be all right that they calmed down enough to notice the ring on her left finger. Tahlia's broken leg and cuts and bruises didn't take away her excitement.

"I'm gonna be a bridesmaid, right?" Tahlia said from her hospital bed. Raven looked at Amari. They hadn't even talked about the date or the kind of wedding they would have.

"Of course," Raven said, taking Tahlia's hand where it didn't hurt. "Just hurry up and get well soon, okay?"

"Okay. Mom, did you see her ring?" Tahlia asked, looking at Clare, who stood close to her head.

"Yes. It's beautiful," Clare said, smiling in Raven's direction. "Now, the doctor said we should leave you to rest. We'll be back to see you in the morning."

"All right," Tahlia said sleepily. Clare kissed her youngest child on the forehead and Raven kissed her cheek. Philip walked up to her and rubbed her cheek.

"You gave us a scare, little one. Thank God you're all right," Philip said. They all wished her a good night and left the hospital room.

"I don't want to leave her alone," Clare said as they stood in the hallway. The hospital was quiet and they saw one nurse walk into one of the private rooms.

Philip put his arm around his wife and Raven watched them. Their love always shone the most in times of crises. Though Clare tended to be the louder one Philip was her rock. He calmed her when there was a storm, and Raven hoped Amari would be that for her. His arm on her shoulder gave comfort.

"God is with her just as he was with her when the accident happened," Philip said. Raven shivered when she heard how close Tahlia's car came to falling off the overpass. Tahlia had crashed when she thought she missed an exit and hit a wall.

"It's unfortunate that your engagement coincided with this accident, but we're happy for both of you. Congratulations," Philip said.

"Yes," Clare whispered, smiling tiredly. "It's almost midnight, Raven. Do you want to come home with us?" Raven looked at Amari. She needed to be with him, but she also wanted to be with her mother. Amari would be leaving again for another game on the road.

"I'll come tomorrow," she decided quickly. She needed to talk to Amari about something important and she couldn't wait until tomorrow. Clare looked at Amari with understanding, though it didn't make her happy. Esther had left to visit Angelo's family and Philip Junior had a speaking engagement in Texas, so Raven was the only other child available.

"Good night then," Clare said and hugged both of them. Raven and Amari watched her parents walk towards the elevator and get in.

"I'm glad you didn't go," Amari said, bringing her close to him. She put her arms around him.

"You'll take me to the city?"

"Wish I could take you to my home," Amari said as they walked towards the elevator. Raven smiled. As soon as Amari started getting the car out of the garage she turned to him.

"I hope you didn't think I was being presumptuous when I said Tahlia could be my bridesmaid. I mean, I don't even know when and what kind of wedding you want," Raven said.

"Hey. That doesn't bother me. I would marry you tomorrow," Amari said.

"Are you serious?"

"Yes. I don't enjoy leaving you alone and going to my lonely bachelor pad."

"You can hardly call that huge house a bachelor pad," Raven pointed out, leaning back.

"I need you with me. Soon." He reached over and grabbed her hand.

"I feel the same. I don't really want a big wedding," Raven said.

"Oh, good, neither do I!" Amari laughed. "I would like us to go away somewhere exotic and get married. Just us two, or maybe our close family and friends."

"A destination wedding? Like Mombasa?"

"Somewhere different. Just you and me."

"Well, and my whole clan. Can you imagine my family agreeing to that?"

"Do they have such a hold over you?"

"No. I do what I want, but in some things, like which church I go to, and Sunday dinners and Christmases, those I don't have much choice."

"Interesting," Amari said.

They drove in silence, Raven sitting as close to him as her seat belt would allow her. When they walked upstairs Raven still had something else to discuss with him as soon as they walked into her living room.

"About what nearly happened before the call . . . ," Raven started. Amari looked at her embarrassed face, his lip lifted in a teasing smile.

"That bad?"

"No! I love it! Too much." She looked down as he took her hands into his, rubbing her new ring.

"You love it?"

Raven still couldn't look at him as she spoke. "I nearly got carried away, and I almost feel God was speaking to me when that phone rang."

"You don't think it matters that we are engaged?"

"I always wanted to wait until my wedding night. I just never thought it would be so hard," she said, looking into his face. His smile made him even more appealing. "And you've been engaged before."

"Uh-oh. That truth is hard to swallow."

"I didn't mean to . . . ," Raven tried to explain.

"No. It's fine."

"I know you're tired. Do you want the couch, or are you going home?"

"I'll stay here tonight, but when we are married you are going to . . ."

"Do it anytime you want?" Raven laughed moving away from him.

"I'll have that in writing," Amari said, plunking himself on the couch.

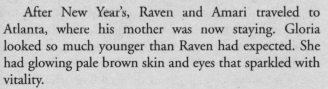

Raven and Amari's best-laid plans for a small, intimate location wedding went out the window before they could even say the word wedding. Clare took the wedding project as if she was running one of her many church fundraisers, with tenacity.

"You have to get married in your father's church. It's tradition," Clare insisted.

Raven wondered when it had become tradition. Only Esther and Angelo were married there. Clare wasn't even married at Calvary Worship.

With Amari traveling so much the wedding plans were left to her. The news even reached the newspapers and reminded Raven again about her fiancé's fame.

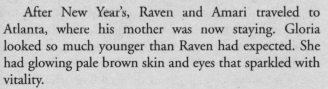

After New Year's, Raven and Amari traveled to Atlanta, where his mother was now staying. Gloria looked so much younger than Raven had expected. She had glowing pale brown skin and eyes that sparkled with vitality.

"Amari has been keeping you a secret," Gloria Thomas said the moment Raven walked into her lovely waterfront home. Amari bought it for her during his third season in the NBA. The house was beautifully lighted and boasted classic furniture and incredible paintings of African Americans in evening attire. The bright colors and warm furniture matched her personality.

"Ma, I haven't kept her a secret. We were just thinking of the best time to visit," Amari said.

"Well, it's good to finally meet you. Amari, you'll sleep in the bedroom downstairs and Raven can take the one near mine," Gloria commanded like an army general. There was no argument there. Amari picked up their luggage obediently. Raven looked at mother and son, noting the resemblance in the striking eyes. Gloria was a shade darker than Amari. She was also several inches shorter than Amari. "He told me about your arrangement. I'll keep him far away from you," Gloria said, and Raven bit her lip with embarrassment.

"It's nice to finally meet you," Raven said instead as they were left alone in the beautiful white hallway.

"Oh, so glad to meet you. I'll have to show you some pictures of Amari that will make you laugh. Come along, let me show you around this house Amari spoilt me with. He's a good child, that one."

The first meeting was great, and from her strong personality Raven knew that Clare and Gloria were probably going to fight about the wedding details. As they talked over dinner, Raven realized Gloria wasn't happy about the plans.

"I would've loved to throw the wedding here. Detroit is not the most beautiful city in the country," Gloria said. "I lived there for many years."

"It's all right, Ma. There's more to Detroit than what the media portrays."

"I don't know."

After dinner Gloria brought out the photo albums. There was a special gold one that showed all of Amari's special moments. His first day in school, his high school and college graduations. Raven froze when she saw the next picture. It was Amari's engagement party.

"Oh," she said.

"That was the woman who almost became my daughter," Gloria said, shaking her head. Raven wondered whether she heard a wistful sigh or not as she kept her eyes glued on the picture on Gloria's lap. "It didn't work out."

"Mom, why are you showing her those pictures anyway? Why do you still have a picture of Monique?"

"I made this album of all the main events in your life. Just because things didn't work out doesn't mean it never happened. You graduated in business but you're playing basketball."

"I have businesses," Amari said. "That's besides the point anyway. I'm talking about a picture and . . ."

"It's okay, Amari. It's no big deal," Raven broke in though her heart was still beating fast. Monique was so beautiful. Raven felt her insecurities rise again. How could Amari go from that gorgeous, voluptuous beauty to her? Monique had light green eyes, gorgeous long, curly hair and breasts that were double her size. The perfect ten. And this woman had lived with Amari.

Raven sat on her bed later that night still seeing Monique in her mind. The other woman who had been with Amari for almost three years. She heard a knock on her door.

"Come in." It was Amari dressed in pajama bottoms and a T-shirt. He leaned against the door looking at her.

"Sorry about my mom and her photographs. She's got about a million pictures of me," he said.

"I liked looking at them," she said, not quite meeting his eyes, her hands smoothing out the down comforter on her bed.

"Hey, I know the pictures of my past bothered you," Amari said.

"How do you know?"

"I could tell. It was over way before I met you," Amari said.

"I know. It's just hard to think you were that close to somebody else," Raven said.

"It wasn't that deep."

Raven shrugged, looking at him. She was torn between wanting to learn more about the ravishing Monique and pretending she never existed. "She's very pretty."

"You are beautiful, both inside and out," Amari said. She shook her head, looking down. Amari lifted her chin so their eyes locked. She could read his eyes and look deep into his soul.

"I can't wait to marry you."

"Me, too." He pulled her off the bed and brought her against him, claming her mouth in a kiss. There was a knock at the door. Amari broke the kiss but kept his hold on her.

"Raven, can I come in?"

"Yes, Ma," Amari said, laughing. Gloria came in holding fresh towels.

"What are you doing here?" Gloria asked, feigning surprise.

"Can't stay away from my fiancé." Amari grinned, his arm still around her. Raven loved to hear him call her that.

"Well, thought you might need more towels." Gloria put the beautiful engraved towels on the bed.

"Thank you," Raven said. Gloria looked at Amari pointedly.

"Okay. I better go then, Raven." He kissed her and left the room. When they were alone Gloria surprised her with her next words.

"I think you are good for my son. He needs a woman of character. I know I just met you, but you have a lot of depth and integrity. I can tell that about a person in a few seconds."

"Thank you," Raven responded, not sure what else to say.

"You will make him happy won't you?"

"I intend to." Raven looked warily at Gloria. Did she mean what she said? Was Monique really a bad person? Was *she* good enough for Amari? Because he was just so perfect for her. Oh, God, he was so thoughtful, so sweet, but confident and sincere.

Later that night Raven lay in the strange but beautiful bedroom and had dreams of women like Monique taking Amari away.

CHAPTER 13

A few weeks after her visit with Amari's mother, Raven wanted to be anywhere but sitting in her car with Candice watching the hospital entrance. She still wondered why she had agreed to this fiasco when she would rather be at home looking at wedding magazines and dreaming of a perfect wedding to Amari. Charles was supposed to come out at 6 p.m. but it was already 6:45 p.m. and there was still no sign of the man. The whole evening had started with a call from Candice soon after she got home from work.

"Raven, you've got to come quick," Candice had said earlier that day.

"Come where? What are you talking about?"

"Charles called again to say he would be home late because of a meeting. I think he's lying. This time I'm going to catch him with his pants down."

"What do you want to do?"

Candice's voice was filled with urgency and determination. "I need you to follow him in your car."

"Why my car?"

"He doesn't know your new car, and mine would give us away. Come on, Raven, hurry up. I'm taking the baby to my mother's and then we can meet at my place."

"I don't know, Candice . . ."

"Raven, you're the only one I can count on. I need you, please hurry," Candice begged before she hung up. Raven had felt powerless to refuse. So here she was sitting in a parking lot on a rather cold spring day. She looked out the window as Candice looked at her cell phone to see if Charles had called her.

"He's rather late coming out," Raven commented.

"He might have had an emergency or maybe he's doing paperwork. Give him a few more minutes, Raven. Don't back out on me."

"I wasn't," Raven reluctantly reassured her friend, looking at the hospital entrance as many people walked in and out of the sliding doors. None of them were their "suspect." This moment reminded her of the many times Candice demanded something outrageous from her when they were little kids. And now ten years later they were still at it, only this time the stakes were higher and Raven liked it even less.

"I just want to see if my suspicions are true. I'm sure if you were in my shoes you would do the same."

Raven knew why she was saying the next thing she did but she did it anyway. Raven had always accepted her role in life as Candice's shadow, and she said what she did to reassure Candice that she was the winner and Raven the spectator to Candice's exciting perfect life.

"I saw a picture of Amari's fiancé. Well, ex."

"What's she like?" Candice took her eyes off the entrance for a second and glanced at Raven.

"Sultry. Yeah, that's what comes to mind. Someone I would expect him to be with."

"But he has you," Candice said, looking away. Raven didn't like the way Candice said that, hoping for some compliment, but shrugged it off.

"I still wonder why they broke up," Raven said, then jumped when Candice slapped her arm.

"Look. There he is talking on his cell phone. Do you think he's talking to her?" Raven watched Charles as he walked out of the hospital in khaki pants and a button-down blue shirt. He had put on weight since the wedding, but had turned most of it into muscle. He looked confident in his appeal and success in life.

"Let's follow him. Start the car," Candice breathed urgently, as if Charles could hear them.

"We can't follow him. He came out alone. You said you wanted to see if he was seeing someone at the hospital."

"Just follow. Go!" Raven started the engine and followed Charles's dark blue sedan.

"Not that close!" Candice cried, grabbing the steering wheel with a vice-like grip. Raven pushed the brakes hard with panic and they both lunged forward.

"You're making me nervous," Raven said. "Just calm down."

"Follow him now. We might lose him." Raven realized there was no reasoning with Candice. Her mind seemed to have left her.

They followed Charles's car for about thirty minutes, twenty of which were on the highway towards Troy. Charles exited the highway and immediately turned into a hotel parking lot. Raven kept back as he parked.

"Oh, no," Candice moaned. "He really is cheating."

"He might have a meeting," Raven said, watching Charles put on a light jacket over his shirt and walk towards the hotel entrance after a furtive glance around.

"Let's go," Candice said, picking up her purse from the floor of the car. Her pretty eyes looked at Raven with urgency. She brushed her beautiful dark hair back with her hands, trying to calm herself.

"No, Candice. I can't come in there. I think I've done too much already. This was a crazy idea."

"Don't chicken out on me now! Let's go. I need to know what's going on," Candice practically shouted.

"Get a private investigator or something. Just don't do this on your own."

"Sitting here is wasting precious time. Now I won't even know where he is, damn it!" Candice got out of the car and slammed the door. Raven remained in her seat, wondering who Candice was. She had clearly lost her mind. She got out of her car and ran after Candice, thinking of how she would explain this mess to Amari.

Inside the hotel lobby they couldn't find Charles. They checked every conference room and finally Raven stopped Candice when she wanted to walk on every floor.

"This is almost ten floors and I have to go. I'm picking up Tahlia. She can't drive since her accident and Amari is coming tonight," Raven said out of breath.

"It's all about you and Amari, isn't it? Never mind that my husband could be somewhere in this huge place doing some unimaginable things to someone and you just think of yourself!" Candice said as tears fell from her eyes.

Raven took a deep breath to quell the anger threatening to engulf her. "I'm thinking of my sister. I must go. You can come with me, or I will have to leave you here," Raven said, looking at her watch. It was already dark outside and she had had a very difficult day at work, and now this CSI moment had just taken its toll.

"Raven, please just wait with me. I can't leave without knowing. I'll never ask for anything else again. Just wait a few minutes. He doesn't take that long anyway."

Raven shook her head at Candice's comment and sat on the overstuffed sofa next to her. They sat in silence in the lobby, Raven staring into space and Candice's eyes glued on the elevators.

"What are you gonna do when you see him?" Raven asked as a way to pass the time.

"I'll think of something. Something he ain't gonna like, that's for sure. What would you do if it was Amari?"

The two women looked at each other. Raven didn't want to answer. She wasn't even married yet and Candice was putting those horrible thoughts in her head. No! Amari would never do that, but Candice's voice continued, cutting through Raven's denial.

"They all do, and Amari, well, women line up for men like him. Fine muscled brother with those eyes and all that dough."

Raven stood up quickly, "I need to go call Tahlia and . . . Amari."

She walked outside trying to still her thumping heart. Candice was just being her usual insensitive self talking about Amari that way. What did she know about men of

God, anyway? Charles never went to church and he never read the Bible according to Candice, so that's why he was acting up. Amari loved God more than he loved anything and he would not disrespect her. She was so sure of it that she decided to laugh at Candice's words and banish them from her heart. She dialed Tahlia's number.

"Hey, sis, I'm sorry I'm running late," Raven began.

"Where are you, anyway?" Tahlia asked, impatience in her voice. She had every right to be mad. Raven looked back at the hotel and froze. Charles was coming out and Candice was already pouncing on him.

"I gotta go," Raven spoke into the phone, walking towards the hotel.

"What's going on, Ray?"

"I'll call you back, T."

Raven closed her phone and ran in just as Candice hit Charles with her purse.

"Where were you? Who was it?" Candice cursed as Charles jumped back from the blows.

"Candice, it's not what you think."

"Almost an hour in the hotel. Do you think I'm stupid. Huh?"

The elevator doors opened and a blonde woman stepped out, but when she saw the scene she jumped back in. Candice ran after her and caught the door before it closed. The hotel concierge was making a call and Charles yelled to Candice to stop, but she was already in the elevator.

"Did you bring her?" Charles challenged, his eyes looking so angry. Raven felt nervous as if he wanted to strike her. She tried not to show her fear. This wasn't her issue. If only she had just left Candice alone. Raven just shook her head and ran to the elevator, but it closed before she could stop it.

"Sir, is everything all right?" the man at the front desk asked.

"It's cool." Charles waved him off even though his voice sounded anything but cool. He looked at Raven again, but Raven would not look at him as she punched the elevator buttons.

Charles turned Raven around to face him and demanded. "What are you doing here?"

She shrugged off his arm and folded her arms across her chest. "Just talk to your wife. Leave me out of this."

"Leave you out? I see you and her sitting waiting for me. What the hell am I supposed to think? Were you spying on me?"

Raven moved away from him, shouting, "Just watch your tone, Charles. You were the one who was doing something wrong, not me!"

"But . . ." Charles was about to rant when the bell rang to signal the arrival of the elevator.

The gold elevator doors opened and Candice got off, seemingly cooler than before, but the fire in her eyes couldn't be mistaken. She was ready to kill somebody, and her disheveled clothes made Raven wonder. Maybe the woman who had been on the elevator was already dead.

Charles turned to his wife. "Candy . . ."

"Save your words, cheater. Your woman told me everything," she spat out, looking him up and down like he was bird droppings on her car.

"What did you do to her?"

"I should've done something, but she's up there cowering like the whore that she is. Raven, let's go."

Candice walked past Charles. Charles stood for a minute, not sure what to do. Run after his wife or go and check on his mistress. He chose wisely as he came after Candice.

"Honey, I can explain. It was a mistake."

Candice ignored him and the few hotel workers who had become their audience and stepped out of the double doors. Raven ran by her and pressed the key to open her car. Charles was still explaining but Candice ignored him completely, her head held high. She got into Raven's car and shut the door on Charles's words.

"Just drive," Candice ordered, sitting back in the seats and folding her arms in front of her chest like a protective shield. Raven reversed and drove around Charles, who kept begging for forgiveness and knocking on the window. Raven watched Charles through her rearview mirror and then turned to Candice. Tears rolled down her cheeks and after a few yards she broke down into heart-wrenching sobs.

Amari put the phone down after talking to his agent. He was always willing to try new things as long as they didn't compromise his beliefs. Don't wanna do anything to upset The Main Man Upstairs. He recalled the work he did for one of the leading banks in Europe, a commercial for a bank and one for a chain of new hotels just to add to the few endorsements he had received. He enjoyed acting and found it came easily since high school. Another chance he had to practice his acting chops was when he had taken part in a few music videos for two gospel artists. That was fun!

His agent asked him if he was willing to try a small part in a movie. Dan Richman and Amari had been working together since he signed with Detroit. Dan was well connected and talked about a new movie starring one of the most successful black actresses, Lexie Hart. Amari had enjoyed a few of Lexie's movies, but always thought her personal life was like a trash novel. She had done such crazy things he wasn't sure which was fact and which was fiction.

His cell phone rang and he picked up after checking the ID. It was his mother.

"Hey, Ma," he said leaning back on his hotel bed.

"Amari. Good game yesterday," Gloria said.

"We lost and my shot was off," Amari complained.

"Your team is still leading the league. How's Raven?"

"She's cool. Spoke to her earlier. And you?"

Gloria sighed and Amari knew that there was a storm brewing. "Fine. Just thinking about that wedding of yours."

"The Davies have taken over. I think Raven decided to let her mom run the show. Clare's in charge."

"She has no right to do that. What kind of woman is she? I know that traditionally the bride's family plans and pays for the wedding, but I would have liked to have a small part. You are my only son."

"I know, Ma. Don't worry. In a way, I am glad I don't have to do much."

"Well, I wish I was doing more than throwing you the engagement party."

"We didn't want the engagement party, too. But we are going along with you. I think you'll find you have a lot in common with Pastor Clare Davies."

"I'm not pushy!"

"But you always get your way." Amari laughed as his mother grumbled in his ear.

"Soon I'll get to meet your future family. So you are sure this time it's for real?"

"Yes, Ma. Raven's the one."

"She's very different from most of your other girl-friends."

"I wasn't in love with most of the other girlfriends. I'm crazy about Raven and I can't wait to marry her."

"Fine. Fine. I don't want to bring up the past, but Monique's mother called me the other day. She still misses you and says Monique misses you."

"We broke up a long time ago, and that's better left in the past."

"I had to tell them about you and Raven," Gloria insisted.

"Good. I'm glad Monique now knows I've definitely moved on."

"What really happened between you two?"

"She gave me an ultimatum. Either I set the date or she walks. I never set the date."

"Why?"

"Ma, I've told you before. We were from two different worlds. It wasn't an easy decision, but let's focus on my life now, and Ray." Amari heard his mother sigh again. Gloria was still not convinced there wasn't some other reason why he broke up with Monique.

To say Monique was beautiful was an understatement. Everybody who saw them together thought Monique and him made the perfect couple. Men and women would turn their heads to look at his beautiful girlfriend. But there was something missing. He had been living with her when he rededicated his life to God. He had just been a Christian in name only without the power or real change in his lifestyle, his ma would always say to him.

Monique was like a ball and chain preventing him from living a victorious life. He met her when he was out with some friends in the music industry in Atlanta. When she walked in glancing around confidently, hair swinging from shoulder to shoulder, he thought she was the kind of girl that frequented the clubs and would get in without a problem. Even though every guy in the club wanted her she had walked up to him boldly and asked him to dance. And the kind of dancing Monique did was a simulation of much more than that, except they still had their clothes on. Of course he was attracted to her but even though she had been uninhibited on the dance floor when he took her home she hadn't wanted to sleep with him. She told him that she would want to see him again. And so they had begun dating. She was a good Catholic girl, she had told him.

"I'm looking for a relationship, Amari. I'm not into casual relationships." That had been the kind of thing he wanted to hear. So the more he got to know her the more he thought she aligned with his principles, at least the principles he had in theory.

"So if you are not into casual relationships what were you doing at the club dressed like you are that kind of girl?" Amari had asked her a year into their relationship when they had taken a trip to the Bahamas. She had planned the trip and wanted to celebrate getting to shoot a commercial. She was a student at the time studying theatre and music. Monique, like most beautiful girls, had dreams of making it in the movies, and commercials were the stepping stone she needed.

"I guess I've studied men. You wouldn't have noticed me so quickly if I had been wearing my thick glasses and a sack, would you?"

"You don't even need to wear that tight white dress to be noticed. You always look great."

"There are many beautiful girls, Amari. I just had to make myself stand out. But I don't want to be used by men for one night stands. I've been there, and I was tired of having relationships go nowhere. So I still go out to meet people, but with you I just knew you were different. I had read your website and you talked about your belief in God. I knew you were not just into playing around."

Amari took this in, surprised. She had done research on him. She had hunted for him like a predator, and she had gotten him. He glanced at her lying on the chaise lounge, her caramel skin glistening from the oil she had applied so her skin could darken. Her bikini left little to the imagination and she looked good, though at times he wished he could cover her up.

So that was the first problem. She liked to show off her curvy body, displaying for anybody who wished to see how sensual her body was. She wore revealing clothes. As much as he felt proud being with her, he also didn't think she could be the mother of his children. They fought about how she would dress when he took her to his mother. She had complied to dress conservatively but with bitterness.

Another problem surfaced. When they met he was not making that much money. He was doing all right, but he wasn't like the other guys with million-dollar endorsements, so her spending was putting a dent in his account. She wanted to wear designer, Dolce and Gabbana, Louis Vuitton, Coach. There were names of every European designer in their closet. That was the other thing, she had gradually moved herself into his condo. Before he knew it, she was living with him, cooking for him and doing everything a wife does. And the spending continued. Renovating the condo, parties, until they were always fighting about money. She wasn't spending her money. She was spending his. Then she wanted to get married. Her mother wasn't happy with the living arrangement, nor was his mother. If he were honest, he wasn't either.

"Amari. It's either you marry me or I walk," Monique had threatened. In the end she had left him to date a rich Atlanta businessman, but that didn't last either.

When he met Raven she was right in every way. She was the missing link, someone who truly shared his values. With her he felt at peace with God. With Monique he had never been at peace, living year after year with her while deep down inside he was tormented. Gloria thought that the main reason he broke up with Monique was because of her ultimatum. The ultimatum had come after he found something shocking in her underwear drawer. A stack of fertility pills. Monique had been trying to get pregnant while he thought she was on the pill. That had been scary, and he really felt like he didn't know her at all.

He was looking forward to a life with Raven, but he had to get through the engagement party his mother was planning for them. She complained about the Davies family taking over his life. Now he focused on his conversation with his mother as she continued her tirade against the Davies clan.

"We are all set then. The party will be at my place," Gloria concluded. "I still wish I could do something at the wedding. You are my only son and those Davies people seem to be taking you over."

"They are nice people and I'll always be your son. Love you, Mom. Gotta go."

"Fine. I'll only feel better after I've met them all."

Amari wasn't so sure about that.

CHAPTER 14

Raven called Candice a day after the debacle at the hotel and left a message. She worried about Candice and Charles and wondered if they would be able fix the huge problem caused by his cheating and getting caught in such a humiliating way. When she explained the situation to Amari on their way to her place after renting some movies, she wasn't sure if she liked his attitude as they discussed it.

"They'll fix it, babe. Some men make mistakes," Amari said, putting in the DVD. The first movie was his choice and the second one was her choice. He liked guns and buildings being blown up and she liked sappy, heartfelt movies. But the good thing was that they both watched each other's choices and still had fun.

"I know. I think Candice is a good wife to him. Why would he do that?"

Amari walked back to her saying, "How do you know how good she is?"

"Even if she's not that 'good' that's no excuse!"

"Hey, Ray, why are you getting so hot and bothered about it? It's not your fault."

Raven shook her head, trying to calm her breathing. "You seem to be defending him. Would you cheat on me if you thought I wasn't a good wife?"

Amari sat next to her and pulled her into his arms planting kisses all over her face. Raven didn't want to, but she couldn't help giggling. "I don't believe in cheating. I am a one-woman man, and when I stand in front of God and say, 'Till death,' baby, I'll mean it. Okay?"

Raven nodded. When he held her so close she couldn't really do that much thinking, and she quickly forgot their discussion.

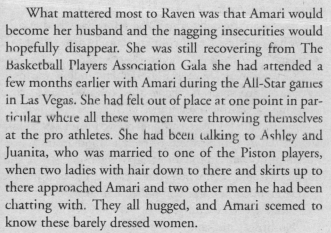

What mattered most to Raven was that Amari would become her husband and the nagging insecurities would hopefully disappear. She was still recovering from The Basketball Players Association Gala she had attended a few months earlier with Amari during the All-Star games in Las Vegas. She had felt out of place at one point in particular where all these women were throwing themselves at the pro athletes. She had been talking to Ashley and Juanita, who was married to one of the Piston players, when two ladies with hair down to there and skirts up to there approached Amari and two other men he had been chatting with. They all hugged, and Amari seemed to know these barely dressed women.

"Better go get your man," Juanita whispered to Raven, one big eye trained on Amari. Raven looked in that direction and gave a smile which they all could see was as fake as those women's hair.

"No. What for?"

"Can't you see the way that one in yellow is touching your man with her multi-colored talons? Are you just going to stand here and watch it?"

Raven felt stupid, out of her depth, and not even sure she belonged at the event with all the glamorous people not just from the sporting world but musicians and actors as well.

"Oh, just come on." Juanita practically dragged her to where Amari stood and thrust her in next to Amari.

"Oh, baby, hi," Amari said and put his arms around her. The woman in yellow stared at her like she was some scum off the street.

"And who the hell is this?" the yellow lady had asked.

"That's his fiancée," Juanita practically growled at the woman.

"Can't a man have some friends?" Yellow purred. Raven couldn't stand it. She writhed out of Amari's arms after quickly saying "excuse me."

She fought her way through crowds until she stood outside where more crowds of people stood around. She was about to walk in the direction of the hotel, where she hoped to find a taxi, when Amari caught up with her.

He grabbed her arm and pulled her close.

"Honey, what's wrong?"

"Nothing," she said.

"That woman was rude, but you do know who she is, right?" Raven shook her head. She did seem familiar. "Sasha. She's just released a new album. I only know coz she told me." Amari paused, looking into her eyes. "I hate to bring you to these things, but it's part of my job.

My agent and sponsors want me out at these things, and the whole team is there, too."

"I know," Raven agreed, looking down. "It just seems so cut-throat. Everybody seems to be competing for attention, for VIP status."

"It's not just the women, you know. The guys are all showing off their cars, their bling," he said. She looked at his casual pants, white shirt and long jacket. He looked so amazing but he didn't wear jewelry. She liked that about him. It seemed that the women revealed as much skin as possible and the men as much ice as possible. It was too much for her.

"Do you want to go, or stay? We can stay together every minute. I would like that. Let everybody know you are my woman."

She had agreed. She wondered if he was really that proud to have her by his side. There were so many, so many beautiful and famous women.

Back in the present Raven shook off those feelings like she would dust off her shoes before entering her mother's house. Amari loved her, and he had proved it time and time again. She had to remind herself every time she woke up and looked at the ring on her finger.

❧

Amari stayed with her until almost midnight and drove home. She didn't get to check her messages until the next morning, and there was one from Candice.

133

Raven called her as she made her way home from the Farmer's Market.

"Hi there," Raven said, watching the traffic on the highway.

"Where are you?"

"On my way home," Raven replied, surprised by Candice's tone. Had something else happened with her and Charles?

"I'll meet you there," Candice said.

Raven drove home, still worried about what could have happened with Charles. Was she leaving him? Had he done something to hurt her?

Raven had just put the kettle on for some green tea when she heard the buzzer at the gate. She let Candice in and then poured them tea. She took a sip as she looked around her place. There was a picture of her and Amari sitting on one of the side tables, and she had finally put up some of her African art. Amari liked to bring stuff when he was on the road, and she had framed one picture he had found in New Orleans. It was a painting of a young girl and boy kneeling and praying in a field of purple flowers. Amari had said that it reminded her of the two of them, when they were young and praying that they would find each other. It always made her smile.

When he said things like that she felt so sure of his love, and when he was close she could see it in his eyes and she wanted to ask, "God. What have I done to deserve the love of this man. This man that you created for me? He's beyond my wildest dreams!"

The knock on the door signaled Candice's arrival and Raven put her mug down and walked to the door after looking through the peephole just to make sure.

"Hi, Candice," Raven said, then closed the door after Candice strode in arms folded over her chest. The anger in her eyes was unmistakable.

"I just made you some tea." Raven walked towards the kitchen and picked up the mug.

"I'm not interested in your tea," Candice said, waving it away. "I came here to talk to you."

"Is everything okay?" Raven asked.

"No! Thanks to you!"

"What?"

"Oh, Raven, you just had to go and blab my business to your mother, didn't you?"

"What are you talking about? What business?"

"About Charles's cheating? The hotel. That bimbo!"

"I-I . . ."

"You make me so mad!" Candice walked around then stopped, raising both her hands. "I could hit you, you know that? Your mother, with her big mouth, was asking my mother about Charles and I? Now everybody is talking about it."

Raven felt her anger growing. As much as she knew her mother had her weaknesses, especially about getting into other people's businesses, she still didn't want Candice disrespecting her. She kept quiet because at this point there was no reasoning with Candice at all.

"I didn't tell her anything," Raven said instead.

"Oh, so how did she know? You must've told someone."

"I had to explain to Tahlia where I was, remember. I should have lied, and I'm sorry."

"It's too late now, Raven. Charles and I had worked it out, but now the whole mess is out with my father and mother involved. All because you couldn't be trusted. You are a terrible friend, and I hope Amari does the same to you and everybody talks about it. You think your life is all perfect, marrying some big basketball star, well, they are worse than doctors. You'll see!"

Candice took a deep breath, her anger seeming to grow with each minute. "You think you are all that planning your stupid big wedding and trying to mess up my life in the process. Well, I'm not going to just watch you do that."

"I said I'm sorry. I wish I could take it back. No need for you to be so cruel," Raven said, tears in her eyes.

"Well, I don't even know what Amari sees in you. If I want to, I can even take him away from you, but I don't need him. I have Charles." Candice walked to the door, then looked Raven up and down like she was dressed in rags.

"Amari must be blind," she spat. She gave a laugh then walked out. Raven collapsed on her couch in tears.

CHAPTER 15

Raven peered out of the limousine on her wedding day. It was just the two of them at last, but still she felt like she was in a dream or watching somebody else's life. If anybody asked her to describe her wedding she would say "magical."

In the end the day had been more than she could imagine. The moment she donned her dress she'd been on the verge of tears. Her mother gave her a classic pearl bracelet as her something borrowed. Before she left her old bedroom a gift in a silk pouch was brought in. When she opened it there was a beautiful white gold necklace with diamonds and the words written on the tiny card brought tears to her eyes.

Hurry and marry me, Amari.

When she walked towards him down the long Calvary Worship aisle tears were already streaming down her face. Amari's eyes shone with tears but he wasn't going to cry in front of all his teammates, his coach and managers. She never noticed anything else as she focused on Amari, her hand on her father's arm. After that her wedding day was a blur of joy, love and ecstasy all rolled into one.

They arrived at Amari's house after midnight. They had decided that their first night would be at his house and then they would be leaving for Mombasa in Kenya for a two-week-long honeymoon. One week was going to be at the exotic island and another week in a game park and then two days visiting different local neighborhoods with friends Raven had made when she visited years before.

The limousine stopped in the driveway and Amari helped Raven out of the car with his right hand. Her gorgeous white dress touched the ground and she lifted as much of it as she could. Amari tipped the driver then they walked hand in hand towards the house, their new home, without saying a word.

"Wait," Amari said, and then opened the door with his key. Before she knew what he was doing he had lifted her up in his arms. Raven squealed with delight as he carried her across the threshold and into the house. Her eyes opened wide when she looked at the beautiful flowers leading up the stairs and the petals strewn on the marble staircase.

"This is amazing," Raven said, looking around from the vantage of Amari's strong arms. Her heart was already racing as he took the steps one at a time with her still in his arms. He kicked his bedroom door, which was slightly open. The whole place was covered with lit candles and there were two vases of flowers. She had seen his bedroom before when he gave her the tour of the house, but that night it looked so different she could have been in another world.

"This is lovely," she said, choked up. "When . . . did you do it?"

"I hired someone," he said, putting her down. "I knew I had very little to do with the wedding, but I'd have a lot to do with this night."

She glanced at him as he walked and closed the door but remained standing in the middle of the room, hands primly in front of her. The nerves and excitement and tiredness all mixed in with Raven's emotions. The bag she had packed for the honeymoon stood in the corner of the bedroom with all the scandalous nightwear that she could buy. Amari stood by the door and looked at her. His gaze seemed to whisper to her, so she moved her gaze from her luggage and looked at him.

"I want to remember you like this for the rest of my life," Amari said as he regarded his bride in her wedding dress standing in the middle of his bedroom, pure, sweet and nervous. If he were an artist he would want to paint her picture. Her beautiful chocolate skin was a sharp contrast with the white dress. In fact, there were many countless moments today that he wanted to paint and preserve forever. But right now he wanted to take off that dress one layer at a time until she stood naked before him and give her a night she would never forget. Tonight he was going to see a new side to her, and he couldn't wait.

Raven saw his expression change and her heart began pounding. This was it. The look he gave her was enough to make the clothes on her body melt of their own accord. He walked towards her and took her hands. Sitting on the bed he brought her next to him.

"You nervous, Mrs. Thomas?" he asked. She shook her head, unable to speak.

"You want me to wait till Kenya?" She shook her head again and he kissed her slowly, gently, until she was the one demanding more, her breaths shorter and sweeter against his mouth. Raven knew from the moment he kissed her that anybody could ask her name and she wouldn't know it, but she somehow gathered the strength to move out of his arms.

"I-I would like to change first," she whispered, smiling shyly.

"That's fine."

"I need your help with the buttons, but after that I'll be fine," she said again and he nodded as he took off the intricate buttons on the back of the dress with shaking fingers. He swallowed hard. Amari wanted to laugh at himself. He felt nervous, too, like it was his first time. It had been a long time and he knew that God had restored his purity with Raven and tonight would be both of their first time.

When the last button was undone she stood up holding the front and walked to her bag that she wheeled into the bathroom without looking back. Her heard water running in from where he stood. Amari got up fast and also made his way into his own bathroom right next to hers.

If she was going to dress up and freshen up, then so would he.

He decided to jump into the shower when he heard her water running and then tried to figure out what to wear. He didn't want to frighten her by being too naked, but he didn't want to be dressed up like he was about to go out to the store, either. Oh, man. He should have done more research on this.

Eventually he settled on wearing a pair of lounge pants and simple T-shirt. He sat on the bed and watched the door to the bathroom, but Raven didn't come out yet. What was she doing, he wondered.

Finally, he heard the door open and out she came. Her hair was now down, in dark swirls, and she wore the most dazzling white nightgown he had ever seen. It was lace from the breast to the knee then some clear-as-day fabric all the way down to her feet. When she took a step towards him her toned leg appeared then disappeared through the slit on the side. Amari felt his throat dry and his mind went blank. He had momentarily lost his ability to speak.

He stood up then walked the rest of the way to meet her. He touched her hair gently looking down the rest of her. She was breathtaking.

"Sorry I took so long," she apologized, her voice breathless.

Amari gave a laugh. "It was so worth it."

She smiled at him, nervousness growing in her like a volcano about to erupt. Esther had told her some details about the first night. She had read some books, but none of them had mentioned the overwhelming feelings rising in her chest. The look he gave her was gentle and reassuring but underneath was that dangerous desire, so evident in his eyes that it took her breath away.

"Mrs. Thomas," he said, then brought her close. Her skin felt just as silken as the gown she wore. He rubbed his hands down her arms and then, as she relaxed, he stepped closer, breathing in her fragrance. When he kissed her he went for her neck and heard her sigh. That prompted him to take her lips in a quickly deepening kiss. He could feel her desire and her heartbeat fast.

He moved back from her. He wanted to take his time enjoying his wife for the first time. The look in her eyes seemed to question why he had stopped. Eager little Mrs. Thomas, Amari thought as he leaned and kissed her shoulder. She seemed to melt under his touch.

Raven felt like she was losing her breath and gaining it at the same time as Amari picked her up and laid her gently on the bed. The way he looked at her made her feel beautiful and shy at the same time. Could he love her that much? With his hands on her body she forgot to think but just feel, as he slowly woke up her body to pleasures she never knew existed, surprising herself as she desperately urged him to come on top of her and into her. It had hurt, that first feeling of him coming into her, but afterwards it was all stars and brilliant lights as she cried from pure, outrageous joy.

CHAPTER 16

Two Years Later

"Tell me more about the movie again," Raven asked coming out of the bathroom dressed in a revealing pink silk nightie. She stood by the light from the bathroom, knowing full well that with the light behind her and the darkness in the bedroom, her body was shown to perfection. She could see that Amari didn't even hear her question. He was staring at her. After two years their desire for each other was still strong.

"Come here," he growled. Raven walked innocently towards him but remained out of reach.

"Don't make me come there," he said. She stood where she was, though every cell in her body desired to be in his arms. She enjoyed once in a while making him chase her. Since their two-week-long honeymoon she had been a quick learner in the secrets of lovemaking and passion. Her desires grew the more she had him. She felt like she could never have enough of him. Maybe it was because he was always on the road, but she wanted him the moment he walked through the door and he seemed to desire her just as much.

There were weekends where they never left the bedroom, satisfying their desires for each other's bodies.

Raven had a new respect and awe of God, now that she was married. He had created sex so that husbands and wives could enjoy each other. And she enjoyed Amari so much, he was fast becoming her favorite pastime.

"You asked for it," he threatened and got out of bed and grabbed her wrist with one hand and pulled her on top of him with the other hand.

"Hey, Thomas," she protested, gazing into his dark, soulful eyes. "Make love to me." Amari was very happy to comply.

Much later, as they lay in each other's arms completely naked and relaxed, she asked again, "Now that you can think straight, tell me about the movie. Did they sign you on to be the star?"

"Not star. I've a fairly big part, but I'm definitely not the star."

"That's exciting," Raven said. "You and Lexie Hart in the same movie."

Amari shifted positions but kept his hold on her body. "She's a very accomplished actress now, if her awards are any indication, and on her way to becoming a producer. My agent says she wanted a certain look for this role and mine seemed to fit. I don't know about the acting part, but we'll see."

"After the screen test, then what?"

"Then I'm off to L.A," Amari said. "Will you come with me?"

"I can visit," Raven said, snuggling closer to him and running her hand across his strong chest. "I was hoping this summer we could go to South Africa on a mission trip."

"I know but this . . . it's what this new talent agency does for you. Raises your profile and endorsement deals. If this movie thing comes together, we may have to postpone the trip to South Africa. Maybe we could do the mission trip next year," he said. "If we are not having babies," Raven agreed, kissing his chest. He pulled her closer and began kissing her again. Raven had been full of wonderful surprises as his wife, and most of them were in his bed.

Their two-year marriage was still in the honeymoon phase and Raven's heart still skipped when he walked into a room. The effect he had on her when she first saw him could still be felt when she was caught off-guard. Even though he evoked such powerful emotions Raven could still talk to him about anything, laughing late into the night as they joked and teased each other.

Raven still had to pinch herself to make sure she wasn't dreaming, but something did bring her back to earth, like learning some of his annoying habits. She didn't like the way he spent so much money on the latest technology. He wanted all gadgets and shoes. They definitely had different spending styles. They also enjoyed different movies and food. And she still could not get used to the social aspect of his job. Public appearances and events still stressed her out. She hated being scrutinized and photographed and talked about, but Amari managed to wipe away her insecurities.

She also had to get used to being talked about, especially at Calvary Worship. For years she had stayed hidden in the shadows of her sisters and her father's church, but now she was easily recognized, especially if she was with Amari. It was still nerve-wracking for her to walk into the church and have so many people turn and look at her. Amari was the one who convinced her to attend church when she would rather stay home and hide.

Another change that came with her marriage was her relationship with Candice. The problems started just before her wedding. Candice didn't want to talk about her wedding, complaining, "All you want to do is talk about your wedding. There are other things in life, you know." And then there was the big outburst she had endured after Charles was caught cheating on her. Candice wouldn't return her calls after that and declined being one of the bridesmaids and eventually didn't even come to the wedding.

However, she was happily married to the man of her dreams now and her best friend's jealousy would not ruin it. Now she had to adjust again. This whole movie business was new to her. With Amari, life would never be boring.

"Lexie!" Renata Stevens cried in shock. "How on earth will you explain to the media why you posed nude for that trashy website?"

"That was a long time ago, and that's your job, Renata," Lexie said, holding her script while sunbathing on the deck of her stunning Malibu beach house. She had the confidence of a woman who knew she had a perfect body and face. She knew that the camera loved her and America and the rest of the world adored her.

Lexie Hart was every bit the movie diva that magazines portrayed, but in the past few years she had been trying to clean up her image with the help of her new publicist, Renata Stevens. It hadn't been an easy job. Lexie's past was as sordid as anyone's imagination could conjure, and cleaning it up needed all the vacuum cleaners and cleaning companies in California. She had done it all and was still doing more. But Renata could make even a former bank robber look like a saint. It was all part of the Hollywood image making and smoke and mirrors that she specialized in.

The reasons people's opinion had changed were walking towards them right now, dressed in matching designer swimsuits.

The six-year-old girls were Lexie's foster kids. It had been a drastic move. After a video of her in compromising positions with a married actor, Lexie had fostered the orphans, Madison and Morgan, to change her image. Their mother had died a year after giving birth and the children had been going from foster home to foster home for four years. Now they were with Lexie Hart. The media was eating up her new role as mom as if she was the first woman to ever foster kids. They were calling her a role model and hailing her as the savior of lost little girls.

The public loved the fact that she had actually taken children that were from the United States and not decided to go overseas to save the children there. And of course black children were the most difficult to place in homes so Lexie and her move to foster the kids had made her a new Mother Theresa of sorts. Renata tried to talk about Lexie and the twins in the magazines as much as possible. She had planned interviews and appearances all to magnify Lexie's good heart.

Now, because of Renata, it was as if Lexie's past had never happened. Under Renata's guidance Lexie had become the most gracious woman to ever walk the face of the earth. Even her wardrobe was more sedate. And Lexie ate up her new image with her caviar and exotic fruits.

"Mommy. Can we go in?" Madison asked, standing close to the pool. Lexie barely glanced at them and nodded.

"Where is their nanny?" Lexie asked, tossing her recently dyed wavy brown hair. "You know I can't watch them and focus on my tan."

"She's coming," Renata said, walking over to adjust the floaters on the girls' elbows. They looked so cute, with their curly hair tied up in a high ponytail. Renata knew that Lexie didn't see their cuteness even though they could pass as her kids. She saw them as a necessary evil, and she would keep them as long as they served their purpose. Renata hoped that Lexie would fall in love with the girls eventually.

"Are you going to swim?" Madison asked again. She was the leader of the two. Morgan was very quiet and just followed her sister around like a shadow.

"Not today," Renata said and added silently, I just got my hair done, no use ruining it with chlorine and goodness knows what other germs are lurking in that water.

"Come, Morgan. Let's go to the stairs. Don't be scared. Remember I be right here," Madison said, sounding like an adult. The tone gave Renata shivers and she was glad to see the nanny, a chubby, cute Mexican lady who spoke very little English, walk towards the girls with their towels and other water toys.

"Madison's so grown," Renata said, sitting back under the huge umbrella. The view from where she sat was breathtaking. She could hear the waves on the private beach and Lexie could certainly afford it.

Lexie had been in the movie business for a long time even though she was only twenty-eight. It was more than her incredible curvaceous body that sold movie tickets. There was something magical that happened on the silver screen when Lexie was on it. Her almond-shaped eyes had the power to hypnotize both young and old alike. She wasn't pretty, or even beautiful. But she was explosive in her sensuality. Everything about her spelled sex, and America was crazy about sex. It had to be in every commercial, every movie, every story and Lexie could sell anything with her body and face. In fact, she had topped the "The most beautiful woman" list several times and the new one, "The Sexiest Body" on *Entertainment News*. The awards and accolades never stopped coming and Lexie still strived for more.

"I don't know how to talk to her. Like a child or an eighteen-year-old or eighty-year-old," Lexie said, putting her script down and chewing on her perfect full lips. Renata looked at the title of the of the script Lexie was reading, *A Lot like Silence*.

"How's the reading?" Renata asked. "Could this be an Oscar nomination?"

"More like BET awards," Lexie said. "I like the story. It's simple enough. Boy meets girl, but girl chooses money over true love and realizes in the end that the boy was the only one who meant anything."

"You know you are the only one who could pull off the life of Catherine Dison."

"Do you think Amari Thomas will test well for screening?" Renata watched Lexie sigh deeply and folded her arms on her full chest.

"He doesn't have to do much. He's in a lot of flash-backs and his looks are perfect for the role. Arresting eyes, mysterious demeanor and chiseled strong body. Of course, it helped his case more because his agent is very good friends with the director and producer. I'm looking forward to meeting him, though."

Renata watched the faraway look in Lexie's fiery eyes.

"He's married, you know." Lexie turned to Renata like she had said something crazy.

"So? Isn't everybody? Besides, I'm not going to do anything. I have worked too hard to change my image to do anything stupid. Renata, give me credit, please," Lexie said.

"I'm just saying." Renata looked at the swimming pool. Somehow she knew she would have her work cut out for her when the movie began. Lexie always had a thing for her costars, and they always seemed to have a thing for her.

CHAPTER 17

Raven watched the end credits of the movie *The Girl In the Mirror* with tears in her eyes. Lexie Hart was a brilliant actress. She had the power to evoke emotion without saying a word. The camera didn't just love Lexie, it adored her.

"She was just as good in *Brown Eyes* last year," Tahlia said, picking up the bowl of popcorn and taking it to the kitchen. Esther stayed on the couch dabbing at her eyes with her fingers. Raven just let her tears roll down her cheeks silently. Tahlia came back and looked at her sisters with astonishment.

"You ladies aren't still crying over that movie, are you? Come on!"

"It's sad, Tahlia, where's your heart?" Esther said.

"It's just a movie," Tahlia told her.

"It's based on a true story," Raven said. "That's what makes it worse. It's crazy to think that twin sisters brought up by different parents both end up with abusive husbands. That's something else."

"I know. I'm sad, too, but you don't see me crying over movies," Tahlia said.

"I think it's because you are a counselor. You've heard it all and now your heart is hard."

"Raven's the one who should be crying. That woman's going to be having some serious scenes with your husband." Esther and Tahlia looked at Raven. Raven raised her eyebrows at them.

"It's just a movie and he's mainly in flashbacks. Besides, Tahlia, you don't even know what this movie's about."

"Lexie doesn't do comedy, I know that for sure. So this movie must be intense and powerful. She stars in mostly dramatic movies and she does them very well," Tahlia said. "So, doesn't it bother you that he gets to meet all these Hollywood women?"

Raven leaned back against her couch. The family room was decorated the way she wanted, it was cozy but chic. That was the room Amari and her liked the most. They usually lay down on the couch reading books or she forced him to do the crossword puzzle with her. On his down time Amari read biographies, and he was reading Nelson Mandela's for the third time.

"He meets a lot of gorgeous women. Women have always chased him, so I'm not going to let that keep me up at night. I think Amari is a lot deeper and stronger than that. Besides, if he cheats, I leave, period."

"Is that what you told him?" Esther asked, staring at Raven.

"No, but I know that I'll never want to share him with somebody else or put up with him seeing somebody else. What about you, Esther?" Raven looked at Esther. Esther took a while to respond like the question was very important to her. Angelo was a very popular man at

Calvary Worship and led the choir that was filled with women, and most of them single.

"I agree with you, though I know breaking up is not always easy. There're so many women who forgive their husbands. God does want us to forgive."

"That's right," Tahlia said.

"I don't know what I would do," Esther confessed, her eyes wide open. "I love Angelo. I don't know if I would just give up on him without a fight."

"Angelo is a great man of God and so is Amari. So we don't have anything to worry about, do we?" Raven said.

"Amen," Esther said, raising her hands up to the sky.

Lexie arrived at the studio early for rehearsals. She wore a white summer dress that made her look like an angel. Her wavy dark hair was pinned up carelessly. The media was there as she walked in. *Black Entertainment Show* wanted to do a sneak peak at the first week of rehearsal for the highly anticipated movie. Her fostering of Morgan and Madison had added to the hype.

"What's your new movie about?" a reporter asked.

"It's a love story with many twists," Lexie threw over her shoulder without breaking her stride. "It's a beautiful story."

"Is Amari Thomas going to be in the movie?" another reporter asked.

"I believe so. We'll see."

When Lexie walked in the meeting room the film crew was already there and so was the director and producer, Mike Stevens.

"How are you, Lexie?" Mike asked. Mike was a giant of a man with a full beard. He always reminded Lexie of a bear. A friendly bear.

"Fine. Trying to adjust to being a mom," she said.

"Oh. The twins. Giving you trouble?"

"No. They are great girls. I will bring them to the set one of these days."

"We would love to meet them. The media kept saying how much those girls look like you. They could pass for your real kids."

"That is wonderful to know. I couldn't love them more if they were mine. I'm truly blessed, Mike." The words slipped from her lips like honey, without hesitation.

"Have you met Amari?" Mike asked.

"No," she said. She could see the back of his head as he talked to another man. Mike called Amari, and he turned. The moment he faced her there seemed to be a flash of silence in the room. She had thought he was attractive on TV, but seeing him in person sent waves of electricity through her body. It had been a long time since a man had made her feel this way. Actually, she couldn't remember ever being this affected this quickly.

"Amari, I would like you to meet Lexie Hart. She will be playing the role of Catherine Dison in *A Lot like Silence*."

"Nice to meet you, Lexie," Amari said, reaching out his hand to shake hers.

"Pleasure to meet you," Lexie said, smiling beguilingly. She wasn't sure which role to play. The innocent lovesick puppy or the seductress. She could pull both of them off very well. She decided to play nonchalance but with a friendly flare. She didn't want him to know the effect meeting him had on her. It was better to surprise him later when there was nowhere to run.

"I've seen a lot of your movies," Amari said calmly.

"Oh. Which was your favorite?"

"*Brown Eyes*."

"I was a young kid then. I hope to tackle more complicated roles than that," Lexie said. "And you? You beat our team in the playoffs."

"I didn't know you were a basketball fan."

"Who isn't? But acting and basketball. How are you going to manage it all?"

"I'm not hanging up my jersey yet. This came up and I want to see how far it will take me. Acting may be a one-time thing."

"I see." Lexie nodded as she had to change her focus from Amari and turn towards Mike, who was bringing the other actors to meet her. He called the meeting to order and rehearsals began. Amari didn't realize how grueling acting was until they took a break at lunch and had to go back to work again until 6 p.m.

"You call this hard? Wait until shooting starts. You might have to spend the night in your seat because you'll be too tired to walk to your trailer."

Lexie took a break before the end of the day and went to see Renata.

"I think I'm in love," she said.

"What? What are you talking about?"

"I've fallen in love. I know it's too early and I've just met him, but I love him."

Renata followed Lexie's eyes to the tall man talking to the director. It was Amari. There was quite a buzz of excitement around him. News of him signing up to play the role of Douglas Perrier in *A Lot Like Silence* had been building for months.

"Him?" she asked, sitting up straighter. Lexie nodded and tapped Renata on the arm.

"I have to have him," she breathed, then sauntered off towards Amari leaving Renata with her mouth open.

"But he's married," Renata finally managed to say, but it was too late. Lexie was already saying something to Amari with her well-manicured hand on his wrist. Renata knew that Amari being married meant absolutely nothing to Lexie.

That evening as Renata was driving home she listened to Lexie's instructions with growing dismay but knew she didn't have a choice but to follow through. A lot of celebrities used that tactic. It was interesting to hear some of them complain about the paparazzi, but some of them even leaked where there would be hanging out at any given time so their pictures could appear in *People* and

US Weekly. Black celebrities had to work twice as hard to appear in the mainstream magazines. It was rare for them to feature a cover magazine with a woman of color or even pictures in the gossip sections. Lexie was unique, though. She had earned more covers than most. Her beauty did transcend color. People of all races could appreciate it because she didn't really look black or white but a mixture of Native American, black, white and Asian. She had a little bit of everything. But when she filled the bubble that said race, she filled in African American. Her soul was African American, and so was her upbringing; everybody knew a drop of black blood in an ocean of white still meant you were black. In Hollywood, in order to get more roles you had to have a look that wasn't too black, and Lexie was that.

Renata punched in the numbers that would start the chain reaction of gossip, news and fantasy. There was a long procession of people used to leak information to the right photographers and journalists and wannabe journalists, the paparazzi.

After the calls she directed her car towards her beautiful apartment. Working for Lexie meant she could afford the nicest places, and the more success Lexie had meant the more successful she became, too. As a publicist and personal assistant to Lexie her job was to work with a team of promoters, magazines and managers just to make sure Lexie's image was the way they saw best to sell movies and generate more money for her and the major studios. Fostering the girls had been Renata's idea. Lexie had balked at the idea of being tied down.

"I'm already the face for so many children's organizations. I speak at fundraisers, I donate millions to African orphans, what more?" Lexie had sulked, pleaded and ranted. "They wouldn't let me be a spokesperson for AIDS because of my past, but I do practice safe sex." She didn't mind giving her money and some of her time, but having kids in her home was huge! Even temporarily. It was too much and she knew she admitted to not having any motherly feelings.

"My mother was never there. She was more concerned with her boyfriends than she was ever with us." Renata listened as Lexie relived her past. Yes, her mother wasn't a good role model. Her mother used men to get what she wanted and Lexie was taking after her, though Lexie would never admit it. Her mother had also sold pictures of Lexie to magazines and conducted interviews that were damaging to her reputation. Mother and daughter had not spoken for five years.

Renata had listened to all Lexie's reasoning but eventually Lexie had come to accept that her image would be worse if she didn't change the public's opinion of her. Renata also pointed out to her that most of the celebrity moms were still able to work, attend parties, date, and still raise a family. Being a single mother with the kids would be a plus and would give her positive publicity for a change and also help the two orphans. They had to make her appear selfless, warm and loving and not the selfish, man-eater that she had been portrayed as before. Renata felt guilty as she thought of Madison and Morgan.

CHAPTER 18

Clare had a secret passion that she never wanted to share with the women she led at Calvary Worship. She absolutely loved magazines. One of her secret dreams was to start her own fashion magazine, but with articles that would interest Christian women of color and uphold the values she knew most women with her beliefs held. Until that magazine was made Clare read a lot of mainstream magazines. She loved Oprah's magazine *O*, of course, but read *Essence* as religiously as her Bible. Her secret passion was the other trashy magazines that told more lies than truths about Hollywood couples. The one she was reading now was making her blood boil. In the "couples alert" section of the tabloid she saw a picture of Lexie and Amari sharing a lunch and smiling at each other like lovebirds. Of course the caption only made her feel worse.

Is Lexie finding a father for her two orphans with a married NBA basketball star?

How could they print such garbage? Not only was Amari married, he was also a man of God, a man who had morals and a man who loved her daughter.

Clare knew Raven would be at the center. Clare decided to visit with Raven at the center. With the new renovations the place was becoming a bigger haven for children. Raven spent most of her time there, and since

Amari left for L.A. Raven was also focused on the huge fundraising gala for the clinic in Kenya. Who could blame her? With a husband who spent more time on the road than at home the girl had to keep herself busy. Her advice to Raven was to have a baby straightaway, but she wanted to wait until after the latest changes to the center were completed.

Clare nearly had a heart attack when she saw the police cars outside the center.

"Oh, Jesus, let my baby be all right," she said as she parked her white SUV awkwardly outside the center. When she opened the door she almost collapsed with relief when she saw Raven talking to the officers, her hands on her bewildered face.

"Mom," Raven said, shaking her head.

"What's wrong?" Clare asked, looking around.

"There was a robbery. I'm just giving a statement to the police."

"Oh, no. What did they take?"

"All the computers and the karaoke machine. I don't know what else is missing." Raven waved her hands around. She was clearly in shock. But she was about to get into an even bigger shock.

"Give us a call if you remember anything else," Officer Owens said, handing her a business card. Raven nodded, grateful for the officer's kindness. When the police left Raven turned to Clare.

"Would you like some tea? I think they left the kettle," she said and tried to smile. It had not been an easy week.

"You could do with a cup, too. This neighborhood is not safe anymore," Clare said.

"I know. I hate to admit it, but I just knew it was a matter of time before they came and took something from us. All around us there have been burglaries in all the businesses. I just hoped they would leave the center alone. We don't make a profit."

"I know, but they don't care. They will steal from anyone. The Bible says the enemy comes to steal, kill and destroy and we are not completely shielded from it."

They entered the mini kitchen. It was well equipped with donated stainless steel appliances. Those may not have been on the thieves' agendas. Raven poured water into two mugs and placed one in the microwave. While it spun around she turned to face her mother.

"What's that you are holding?" Raven asked, looking at the magazine her mother held. Clare looked at it as an afterthought. She had forgotten her reason for dropping by her daughter. Raven caught the expression on her face.

"Is Amari there?" she asked, stirring the teabag then handing her mother the green tea they both liked. "He is, isn't he? Is Hollywood already hailing him as the next Denzel?" Raven reached for the tabloid excitedly, then immediately saw the picture of Amari and Lexie. Her smile froze on her face as she saw them, and then she tossed it on the round table in the corner of the kitchen like it had burned her.

"That's his co-star." Raven shrugged and then began making another cup of tea as Clare's eyes bore on her back.

"That's not what the caption says," Clare insisted.

Raven turned to face her mother, feeling the tension headache building up but trying to remain nonchalant. "I know. Mom, you should know that tabloids would say anything to sell magazines."

"I know, but have you spoken to him about it? What does he say?"

"There's nothing to talk about. He's shooting a movie. I'll go and visit soon."

"I don't know how you can be so casual about this. Didn't I just say, 'The enemy comes to steal, kill and destroy?' And you are just being unconcerned about your husband and this movie Delilah."

"I'm not being casual about it, Ma! What do you want me to do?"

"Don't talk to me like that, Raven. I rushed here to help and you speak to me like that. I won't stay here and listen to a disrespectful daughter." Clare smashed the teacup down with a splash and picked up her purse.

Raven watched her leave and felt a pang. She wanted her mother to leave, but not like this. The picture with Amari and Lexie had shaken her, but she didn't want Clare to know how much it bothered her. After a few minutes Raven picked up the tabloid and walked to the office. She threw it on the cluttered desk, which was now missing a computer. She stared at it from her chair, then leaned over and grabbed it again. Lexie was looking at Amari and he was looking at her. She picked up the phone, not caring that it was early in California. She had to speak to Amari and hear his voice. He would make all those rumors go away.

"Baby," he answered in a sleepy voice.

"Hey, you," Raven said, sitting on the chair and turning over the picture of Amari and Lexie. She didn't want to look at it, but her eyes were drawn to it like it held an invisible magnet.

"How's it going?" she asked. "Did I wake you?"

"Yeah. What time is it there?" He cleared his throat. She pictured him lying in bed and sitting up, the sheet falling off and showing his chiseled chest.

"Noon. How's the movie business?"

"Interesting. You should come visit."

"I'll take time off this week. I'll be there on Thursday."

"You sure, baby?" he asked. She felt reassured just hearing his deep soothing voice. The sleepiness was gone from it now and it exuded confidence and love.

"You don't want me to come?" she teased.

"You know I've been on to you about coming here. I want you in my bed, sweet thing," he said, and she laughed, forgetting the magazine and all the computers that had been stolen from the center.

Lexie's disappointment was deep on Friday morning. When one thing goes wrong then two or three follow, she thought grumpily as she sat in makeup having her already lovely face made even more perfect by the experts. First, her plans to seduce Amari that weekend were foiled by the untimely arrival of Amari's unattractive wife. When Lexie heard that Raven was arriving she expected to see a model or some type of long-haired, light-skinned woman much like herself, but no. Well, she didn't really get to look at Raven up close. Raven stayed on the periphery of the set that morning and left before Lexie could meet her. Besides, Lexie didn't feel like going around introducing herself to a woman whose husband she planned on stealing. Not only that, she didn't really feel like fawning over Raven. She was Lexie Hart, and Lexie Hart didn't run after people. They came to her.

"Renata, can you go and check out Amari's wife? See what she's like," Lexie asked as she wrote some notes on her script.

"Why don't you go and meet her. She's on the set."

"I have to finish this. Just go. Please."

Lexie rarely said please. Renata didn't want to argue, so she went around looking for Amari and his wife. She found them walking through the set. Amari was giving Raven a tour, holding her hand. Raven wore a wrap dress that hugged her body to perfection. Renata decided to assess the couple before she went to introduce herself. Raven reached Amari's shoulders and her hair was tied at the nape of her neck. From her profile as she looked around at all the lights she looked nice. A nice, kind person. She had the full, pouty lips. She wouldn't make it in Hollywood or any movies, really. Most of the women who made it in the movies had a certain color. She would be too dark. They made an attractive couple, and Renata could sense their closeness as they gazed at each other and held each other close. When Raven and Amari turned to face her she was struck by Raven's eyes. That was where her power was.

"Renata. Come and meet my wife," Amari said as they walked towards each other and shook hands.

"Renata works for Lexie," Amari added.

"Nice to meet you," Raven said. "I've never been on a set before, and never knew they would be this huge."

"A movie is quite a big production. Bigger than life," Renata said.

"It must be exciting," Raven said. Amari pulled her close.

"It is," Renata said. Renata liked Raven already. Her innocence. Genuine pleasure at what she saw.

Before Renata could talk to the couple more, other people had arrived and Amari began to introduce them to Raven. Renata left to give her report to her boss where she hid in her dressing rooms.

"She seems nice," Renata told Lexie a few minutes later. "Young, friendly, adores Amari."

"I thought she would be different. She doesn't seem like his type at all. What on earth does he see in her?"

"Some people see beyond what's on the outside," Renata said. "Besides, up close she's striking. She has powerful eyes and a dazzling smile. There's something about her that you can't see from a distance."

"I doubt it," Lexie argued.

"There's something likeable about her. A warmth that is so rare in our business," Renata continued and saw Lexie fume.

"Well, warmth or not, men need heat, beauty, passion. I'm sure Amari will agree with me," Lexie said, then picked up her phone. "It's only a matter of time. The times I've spent with Amari so far have been very interesting. I can tell when a man is interested in me, and as you know, Renata, I've never met a man that I can't seduce."

"Amari might be your first. He loves his wife," Renata said but regretted it. The challenge only made the gleam in Lexie's eyes brighter. Renata didn't even want to bring up her image and what breaking up a happy marriage would do to it. Lexie got what Lexie wanted. Lexie had worked hard to get where she was, both in and out of some famous men's beds, and if there was one thing Lexie liked to hear, it was the word "No." She would go to any length to make sure the "no" became a "yes."

CHAPTER 19

"I'm so glad you made it back," Raven said to Amari as they dressed in their bedroom. Raven's outfit reminded Amari of an African princess or queen. She came to him and straightened his tie.

"I'm proud of you for putting this together," Amari said.

"I'm glad it's almost done. Then I can come and spend more time with you in L.A."

"So how much money do you think you'll raise?" Amari asked.

"The admission receipts alone will raise about $50,000. And then the auction for the African art, who knows."

"I tried to get Lexie to come but she couldn't. However she did say she would send a donation and also got a few of her friends to come."

"That's nice of her."

There was a knock on their door.

"Are you guys ready?"

Raven opened the door and Tahlia came in. She was staying with them for the weekend. She was also dressed in an exquisite African outfit.

"Look at you. That's amazing," Raven said.

"And authentic, too. My Nigerian friend had it sent from her royal family."

"I hope your royal friends will buy some of our African art."

"Of course they will. They are rich. So is Lexie coming?" Tahlia turned to Amari.

"No. I'm afraid not," Amari said.

"Too bad. Anyway, we better get going. The limos are outside."

Raven and her family were the first to arrive at the Detroit Institute of Arts where the event was taking place. Amari met Josh Hardin for the first time as soon as they entered the museum.

"This is our very good friend, Dr. Joshua Hardin," Clare said. Clare looked amazing in her royal regalia along with a beautiful headpiece that almost touched the ceiling.

Since the picture in the article about Amari, Clare's attitude towards him had changed. Clare's new attitude towards Amari strained her relationship with Raven, too. "It's good to meet you," Amari said. Raven hugged Josh.

"It's great to see you again," Raven said excitedly, then turned to explain to Amari about her trip to Kenya years before. While in Kenya she'd met Josh and worked in his hospital. Amari liked Joshua Hardin. The older man exuded confidence and warmth. He didn't look his forty years, but the maturity and steadiness in his manner was hard to miss.

"I'm glad you saw our humble clinic. It's grown a lot since you were last there, Rave," Joshua said. "I hope you'll come again."

"Joshua runs a mission hospital and church on the outskirts of Nairobi," Philip explained to Amari. Philip reminded Raven of James Earl Jones in the movie *Coming to America* in his over-the-top outfit.

"You are living in Africa?" Amari asked, surprised. In the two years they were married, Amari had heard about Josh but never met him. His travels meant he missed meeting many of Raven's relatives and friends.

Joshua nodded. "It's my second home, you could say. When God calls you, nothing else in your life will satisfy but the fulfillment of that calling. This is my sixth year running that hospital and God has provided and fulfilled his promises in the lives of many people who need help."

"What's it like living over there?"

"It's great. Once it's in your blood it's hard to leave. The needs of the people keep you going back so you can save one more life, give hope to mothers and children," Joshua explained. "It's something to see." Amari listened with interest and Raven could see the wheels turning in his head. She knew that they would be making a trip to Africa very soon.

"We better get inside," Clare said. "Esther and Angelo will be here. Joshua can continue to inspire us all as we get ready for the big night."

"I feel like what I do at the center is nothing," Amari commented as they walked through the beautiful building surrounded by artifacts and art from all over the world. "You have given your whole life to serving people in Africa and I just volunteer and give a little bit of money to some charities."

"Don't call it nothing, my man. I think we all have different purposes. We can't all be missionaries in the

African desert or in China, and we can't all be professional athletes who influence the lives of many young boys who want to be stars. I've read about you, Amari, and you are different from most of the professional sportsmen I read about. I think that's important, too."

"I don't know. I think God wants us to show him that we can give it all up for Him like you did. The rest of us just want to keep our comfort, hold on to our money, hold on to our habits."

"Do you know the mark of a good Christian?" Josh asked. He didn't really seem to want an answer. "It's here." Josh put a fist near his heart.

"That's true. More than the head."

"The question is do we love Jesus. Are we doing what we are doing for His glory or our own?"

"Man, that's deep. It's worth asking yourself, though," Amari said, and everybody nodded.

Raven glanced at Clare who tried to stop her eyes from rolling. Amari was different. Clare made it seem like he was a hypocrite, but she knew that Amari more than anything feared God. Not that 'I'll go to hell' kind of fear, but a healthy fear that was more filled with wanting to please God and do what God commanded him. Even the movie he had accepted had the values he wanted to portray. He did not compromise on that.

The band that had been hired began playing African jazz just before the doors opened to all the invited people. Raven had inspected all the food and the decorations and was pleased with how everything looked.

Before she could dwell on her mother's attitude it was time to greet the guests who had paid more than five hundred dollars to attend the evening's event. She had to give it her best and not worry about what her mother thought of Amari.

❧

It rained heavily two Sundays after Amari left again for California. But Raven knew that the storm outside was nothing compared to what was going on in her heart.

What *was* going on? Why was she hearing rumors about her husband and Lexie Hart, of all people? And why was she letting it get to her? Amari had warned her about the media exaggerating and even making innocent meetings seem clandestine. Still this latest group of rumors were really affecting her. She was pushed over the edge when she got home after church.

The house she now called home was new, a present from Amari, but still the past few months and years they had spent very few days together in it. During the season Amari was on the road sometimes for six days out of the week, and this second summer together he was in California making a movie with the woman who was always listed as one of the top 100 most beautiful women in America.

When she walked into the kitchen the phone message light was blinking. After putting her purse on the counter she pressed the voicemail button.

"Hi, Raven. It's Candice. I know it's been a long time, but I just wanted to touch base and find out how you are doing. Give me a call. My number is now 248-929-0114. We moved. We now live in Bloomfield Hills. Call me."

Raven repeated the message and then wrote down the number, her heart lifting a little. Candice had called. She had not spoken to her friend in two years! Raven walked upstairs with Candice's number on a piece of paper, questions whirling in her head.

Should I call her? Why is she calling me now after all this time? She walked into her bedroom and slipped off her shoes. Lying on the king-size bed she picked up the phone beside her bed and dialed Candice's number. Raven recognized Candice's voice immediately.

"Candice, it's Raven," she said, staring at the high ceiling and skylight above her bed.

"Hi, Raven. You got my message?" Candice's voice hadn't changed much, though Raven picked up a distance in her tone, like someone reading the news and not wanting to show any emotion.

"I just walked in."

"I thought you would be at church. I was watching one of those BET celebrity programs and thought of you," Candice said.

"Oh. How are you?"

"Fine, Raven. We finally bought the new house. Charles's doing very well at Beaumont. Might even open a practice with several African-American doctors. You should come and see our house. Right by the lake. Finally things are beginning to look up."

Raven looked out the window at the view of the lake outside her bedroom and curled herself into a ball. Lake views were no guarantee of anything.

"I'm glad to hear that," Raven said. "How's Junior?"

"Great. I'm expecting. It's a girl. Charles and I are very happy."

"Good." Raven wasn't sure what to say to Candice after all this time.

"Well, I just wondered if you were okay? I heard you and Amari were breaking up." Candice's words had Raven sitting up abruptly on the bed.

"What?"

"Well it's all over the media about Amari and his new girlfriend, Lexie. I just had to call. At first I thought people were just making things up, you know, saying that Amari left you and went to California to be with his girlfriend. I even saw pictures of them together in a restaurant, and on an entertainment news show someone asked Lexie a question about Amari. She just shook her head and didn't answer. What are you going to do, Raven? Are you going to let him treat you like that while you are still married?"

Finally Candice stopped talking. "It's just media, Candice. Don't believe everything you read," Raven admonished, trying to convince Candice and herself. Still her heart began throbbing.

"So you guys are still together?"

Raven took a painful breath and spoke as calmly as she could. "Yes. We are."

"Well, if he's going to leave at least try and have his baby first so you can have some link to him. I always knew that you couldn't trust athletes. They have too many women throwing their bodies at them, and some of those women look like models. Some of them are."

"It's fine. Anyway, Candice, thanks for calling. I have to be at church," Raven lied, taking another deep breath, glad nobody could see her face. Her temples were beginning to hurt from the pressure building in her head. Candice's voice sounded so far, like from some deep dark tunnel. Focus. Focus.

"All right. I'll be in touch," Candice said and hung up the phone. Raven ran to the bathroom and threw up.

CHAPTER 20

Lexie lay in bed, physically satisfied, but something was wrong. Usually after her essential trysts with Jerome, she would be completely contented and relaxed. Jerome was a great lover who she met with often. Jerome was married and therefore perfect because he wanted to be as discreet as possible, and so did she. But, she wasn't feeling guilty or worried about Jerome's pregnant wife or their two daughters. As long as she could keep it a secret she didn't worry about the other woman.

Amari

Amari Thomas was the biggest problem in her life right now. She couldn't stop thinking about him even when she was with the most accomplished lover she had ever had.

Amari didn't even seem remotely interested in her because he seemed to spend all his free time calling his wife. The few times they had eaten together she had to concoct some story about needing his input on something.

In all the movies she had done in the past, most of her co-stars adored her. Some of them were like crazy fans who wouldn't leave her alone. They offered her roses, sent diamond necklaces to her dressing room and made fools of themselves. She was used to being adored. She was used to men tripping over their feet when they saw her walking in their direction.

Amari. Well, he was really different. She knew he thought she was attractive. She had seen it in his eyes, but he still remained distant.

Out of reach.

After her meeting with Jerome in the hotel she made her way home. She never liked to take her lovers home. She didn't mind meeting in their apartments or their homes but now, with the twins, she had to be careful with what she did. She didn't relish getting any more headlines that would make Renata rant and rave.

Madison and Morgan were upstairs in the playroom when she got home. She went into her lounge and poured herself a drink. Surrounded by all her luxury she suddenly felt very lonely.

She turned when she heard feet coming down the stairs. They were definitely little girl's feet. It was Madison, the leader of the duo. She hesitantly walked towards Lexie. Lexie knew the kids didn't know what to do with her. They sometimes feared her and they stayed out of her way or they followed her around, mesmerized by how she dressed, how she talked.

"Are you okay?" Madison asked. Lexie looked at her, surprised. Madison was a tricky one. She acted much older than her years.

"Fine. How about you."

"I'm fine. I was teaching Morgan how to draw," Madison said importantly.

"What did you draw?" she asked.

"We were making you a card. You don't seem very happy these days."

Lexie shook her head. How intuitive the girls were. She was in love, and her love was not reciprocated. "Well, I am a little sad."

"Why? Do you miss your mommy?"

Mommy. She did not miss her mother. Her mother had betrayed her so many times that she had lost count.

"No, Maddy. I just like this boy and I don't think he likes me."

Madison wrinkled her nose like she had said something distasteful. "You are beautiful. He'll like you."

"I hope so," Lexie said, then took a good look at Madison. She stood there barely reaching her waist but there was a wealth of wisdom in her eyes.

"Can I give you a hug?" Madison asked. Lexie stood for a minute, surprised. She hardly hugged them. She barely had any contact with them. She nodded.

Madison walked towards her and put her arms around her waist. Lexie reached around her, feeling her tiny shoulders, and felt something shift in her heart.

CHAPTER 21

Amari's hotel phone rang until it went to voicemail. Raven tried his cellphone for the fifth time but all she heard was the prerecorded message. Angrily she tossed her phone on the carpet and wiped the angry tears from her eyes. Everybody was calling her except her husband. She had to speak to him, but the longer she couldn't get hold of him the more worried she became. She had called in sick at work and now sat drowning in her shock and confusion.

This can't be happening.

Was Amari really leaving her for that actress, and without even a hint or a word to her? Everybody else seemed to know what was going on but she had no idea who could tell her what Amari and Lexie were up to all the way in California. She had no way of finding out short of getting on the next flight to L.A and humiliating herself further.

Oh, God, please tell me that this is all just some crazy rumor and Amari is coming back to me soon and that he still loves me. Father in Heaven, you know me. I couldn't handle it if he left me. You know me, God. You know how weak I am, so insecure. And Amari knows that this would kill me so it can't be true.

Raven sobbed into her pillow, and then jumped when the phone rang. Controlling her crying she picked up the phone hoping it was Amari.

"Ray?" It was Esther, and that made her almost want to burst into fresh tears.

"Yeah, it's me. What's up?"

"You didn't go to work?"

"I don't feel well." Raven coughed and wiped her tears with the sleeve of her robe.

"Oh. Can I come and see you?"

"Aren't you working today?"

"Yeah, but I'll be over anyway. I've been hearing some things . . ." Esther began to speak tentatively, but Raven cut her off quickly.

"I know. Come over."

Esther arrived with breakfast of French toast and coffee. The scent wafted to Raven as she opened the door to the house and let her older sister in. Esther glanced at her, and then walked into the kitchen.

"You hungry?"

"No. Not really," Raven said, sitting on the bar stools by the gleaming black granite countertops while Esther took out the plates and silverware. She served golden toast with whipped butter and fruit and then reheated some coffee in the stainless steel microwave. The kitchen was very modern and spotless, just like the rest of the house. She realized that when Amari was away she rarely cooked. When he was home they cooked together sometimes or ordered from their favorite restaurant. Once in a while he even hired his favorite chef to create dinners for them right in their own kitchen.

Raven couldn't help noticing that it had been a while since they had spent time together. So she kept busy even though many well-meaning people told her to follow her husband all over the country.

But I want to be a woman who has more in life than just chasing a man around the country making sure he behaves or making sure he doesn't stop loving me. What did I do wrong?

Esther's voice cut through her descent into panic and despair. "Just have a bite," Esther insisted, cutting her toast into squares like she would for a child, then put a piece in her mouth. "Yummy." Raven tried to smile but her eyes drifted to the phone.

"Have you heard from Amari?" Raven jumped at the question, and then turned her eyes on Esther.

"No. Well, not since Saturday. I guess you've been hearing all the stuff about him?" Esther nodded. Raven fought very hard for self-control, but her mind was on the edge of falling into a dark, ferocious tunnel full of nightmares and loss. She could sense it pulling her away from the presence. But Esther continued to talk, keeping her sane but wanting answers she didn't have.

"What's going on? I mean Amari would never do that. Do you think people are doing this for the sake of writing stories? Movie publicity? You can sue them for slander . . ."

"I don't know," Raven responded, swallowing hard. "It's all over some tabloids that they are together and even on the entertainment news. They are saying he's left me." Esther saw the tears in her sister's eyes then moved close and brought her into a hug. Raven remained stiff, not wanting to give in to the confusion and loss she was feeling. If she gave in to the despair and fell in the pit she was afraid she may not be able to pull herself out again.

"Oh, Ray. I don't think Amari would do that. He's a dignified, God-fearing man. He loves you. I know he loves you."

"I don't know. It's so—so embarrassing having people call me with all these things," Raven sputtered. "Even Candice called."

Esther scowled then demanded, "Candice? What did she say?"

"She's not surprised, of course. First she told me how great her life was, then she told me how mine was falling apart. How my husband was leaving me." Raven broke down, sobbing.

"Oh, Ray, it's not true. We need to pray that the enemy stops attacking you. You know the enemy comes to steal, kill and destroy, and that's what the devil is trying to do to you. Let's pray that this all goes away."

"I can't even pray now, Esther. I just feel numb. I think my marriage is over."

"Don't say that, Ray."

"I can feel it. The woman he's working with, this Lexie Hart, if she wants him then she already has him! That's what some movie stars do. They break up marriages without even blinking, and it's happening to me. Only my husband doesn't have the guts to call and tell me. He's letting me suffer and have people tell me things while he hides out in L.A. with Lexie Hart!"

As Raven's voice grew louder she moved away from Esther's embrace and walked to the kitchen chairs. She held one chair but could not sit down.

"Oh, Raven, surely you don't think Amari would do that. That is too typical and Amari doesn't do anything typical. He's different. He's strong. You have to believe in him."

"Then why is his phone off? He must know I would need to talk to him. We talk every day or at least text, but for over twenty-four hours, nothing."

Raven walked to the kitchen doors. She slid them open and stumbled out like someone leaving a burning building and needing fresh air fast. Esther followed and stood with her out in the sunlight and looked at the beautiful garden. The trimmed grass stretched all the way to a man-made beach that ended right by a lake. Raven stared unseeing at the gleaming blue water with white shimmers from the sun. She took another deep breath then wiped the tears away.

"Don't jump to any conclusions Raven," Esther began to speak but was interrupted by the phone ringing. She grabbed the phone from the kitchen then took it to Raven. Raven pressed the talk button.

"Hi, Ashley," Raven said and smiled weakly at Esther. Esther sat on the garden chairs and watched her sister.

"You'll be in the neighborhood?" Raven asked and Esther raised her eyebrow. "Fine. I'll see you then."

"Who was that?" Esther asked after Raven took the phone from her ear.

"A friend. You remember Ashley? She comes to our church. You've met her a few times. She works at the Pistons public relations office. I guess she has some more news for me."

"So what are you going to do today? You can't just sit here and do nothing," Esther said.

"Not really nothing. I'm losing my mind, and you are here, too." Raven gave a small smile.

"Yes. Have to make sure you eat. You are looking too skinny! Come on. At least come and taste that French toast. It is to die for."

After Esther left, Raven tried Amari's phone one more time with no success then roared out of the house for a strong session of kickboxing. Walking through the gym she couldn't help overhearing a sports channel reporter who was interviewing a fan.

"What do you think about this news about Amari and Lexie?" the man with the microphone asked.

"All I can say is it's strange that everybody says how straight an arrow he is, all Christian like, refusing to go to strip clubs, but he sure doesn't seem to mind having Lexie strip for him . . . while his wife's at home . . ." Raven walked briskly past the TV and left the gym, not sure if she was dreaming or if she was awake.

Ashley arrived after Raven had showered and changed into jeans and a T-shirt.

After a little bit of small talk Ashley came straight to the point.

"I'm here to talk to you about Amari. I've been hearing all these rumors, too, and, well, some of them

SHOW ME THE SUN

sound like facts." Raven's heart froze at those words but she hoped it didn't show. Ashley wasn't the type to gossip. She wanted to keep what little dignity she could. She didn't say anything and gave Ashley the expression that she wanted her to carry on.

"I'm here as your friend, Ray. I've admired you as a friend, especially the way you handle your life. You and Amari are both so down to earth. You care about the community and live your lives admirably."

"Thanks, Ashley," Raven managed.

"But I'm sure you know that with the life Amari leads some woman or other is bound to end up in his bed." Raven nearly jumped from her seat. Her skin went cold and her heart started racing.

"I have some inside information on what goes on and I've been friends with one or two wives who are involved in this business. Trust me, I know some of them tell me things or share what their husbands can be up to, on the road and so on. It's kind of understood."

Understood? What kind of ridiculous crap is that? Raven raged inside but kept a small and distant smile on her face.

"Strange, isn't it," Raven commented quietly.

"I know. I know you, and I don't agree with it, but I'm sure you've spoken to Juanita, too." Juanita was married to Blake Williams, who was now playing for the Chicago Bulls. Juanita continued with her marriage as if nothing had happened and even kissed her husband in public a few weeks after the whole incident swirled

184

around the city. Why should she worry about Amari and just one affair?

Because he's going to leave you, a voice said, and Raven looked back at Ashley as if she had spoken Raven's thoughts out loud.

"Call me if you need to talk, Raven. I know it must be hard for you," Ashley said sympathetically. She looked genuinely concerned, but Raven wasn't going to talk to anyone outside her family until she spoke to Amari. She watched Ashley's car disappear as it turned left at the end of the drive. The house phone rang and she broke out in a sweat when she saw Amari's name on the caller ID.

"Raven?" Amari's voice reached her and caused her heart to beat even faster. She had rehearsed what she would say to lead to the conversation about Lexie, but now that he had finally called all her calm words left her mind.

"When were you going to tell me?" she screamed instead.

CHAPTER 22

"It's not what you think," Amari pleaded.

"You don't even know what I'm thinking." Raven listened to the silence, wondering if he had disconnected the call. She was relieved and her anger increased when she heard him clear his throat. This was her Amari, but right at that moment she felt like she was talking to a stranger, an unknown person who she once knew but didn't know anymore.

"I've been trying to call you. I've heard all about you and Lexie, Amari. Your secret is out."

Amari began his explanation, but nothing eased the pain in Raven's chest. "I turned my phone off because somebody leaked my number and reporters kept calling. The media is exaggerating. We just work together."

"Oh, come on, Amari. I'm your wife! Very reliable sources tell me something is going on between you and your co-star. Pictures of you and Lexie don't lie. Please save us some time and just tell me what you want."

"Let me come home so we can talk in person." She listened, loving his voice but realizing he was no longer her safe place. He was hurting her ten times more than all those people who had called her names, and who had made her feel like she didn't measure up to the world's standard of beauty.

"No, Amari, I want to know now, this minute. Are you in love with her? Do you want to be with her?"

"No! It was a mistake."

Raven had been standing in her bedroom, but at his words she sank to the carpet holding her stomach as if she had been shot.

"It didn't mean anything," Amari said when she didn't respond. "Raven, are you there?"

"What didn't mean anything?" She wished she could look into his eyes and read them herself. For all she knew he was with Lexie right now, holding her long, manicured hand. They could be lying in bed together plotting what to say to her, gullible naive Raven.

"I can't discuss this on the phone, Ray. I'll be home on Friday," Amari said.

"Don't bother coming here, Amari. I don't want to see you."

"Come on, Raven. We need to talk. The phone makes everything sound worse, but I'll speak to you this Friday. I'll explain everything."

"I said I don't want to see you. I think we should separate for a while," Raven said, her voice getting colder as her heart froze.

"Rave. What do you mean, separate? I love you."

"Good for you, Amari, but I mean it. I don't want to see you until I'm ready. Don't come to my house, don't call me. Just leave me alone!" Raven then threw the phone against the wall, where it left a black mark and fell to the floor. The phone rang immediately, but Raven went and pulled all the phones off the hook, almost hurting her hands in the process. As she walked around the massive house Amari's words kept hitting against her brain.

It was a mistake. It didn't mean anything. It was a mistake. It didn't mean anything.

Raven feared that Amari would come back to their home so after talking to him she packed her bags and moved in with her parents. She went to her old bedroom on the corner of the house overlooking the driveway. Philip gave her space and Clare hovered over her treating her like an invalid. She told them both she didn't want to talk about Amari just yet and didn't want their advice. She wanted time to think without people telling her the latest news about Amari and Lexie. Just the way the news did when a terrible tragedy happened. They talked about it every minute, adding an extra word, adding the latest information just to make their audiences feel worse. That's what all those well-meaning calls were doing to her. They were killing her one word at a time.

The worst weekly tabloid even printed pictures of her wedding to Amari, calling her the jilted wife of the famous basketball player. They had headlines screaming LEXIE'S FALLEN IN LOVE WITH AMARI AND WANTS TO HAVE HIS BABY!

That headline felt like a stab in the heart.

On Friday Clare came upstairs after Raven had taken her shower. When Clare knocked, Raven was sitting on her bed, flipping through a home decorating magazine without seeing much.

"Can I come in?" Clare asked.

Raven turned to look at her mother. "Sure, Mom," Raven answered. Clare walked slowly into the room and sat on the bed.

"Amari's here." Her announcement made Raven's scowl deepen.

"I said I don't want to see him," Raven said, her eyes appealing to her mother for understanding. Her heart was racing and she felt sweaty and hot all of a sudden.

"Honey. You should at least talk to him. He's still your husband," Clare reminded her, taking her hand.

"Mom, please. He stopped being my husband when he betrayed me."

"Come on, Ray. You are not the first person that this has happened to. You of all people should realize how lucky you are to have a man like Amari."

"What do you mean 'you of all people,' Ma?" Raven demanded, her anger showing in her brown eyes.

"I'm just saying he's willing to explain all those tabloids. Why don't you give him a chance?"

"Just say it. I'm not pretty enough for him and I should be grateful that he sleeps with some pretty actresses but still comes back to me, right? Is that what you mean, Ma?" Raven's face was very close to Clare's and Clare stood up, moving away from her.

"I can see you are not being reasonable, and it might be better if he doesn't see you anyway at this moment."

"I'll talk to him when I'm ready, Ma. Just tell him to go away right now."

Raven walked to the window and her heart ached as she looked at Amari's black Escalade in the driveway. After a few minutes she saw him walk out and get back in his vehicle. She almost cried out to him. She missed him. She would do anything to erase what had taken place but she couldn't. He had betrayed her and she couldn't trust her heart to hope and believe that he really loved her. She could only take one heartbreak at a time.

Amari was back filming the final few scenes while also getting ready for the new NBA season that would be starting in the fall. How long could she keep avoiding him? Why couldn't she face him? What was she going to do?

Her decision came quicker than she would have liked. While at the checkout counter two magazines had Lexie Hart on the cover holding the twins with the screaming headline *Lexie Hart Pregnant!* and another one saying *Lexie Hart and Amari Thomas Expecting Their First Baby!*

After reading the headlines she didn't know how she managed to get home, but when she did she called her father at his office.

"Daddy. Please come home now. I need to talk to you." Philip was home within twenty minutes with Clare right beside him.

"What is it, Rave?" Clare asked, walking towards her where she sat on the couch, her legs under her. Her eyes were red from crying and a box of tissues sat on the floor. "Mom. Dad! Help me get a divorce lawyer. It's over."

CHAPTER 23

"Oh, my God, what have I done?"

"Amari. Don't ask God what you done, you did it yourself!"

"Ma, I know I did, but I don't know how it happened." Gloria rolled her eyes then put the macaroni and cheese in the oven. Amari stood in front of her looking like a lost little boy. Her heart broke for him, and at the same time she felt like wringing his neck. He was lucky the island in the kitchen separated them. Her whole family was going to be there for the family barbecue at her house and she would have to put up with more of their questions and comments. She made sure Amari made it home because she was not facing her nosy relatives alone. If anybody asked her anything, she would point right at her son's head.

"What's Raven saying now?"

"Divorce, Ma. She wants a divorce," Amari said.

Gloria shook her head and clicked her tongue, closing her eyes as if that would make the whole situation disappear. "I suppose she wants you to pay her alimony?"

"She doesn't want anything from me, Ma. Raven is not like that. She-she's the best thing that ever happened to me." Now Gloria reached over and hit him on the arm.

"Ouch, Ma." Amari pretended to be more hurt than he really was.

"So now you care about her?" Gloria questioned her son. She hurt for him, but she still wondered why Raven was being so difficult. Amari clearly loved her, not Lexie. Gloria hadn't spent much time with Raven. They lived too far from each other and had separate lives. But there were some things that annoyed her about Raven. Her desire to wait to have children, for instance. The way her parents seemed to want to control her, and now Amari, too. Especially Clare. She resented that. She also wished that Raven would visit her more often. Despite all the misgivings, she still loved Raven because Amari loved her. She looked at her son now as he professed his love for his wife.

"I always did, Ma. I always cared about my wife."

"That was a pretty great way of showing her." Gloria took the bowls she had been using and dumped them in the sink, and then continued to wipe the counter.

Amari perched on the edge of the stool and looked at his mother, shaking his head. Gloria continued to speak.

"I love Raven. She's like the daughter I never had. She's respectful, loyal and honest. She's like a breath of fresh air. Now this Lexie person, she's like Monique as far as I'm concerned with her calculating ways and her self-ishness."

Amari rubbed his forehead and shook his head at the same time. He looked at his mother, not sure what to say. Nothing he could say would make everything all right.

"It's a pity, son. Do you want to divorce her?"

"No." The word came out as a groan.

Gloria looked at Amari surprised. "Don't you want to be free to be with Lexie?"

"No."

Gloria shook her head again. "Son. So you want to keep your wife?"

"I love Raven. She won't even talk to me. Maybe she'll talk to you."

"What can I say?"

"Nothing, Ma, don't worry. I'm just thinking out loud."

"Well, if you want that woman then you better get her back. I didn't finish my good heel for nothing dancing at your wedding only to have you divorce before you even give me a grandchild."

Now Amari looked at Gloria with strain in his eyes. Gloria started shaking her head again.

"Don't tell me that Lexie is really pregnant," Gloria said. "I read about that but I didn't believe it. Is she with child?" Amari just stared at his mother, his lips pressed together. "Answer me Amari. Is she?"

"I don't know, Ma. I really don't think so. I don't know."

"How can you not know?"

"I haven't spoken to her since the movie wrapped. I didn't even stay for the wrap party. Of course the producers are not happy with me right now. The only thing I care about is getting Raven back."

"Oh, you really mean that, don't you? You really love that girl, son?"

"I do."

"Then do everything in your power to win her back. You're going to have to give up your pride. Can you do that?" Gloria looked into Amari's sad eyes and knew her answer.

❧

Lexie read the latest tabloid and grinned wickedly. She couldn't help it. She liked it when her plans started to fall into place. Her tireless planning and plotting were beginning to pay off. Her hard work was being rewarded. It felt so good!

The media had helped make her dreams come true. She knew their power. They could make or break anybody's career. The media was a machine that could make even mediocre movies into blockbusters. The media could make relationships or destroy them. It was all about image, reputation, just smoke and mirrors and getting the public to eat it all up like caviar.

She loved seeing her face in magazines. No, it was more about being loved by the public, and she had to admit, it was about vanity. When celebrities had babies they couldn't wait to sell their pictures for magazines. They sold wedding pictures and the public ate it all up. As a black woman she knew that it wasn't easy to make the tabloids. She was one of the lucky ones that the media were interested in, and she had worked hard to get it that way.

She dropped the magazine on top of a script she had been reading. That magazine had a white person on the cover, of course, but inside there was a page about her and Amari. This hadn't really come up by accident. She had made sure that the right people heard so she could get some print space and then act shocked when interviewed.

Lexie walked to her luxurious bathroom. She loved the tropical feel of the room, the huge tub that she filled with water and bubbles, using products from her favorite spa. After undressing she lay back in the warm water and let her mind wonder to the night she had finally seduced Amari. It hadn't been that hard once she had him. The hard part was winning his trust. What helped was the element of surprise. In the beginning she never wanted him to know her intentions. She wanted him relaxed around her, acting like a coworker when in fact she was weaving her web and entangling him in it. The lunches seemed innocent enough but he didn't know about the photographers capturing every moment. They became friends fast. She made friends with males very easily. She had to admit she didn't have any female friends. The only women who were close to her were those who worked for her. Once Amari was like a buddy, she was ready for the next step.

Her toughest challenge was to get Amari alone. She knew that once that happened then the battle was over. He would have nowhere to go.

It wasn't easy to decide how to lure him to her place. She thought of many different ideas but eventually settled on a private dinner.

"Amari, you should come over tonight. I'm having a few people from the set over for dinner."

Amari liked the sound of the few people. He agreed to arrive there around 8 p.m. When he arrived at Lexie's house he was surprised to only find Renata and Tony Madiland, Lexie's agent, as the only other guests.

"Welcome, Amari. My other friends cancelled last minute. You don't mind, do you?" she had asked.

"No, it's fine."

The chef had created a wonderful dinner of decadent sea food. They talked about the movie business mostly. Renata suddenly had to leave and that left him and Tony, who had a lot of ideas for other projects that Amari could get involved in.

"I'm hearing a lot of good things about you. The movie business can be a great stepping stone to other things and vice-versa. It's all about getting the right exposure."

"You don't have to convince me," Amari said. "I know the power of the media but I want to use it for good. To be a good role model but also to create opportunities for children who otherwise wouldn't have that chance."

Lexie liked how the evening was going but almost panicked when Tony announced he had to leave and Amari also stood up.

"Amari, do you have a few minutes? I wanted to show you how that scene worked out. I managed to get an advance of the scene from the director."

Amari hesitated for a minute, and then nodded. "I have a few minutes."

"I'll just walk Tony out," Lexie said, taking Tony to the door. Amari was sitting down when she came back a few seconds later. She liked the way he was dressed. He wore a white shirt and loose-fitting slacks. She watched him for a few seconds, her desire brewing. At last.

"We can take a look at it in the theatre," Lexie said casually.

"You have your own movie theatre?" he asked, walking into the darkened room at the corner of Lexie's mansion.

"Yes," she said breezily, though inside she was knotted up with tension. It was hard to act nonchalant when just his presence turned her knees to butter and she wanted to pull him close to her and give herself to him. She wanted to do things to him that his ugly wife wouldn't even know how to spell. And when she was done with him she wanted him to keep begging for more, and she would gladly oblige.

"When I can't get to the movies this is just as good, and my family loves camping out in here."

"It's cool," Amari commented, then walked and picked up the remote. He pressed a button and the curtains began to open slowly, revealing a dark screen. "This would be great for the center. The kids would totally love this."

Lexie walked towards him and, while he still held the remote, she pressed a button and the screen came on. She didn't want to talk about his center and then his wife.

"It's custom-made. It has surround sound and other features that I specifically asked for. Here, press this."

Before dinner Lexie had taken a long, luxurious silky bath that left a soft fragrance and made her skin soft to the touch. Her hair stylist and makeup artist had all been called to work on her as if she was going to the Oscars. Her perfume was discreet, but with each turn she hoped he would be seduced, especially now that they were alone.

The music came on from all around the room and Amari turned around, impressed.

"I see you like your technology," he said gruffly.

Lexie took the remote from him then put it on the ground as jazz wafted from around the room. She pressed herself against him.

"What are you doing?" he asked, holding her elbows. Amari leaned back from her.

"This," she whispered, looking at him, then pressed her lips against his. He was shocked for a moment and just remained still. When he recovered he moved her back, but the way her legs were somehow tangled with his they both fell against the couch with Lexie on top of him, her eyes filled with desire. Somehow Lexie knew that she had to get him the first time she tried or he would put up his guard, and tonight was perfect for many reasons. She was going to do everything in her power to get him, and she had a lot of power.

"Lexie," he began, then stopped when he felt her hands touch him intimately.

"Shhh," she said, her lithe body straddling him. Her explorations were deft and expert and when she slid down his chest, Amari lost all control.

Lexie was disappointed that Amari didn't stay the night. He had left with a barely audible excuse an hour later. Her success in seducing him left her with a glow that could surpass any frustration she might have at him for leaving so quickly. When she lay in her bed she thought of him and wanted him with her. She knew from the moment she met him that he was the kind of man she could love. Seeing him for the first time had sent electric waves through her body. She had never felt like that about anybody. For the first time she wanted a man for himself and not what he could do for her, and she would do anything to hold on to him.

CHAPTER 24

Staying home and hiding from the public was making Raven feel worse, not better. Even the kids at the center knew about Amari and Lexie. They regarded her with sympathy and the curiosity usually reserved for animals at the zoo. Despite all the uncomfortable questions, staying home was just as bad. She was haunted by feelings of insecurity, anger and loneliness. And to make matters worse, she missed Amari.

"What's gonna happen with you and Thomas?" Jalen, who was now a sixth-grader, asked when Raven braved a visit to the center. Math was still his difficulty, but with the support at the center he was able to maintain good grades.

"We're fine." She smiled broadly, her head hurting with the effort.

"Is he having a baby?"

"No. No. That's just lies," Raven blurted out, then calmed down when she saw Jalen's confusion. "Here, why don't you focus on this problem there? I'll be right back."

Raven walked up to a fellow instructor in their small media center.

"I think I'm gonna go home. Will you be okay on your own?"

"It's going fine, Ms. Thomas. There are only ten of them today, and we'll be done soon." Raven thanked the young man and walked into her office. Her cellphone rang just as she picked up her purse. She didn't recognize the number but pressed the talk button anyway.

"Hi, Raven, it's Juanita."

Raven searched her mind. Juanita? Who was Juanita? "I'm sorry, who's this?"

"Juanita. Blake Williams's wife."

"Oh."

Raven recalled the story about Juanita's husband and the affair he had. She couldn't remember the details and she felt a mixture of emotions, but the one that stood out the most was dread. Was Juanita calling to welcome her to the club? They'd met a few times. Juanita was beautiful and classy, and still she had been cheated on. And what did the statistics say? About half of all marriages had infidelity, and half of those ended in divorce.

"How are you?"

Raven sat down, preparing to hear the worst. "I'm fine. Fine."

"I just wanted to call you to support you. I also had a very public situation."

Raven smiled, but the tears filled her eyes. Yeah, public was the word. The whole world knew that she had been betrayed and would probably lose her husband with a huge audience. In bold headlines and glossy magazines.

"Thanks. It's a nightmare," Raven sniffed. "I can't escape it."

"I know. I had women laughing at me for staying with Blake after the story broke. They obviously assumed I was a gold digger wife of some sort, but what about the woman who had tried to steal my husband? I lost my respect, but you know what, I held my family together."

"Good for you."

"I had kids. I couldn't break that up. But sometimes as women we tend to put each other down. I wanted to support you because out there our husbands are being preyed upon. Now the problem is it's not just all the millions of single mothers and sistas we have to worry about taking our men, but the white girls, too. They are after our men! They have to be that much stronger and we are just unfortunate because our thing was so public but it happens to many people not just professional athletes."

"I guess," Raven said, not sure how to respond and still not sure what Juanita really wanted to communicate to her. Everybody had something to say. Her family, friends, enemies and even strangers.

"You should forgive him. That's what I did when my husband left me. I forgave him and then the healing could begin. What I want to say is, don't let Lexie win. She's a homewrecker. Don't let her break up your family. I know her personally. She's a vulture, and Amari's too decent for her."

As Raven listened to Juanita's husky voice, questions ran through her head. *How did she get my number? How does she know Lexie? Is Lexie pregnant? If so, what was the point of fighting?*

"And Raven, have a baby. Why haven't you had a baby with your man?"

"We were . . ." Raven was about to tell her that they were going to start after the movie wrapped, but what was the use? That sure was water under the bridge.

"It's okay. You can still save your marriage. Women like Lexie can't go around thinking they can just wreck homes and go on to live happily ever after with our husbands. She thinks she's something special, but she's not, you hear me? Look at the woman who had an affair with my husband. Well, where is she now? Nowhere. I am still Mrs. Williams and we are a family. She was just trash and belongs in the garbage where she is."

Raven listened to Juanita's strong, authoritative voice, frozen. She finally forced her voice to reach Juanita's ears. "Thanks, Juanita. I appreciate your help, but I need to go."

"You are welcome. I'm praying for you. I support you. Don't worry."

"Thanks."

Raven put her head on her desk and cried.

CHAPTER 25

Philip finished writing some notes for his sermon, and then picked up the phone after the third ring.

"Dad, it's Amari." Philip leaned back into his chair and glanced at the picture of his children on his desk. Raven stood next to PJ, smiling into the camera, looking very different from her other sisters. He pushed the thought that came into his head aside. Now was not the time. The reason he had been thinking of the past so much was because of Clare's words the night before. She was the one who had him second-guessing everything.

"Good evening, son. Are you in town?"

"Yes. I just flew back from visiting Ma. She says hello."

"Good. How's she doing?"

"Fine. Wants me to fix the mess I've made."

"I see," Philip said, wishing he had not answered the phone.

"Is Raven home?" Amari said.

"No. She just left." Philip sighed. He listened to Amari's sigh.

"She tell you to say that?"

"No. She just left," Philip insisted. "That's the truth, son." There was silence on the other side. He imagined Amari thinking of something to say. After a while Amari spoke.

"I wish she would speak to me. It's hard not seeing her and not having a chance to ask for forgiveness in person. I miss her."

"Give her time. She's still hurting and needs time to process." He also wanted to add that she was carrying her anger around like armor, but kept quiet.

"I'm just worried that the longer we stay apart, the harder it'll be for us to work things out." Philip digested Amari's words and came to an instant decision.

"Where are you?"

"I'm staying in a hotel. Not far from there. I was going to try and come around later."

"Well, if you want to see her why don't you go to your house?"

"You mean in Lake Point?"

"Yes. That's where she's headed."

"She's moved back in?" Amari said. His pleasure filtered to Philip's ears.

"Don't get excited yet, Amari. She went to get some more of her stuff."

"I wish she'd move back in. I better run then. Thanks. Dad. You're the best," Amari said and hung up the phone.

"Who was that?" Clare poked her head around looking like she had just stepped off a fashion magazine. How did she manage to tantalize his senses after all these years?

"Amari." Philip watched the look of distaste on his wife's face.

"What does he want?"

"To make things right with his wife," Philip said.

"I hope you didn't tell him where Raven was, did you?" The look on Philip's face was the answer she needed. "Oh, you foolish man. He will just hurt her again. Why are you giving him a chance?"

"We all deserve second chances. Don't we, Clare?" He saw her eyes widen and her lips curl. He had touched a nerve. He wished he had never had to bring up the past, but now Clare with her negative attitude was forcing him to open up that Pandora's box.

"That's low and you know it," Clare said, folding her arms in front of her chest.

Philip got up and rushed to her quickly.

"I'm sorry, Clare. It's just that this whole thing is beginning to weigh on me. I think these children need to see each other before making any serious decisions." He held her arms but Clare remained stiff and cold. What he had opened up was no laughing matter, and he would have some work cut out for him getting back into his wife's good graces.

The house looked the same. Just lifeless and deserted. A house was nothing without the people inside to make it breathe and fill with memories. The pleasure it once gave was gone. Raven closed the front door and looked up the stairs leading to her bedroom. Her pulse quickened when she recalled how countless times after seeing Amari after a long road trip they never made it up to their bedroom but would ravish each other right there on those stairs before taking the passion up to their bedroom.

Shaking her head vigorously to clear the images she walked into the living room. She used the remote to turn on the stereo, and one of the twenty CDs loaded and began to play a Luther Vandross ballad. She clicked again until an upbeat praise gospel compilation came on. She couldn't handle any love songs right then.

Glad that the silence was wiped out by the incredible voice of Fred Hammond, she walked up the stairs to the bedroom she and Amari once shared. It looked neat as if nobody lived there, as if it was used for display not for making love and sharing a life with a man that you loved. She walked up to the bed and ran her fingers over the silk bedding that matched the window treatments then proceeded to her closet.

Once there she pulled up a chair and reached for the velvet box next to her hat box. This box held important letters and cards, mementos she held dear to her heart. She always used to tell Amari that if there was a fire she would grab that box and run. She dragged it to the bedroom and sat on the bed. The first thing she picked up was a magazine featuring a story on Calvary Worship. Her father's church was named one of the ten biggest churches in America, with a membership of close to twenty thousand. In that issue there was a picture of Amari and her, arms around each other. She put that down then picked up ticket stubs for events they had attended or invitations she had designed for fundraising projects that Amari and her worked on in their first year of marriage. Looking at everything she couldn't believe that they wouldn't be making any more. That this box would be it.

"Raven!" The voice from the door made Raven scream and drop the velvet box to the ground, spilling its contents. Relief replaced her fear when she saw Amari walk towards her, but immediately her anger took over.

"What on earth," she cried, standing by the bed with her hands over her chest. Amari could see the fierce expression on her face.

"Sorry. I'd been calling and wasn't sure where you were," Amari apologized and picked up the basket. She swatted his hand away and grabbed the basket from him with so much force she fell against the bed.

"Are you okay?" he asked.

"I'm fine. You scared me." She stared at him, trying to control her breathing. She felt weak and nervous at the unexpected sight of him. "What are you doing here?"

"Looking for you," Amari said.

"How did you know where I was?"

Amari wanted to lie but instead he just gave it to her straight. "Your dad told me."

"Oh, I should never have told him," Raven muttered under her breath, picking up the scattered papers, glad for the diversion.

"Let me help you," he offered bending down and picking up their wedding invitation and looking at it. She quickly snatched it from him.

"It's fine. I don't need your help," Raven maintained angrily. Her heart was now racing for a totally different reason. Amari stood up and she looked at him from her crouched position. He looked so good it unsettled her. It was bad enough he had just barged in without any warning. The first time she saw Amari again she had wanted to be looking gorgeous, not dressed in sweats and her hair tied up in a ridiculous green scarf! The thought of how ridiculous and pitiful she must look to him made her blood boil.

"Listen, can we talk?" Amari asked, standing a few feet from her. She glanced over his clothes, taking in the casual loose fitting pants and a crisp blue shirt. He smelled good, too. Her desire for him was instant. She missed the feel of his lips on hers, his hands on her body, but she would rather die than let him know it.

"Just leave, Amari," Raven begged instead.

"I'm not gonna leave until we talk," Amari promised firmly. "This silent treatment's gone on long enough."

"All right. Fine!" Raven said, one hand holding her velvet box like a shield and the other one raised to stop Amari from speaking again. "Just wait for me downstairs. I'll be there soon."

"Five minutes?"

"Ten. I just need to gather my things and I'll be there," Raven said, now holding the box with both hands. Amari ran his eyes over her body, then nodded and stepped back.

"Fine. See you down stairs."

Raven stood on the spot until the door was closed, then quickly returned the box into her closet and grabbed her purse. She was not going to talk to Amari today.

Who does he think he is? She fumed looking around for a way to escape. She looked at their balcony and slid the door open. She stepped outside and closed the door.

Looking down she realized there was no way she could get away from him without him seeing her. She felt foolish wanting to run away from her own husband, but with the way her heart was racing when she was in front of him there was no way she could talk to him without losing her mind. When she saw him it would be when she was ready, on her terms. She was as ready to face Amari now as a person ready to face a pride of lions.

Just go back and tell him to leave you alone, Raven tried to reason with herself. She walked to the door and tried to open it. It wouldn't budge.

Oh, no, I'm locked out, Raven thought, fighting with the handle. She looked down at the ground and realized the only way she could get back in was by calling Amari, even though he was the last person she wanted to call for help. She stood on the balcony looking at the beautiful view of the driveway, and then walked 'round the back to look at the lake. She had no way out. She could stand here forever in the heat and still Amari would be the one to save her from her stupid plan. After a minute she took her phone out of her purse and dialed the house number.

"It's me," Raven said when he picked up.

"You still coming or what?"

"I'm locked out," Raven mumbled.

"What?"

"I said I'm locked out, come and open the door for me," Raven said, and then snapped her phone shut.

In a few minutes Amari stood in their bedroom, then burst out laughing at the sight of her standing on the balcony holding her purse.

CHAPTER 26

Raven glared at Amari. That stopped his laughter quickly as he unlocked the sliding doors. He stood close to the door, and that made her edgy. The uneasiness annoyed her. She had been so certain that he no longer affected her, and to find that he did angered her.

"Thanks," she said reluctantly and walked past him. He turned his shoulders a little to let her through.

"Were you trying to run away?" Amari asked, closing the sliding doors and turning to face her.

"I have to go," she said, standing by the bed. Amari closed the gap between them and stood right by her.

"You said we could talk, Raven."

"There's nothing to talk about . . ." She stopped talking when he moved close to her. He held her arms and she didn't know how to react. She stood frozen.

"I miss you, Raven. I –I need to be with you, to make things right." Amari touched her face and she looked down. "I'm so sorry. I'll do anything to make it right between us again."

"Amari," she said but stopped again when he lifted her chin. Before she could protest or move away his lips were on hers, strong, demanding, hungry for her, just as she remembered but somehow more intense. He had taken her by surprise and she went weak, leaning into him, loving him, forgetting what he had done with . . .

"No," Raven cried, moving away from him. "Don't."

"Raven. I need you."

"I don't want you near me. It's over between us," she said, moving towards the door and rubbing her treacherous mouth.

"Let's talk, Ray. I made a huge, terrible mistake." His eyes were so sincere. It would be easy to just run into his arms and accept the flowers and gifts he had been sending her way, but the headline about a possible baby with that woman made her stomach turn. She couldn't bring herself to discuss that with him. She wanted to run, run as far away from him as humanly possible.

"I'm leaving, Amari. Just sign the divorce papers." She walked out the door and started running down the stairs.

"Raven, wait," Amari called, going after her, but by the time he reached the bottom of the stairs she was at the door. He caught her before she pulled open the wooden doors. He turned her around to face him.

"Raven, you can't keep avoiding me," he said, barely out of breath while she panted from the effort.

"I can do whatever I want."

"Are you trying to punish me? Because it's working."

"No," she said, leaning against the door, out of breath. He kissed her again and he knew she couldn't resist him. He kissed her neck feeling her breath, still fast from the combination of exertion and desire, fanning his cheek. He claimed her lips again.

"I need you. You are my wife. I can't lose you," Amari groaned in her ear, running his hands over her back and pulling her close.

"Amari," she said, but all he did was silence her with more kisses. She had missed him more than she even knew, but her response to him let her know that they were meant for each other. Their desire for each other was still strong and powerful. When her purse fell to the ground she came back to her senses. She had to wake up from this dream, because that's what it was. It was over between them.

"Stop," she said firmly, and he did though he still held her. He looked at her through heavy lidded eyes that always had the power to make her heart race. He knew that.

"Is that what you did with Lexie, Amari? Did you kiss her like this and take off her clothes and have sex with her just as we almost did?" She watched him recoil with disgust. It was like she had poured icy cold water on him. He hadn't expected that from her.

"That's not how it was," Amari said coldly. His face reflected both passion and anger, and was a mirror image of how Raven felt.

"Spare me the details, Amari. Never touch me again," Raven spat out and opened the door. This time Amari didn't try to stop her.

Lexie laid back in the creamy bubbles, letting the smooth warm water ease away the tension. Nothing was going as she had predicted. She didn't want to doubt herself and the power that she knew a woman of her beauty and brains possessed, but Amari was becoming more of a challenge than anticipated. She had hoped that Amari would be by her side when she did the interview she was about to hold with *Challenge,* the new fashion magazine. She wanted to reveal her upcoming nuptials and also announce the addition to her family. Now all the answers she had prepared would have to change. She had to come up with some other answers to the questions the writer had given her in advance.

Sinking her shoulders deeper into the water she played in her mind all that had happened since she met Amari. It was like a movie that she would never know the end to. All her plans had finally led to the seduction, the remembrance of which caused her to sigh contentedly. Oh, after that she had played the media; the hints dropped around the right ears to the right editors had definitely contributed to her story reaching headlines. The divorce news had reached her, but still Amari had not made a commitment to her. What was preventing him from cutting his cords with that boring wife of his?

Later that day, as she was getting her hair and make up done for the photo shoot and interview, Renata arrived with her ever-present leather briefcase. She wanted to go over the interview questions with Lexie so she wouldn't say anything that might give her problems later on in life. In the past Lexie had been eager to blurt out anything to reporters, and some of her careless words came back to haunt her. She'd hired Renata to make sure she didn't sabotage her new squeaky-clean image.

Lexie listened as Renata mapped out her schedule for the next few weeks. It was a rigorous itinerary, but Lexie was now a pro. The only thing Renata was worrying about was the scandal. How on earth could she spin that whole affair in a positive light? Renata decided Lexie would just have to ride the wave of public opinion.

The photographs were taken and Lexie made a decision that might have been a gamble. So far her pregnancy had just been speculation in the tabloids. Now it was time to play the card she had been holding close to her chest. Amari might kill her, but he left her no choice. She was not going to be a single mother much longer, especially when her own biological child was on the way. Now, an hour into the interview, the questions she had been waiting for were broached.

Interviewer: Ms. Hart. There have been so many rumors in the tabloids about you and one of your leading men. What do you say about that?

Lexie: I also read them. All I'll say is this. Whatever is happening between us is something I'd like to keep quiet. We still have to work through some issues.

Interviewer: What about the baby rumors?

Lexie: You have put me on the spot. To deny it would be the easiest thing, but I always want to be a woman of honesty and truth.

Interviewer: So you are pregnant?

Lexie: May I not answer that for now?

CHAPTER 27

"We'll go to church together and you can hold your head up high."

Clare woke up determined to get Raven up and about, and especially to church. She had found her daughter lying staring into space. Clare was sure that she wasn't getting much sleep.

"I don't know, Ma. I just hate everybody talking about me behind my back, whispering about me."

Clare cut her off at once. "No. It's not your fault, so don't act like you did anything wrong. Get dressed and we are going to church today. At least the first service."

"Do you think it's a good idea, Mom?" Raven sat up straighter. Her hair was a huge mess around her head. Clare held her tongue. She was about to criticize, but she knew that would ensure a fight and worsen their relationship.

"It is. I don't think staying cooped up in the house all by yourself will make you feel better. You will get stronger when you learn to face the world, face the problems headlong. Don't hide."

Mother and daughter regarded each other. Clare tilted her head sideways regarding her. "I'll help you choose something to wear if you like. Come on, get out of bed."

"Give me a few minutes, Ma. I'll be ready soon."

Raven dressed in a dark pencil skirt and white volu-
minous blouse and silver stiletto sandals. She worked
hard on her makeup and tied her thick hair back in a
tight chignon. Her image brooked no nonsense, and
that's exactly how she wanted to appear. Nobody at
church would mess with her.

"You look great," Clare said as Raven glanced at herself in the mirror one last time.

"Thanks. I don't feel great. Now you look incredible."

"Thank you."

"I sometimes wish I looked more like you."

"That's nonsense, Ray. What's wrong with the way
you look?"

"You know. As much as we think we've progressed as
a race we still are judged by our skin color, hair texture or
so many little things."

Clare sighed, and then turned Raven around to look
at her.

"Darling, look. We all can't look the same. I've
watched you for years try and compare yourself . . ."

"I wasn't the one, it was other people!"

"Still, Ray. You never really take compliments. Even
now, I can tell you still think you don't deserve Amari. I
want you to stop it! Stop it!"

"Ma!"

"No, Raven. Sometimes I think even your choice to
leave the church is all to do with this, this outside exte-
rior when inside you are so much better than all of us.
You do so much for others. Your whole life is about

serving. Don't listen to what people say. I think I want you to stand tall, not because of what you look like outside, but who you are inside. And besides, I want you to tell yourself you are beautiful and mean it. If you believe it then everybody else will, too."

"I don't want to talk about this, Ma. Let's just go."

Clare sighed again, not sure she should say this. "I was the same, Ray. I never thought I was pretty enough."

"Oh, not you, Ma. You've always been . . . so beautiful. Everybody copies your style, hair, makeup . . ."

"Yeah, but it's different from you. For me it was because I never really knew my father, just knew of him. My mother was too busy with her own life to care for me. I just felt unwanted, and because of that made many bad choices in school . . ."

"Really?"

"Low self-esteem comes in many forms, but we have to let it go, not let it control our lives. At some point you have to say, 'Yes I deserve the best' and 'Yes, I am beautiful and nobody can tell me different.'"

"I'll try." Raven smiled, feeling closer to her mother than at any other time in her life. Clare had insecurities, too? Clare Davies, her stunning mother, had felt not good enough, too?

"Good. Let me get my hat from upstairs."

Clare walked out and Raven looked at herself, really studied herself anew. Her skin was glowing, her eyes very pretty and expressive. She knew she was kind, caring and smart. She looked great and her legs were toned and shapely. She smiled, trying to be kind to herself. She should be kinder to herself because she only had one life to live and she would learn to be the voice of encouragement amidst life's criticisms.

They arrived at Calvary Worship early and Raven hid in her father's office while everybody went to a pre-service prayer. She didn't want to be a part of that yet, though lately she had been feeling a call to get involved in something with her family. They were constant and true and wouldn't hurt her the way Amari had done. The past few weeks had given her time to reflect, and she was beginning to accept that her fear of failure was what kept her from finding her gifts to use in Calvary Worship or any other church. Clare was right. It was time to stop hiding.

After the prayer session Esther came back to get her from Philip's office.

"Let's go in," she said, and they walked together in to the service. Angelo led praise and worship and, during the fast song, Raven was very conscious of the eyes on her back. She had to fight the urge to leave. The worship song reminded her of God's love and she felt tears sting her eyes as they sang, "I trust you, Lord. Even when I don't feel you near."

Oh, Father. I've been so focused on my own problems when you died for me. For me that I should live free and with joy. Forgive me. Forgive me.

Raven's head was bowed when Pastor Davies walked up to the podium. When she looked up she almost died of shock. Amari stood with her father, right there in front of the thousands who attended church that Sunday. *Oh, my God. What's going on? Let me disappear, please. Don't let him talk about me.*

The music stopped and everybody in the church seemed to take a collective breath of shock. Everybody knew about Amari and her. Everybody knew about their lavish wedding two years before, everybody had read magazines that made a mockery of her marriage, and now the object of her shame and anger stood right in front of her father's church.

Pastor Philip Davies began to speak. "Before we start service my son, my daughter's husband who some of you know, Amari Thomas, wanted to address the church as part of our testimony time. Please allow him to speak his heart for a few minutes and then we will get on the word, which I am excited to say today will be given by our associate pastor, Simon Pauling."

"Good morning, church," Amari began. The congregation said a united 'good morning.' Raven's mouth was dry and she knew that she couldn't leave. She was stuck in this nightmare. She remembered the dream she used to have when she would suddenly find herself naked in front of people from church. Someone had told her that that dream meant that she felt inferior to whoever saw her naked. There were a lot of people in that dream. At that moment, she felt naked and unable to hide her shame from the rest of the church. The buzzing in her head and the sweat in her palms was evidence enough that she was about to be humiliated.

"I would like to thank Pastor Davies for allowing me to speak to you all this morning." Amari paused and looked around at the congregation. He seemed calm and humble at the same time. "I remember two years ago when I married my lovely wife Raven. You all wished us well."

Amari stopped. Raven began to tremble. Clare held her arm as if she knew Raven was about to get up and run.

"I also know that most people in this building have read some incriminating stories about me in the press. All I want to say is, yes, I made a mistake, but the press exaggerates. I want to say in front of everyone that respects the Davies family that I love my wife and I pray that she'll forgive me. I sinned against God and I ask the forgiveness of all the people I may have offended because of this mess. Thank you for your time."

Amari handed the microphone to Pastor Davies as the church applauded and gave him a standing ovation. Raven wanted to die. She tried to remain seated, but a burning feeling in her seat sent her to her feet. Struggling to move away from her mother's grasp, she ran for the exit.

"Raven!" she heard Amari's voice but she continued to run as all the worshipers stared and gawked. Even if her life depended on it she could not remain in that sanctuary. Nothing could keep her sitting while her blood boiled and her body soaked in sweat. She finally reached the door and escaped outside, promising herself that she would never set foot in her father's church again. Once outside she took in a deep breath and looked around for a place to go. Of course she had come in to church with her parents so didn't have a car.

She started walking towards the exit to a major road when she felt Amari grip her arms.

"Ray," he said. Raven shook her head, turning away from him. Her face was awash with tears and she didn't want him to see her cry. "Look at me."

She shook her head, looking down and taking a deep breath.

"Honey . . . please."

His voice cracked with emotion. She turned to him. His head was blocking the sun but she could see the moisture in his eyes. Her heart broke, but she told herself she was being weak again.

"What, Amari? What you did . . . in there," Raven stammered, pointing towards the church building behind them.

"I'm trying to reach you. I—heard about what people were saying in the church, calling you, calling your family. I wanted to put a stop to it. They need to know that I was wrong and I am sorry."

"Good for you, but now they'll focus on it even more. I mean what . . . You know what, I don't even want to talk to you right now."

"Ray. I've been trying to talk to you for weeks. Don't you think you've been silent for too long?"

"What's there to talk about?" Raven broke in, folding her hands in front of her chest.

"I feel terrible." Amari began, and then held up his hand. "I was awful. I made a terrible mistake. I was weak, the whole thing was pathetic, but I want us to talk. I need a second chance."

223

"I don't know. I just want to get away from here right now. I—I don't want to be here and I didn't bring my car."

Amari sighed, frustrated. She wasn't making it easy on him. He felt her pain. He was ashamed. He had let so many people down. The young men who looked up to him. The whole church who thought he was different and would be a faithful husband. A godly man.

"I don't want a divorce, Ray. God hates divorce."

"If you are going to quote the Bible then read Matthew, Amari," Raven scolded, her anger building. "What you did is grounds for divorce. Unfaithfulness is what God hates more!"

"Okay. Okay, you are right. I deserve every bad thought you have towards me, but can't we go somewhere and talk?"

"No." She shook her head, looking at the ground. She noticed some people staring at them as they walked towards the church, almost an hour late for the service.

"I just want to leave. Maybe we can talk later. Right now I can't even think straight."

"Fine. Why don't you take my car? I'll find my way to pick it up later. But you have to meet with me tonight. We can go somewhere and talk."

"In public."

Amari laughed at that, but saw that Raven meant business. "Are you sure?"

"I mean I don't want to be alone with you somewhere, like, the house. Okay, I'll see you then. Can I have the keys?" Raven held out her hand.

"All right. I'll pick you up at seven or eight, whichever you prefer." He held the keys away from her reaching hands.

"Eight's fine."

He handed her the car keys.

"I'll walk you to the car," Amari offered. She had no choice but to agree. She didn't say a word to him all the way to his Escalade. She got in and closed the door and drove away without glancing in his direction.

CHAPTER 28

Amari arrived at the Davies house a few minutes before eight. It felt like a date to him, and he was nervous. He had planned the whole evening out, and it had put a dent in his bank account. Still, the excitement and butterflies made him feel like a little kid. The sun was getting ready to set but it was still a warm, perfect evening, perfect for his plans.

He stepped out of the car and tapped the limo driver's window.

"Will be back shortly," he said.

He rang the doorbell and Philip Senior opened it.

"Hello, son," he greeted him, and then winked. That said it all. Philip was happy that he and Raven were moving in a more positive direction.

Amari had just sat down when Raven walked in. Amari immediately stood up, glancing in her direction. God only knew how much he loved her. She had dressed simply in a knee-length cotton dress. She had lost weight, he suddenly realized. She looked so small and vulnerable as she walked towards her father and kissed him on the cheek.

"I'll be back soon, Dad. Amari and I just need to talk."

"That's all right," Philip said. In a way he was glad Clare wasn't home. She had a meeting with Esther and her youth group. She might have said something to spoil the evening which seemed calm, considering.

"Good night, Dad."

"You kids have fun," Philip said, but the look Raven gave him told him not to be too hopeful. She walked ahead of Amari towards the door and Amari ran to open it as if he was a hotel bellboy.

When she stepped outside she was surprised to see the black stretch limousine parked in front of her parents' home.

"What's going on?" she asked, turning to Amari questioningly.

"I didn't have my car so I got this instead."

He could tell that Raven was about to say something, but he could see her make the decision to remain silent. He had counted on that. He didn't know what he could've done if she had refused to go in the limo.

Once they were settled into the car, the driver left the Davies' driveway smoothly and then, after a few minutes, entered the freeway.

Raven looked out the window, but didn't say anything for a while. He watched her profile, loving the fullness of her upper lip. He knew she had questions as he sat opposite her. The limo reminded him of their wedding night. He wondered if she remembered, too.

"Would you like a drink?" He held up a bottle of white wine for her view.

"Where are we going?" she asked instead. Amari replaced the bottle.

"I thought dinner on the lake would be good," Amari said. He wished he could figure out what she was thinking, but she wasn't giving much away. He couldn't wait till they got to their destination. He hoped she would be impressed. "First, I wanna say thank you for coming out with me."

"That's fine." She waved his thanks away like it was a fly.

"I've missed you."

They looked at each other. His eyes were sincere. She wanted to believe him, he could tell.

"This is hard, Amari," she said.

"It's me. I feel like I'm making you nervous. Like you are with a stranger."

"I don't know. I thought I knew you, but I was wrong."

"You were not wrong about me, baby. I'm still the same man. I just made a horrible mistake."

She didn't disagree with him. They arrived at the lakefront.

"Come on." Amari reached for her hand but she shook her head and made her way towards the door. She got out and stood on the tarmac.

He gestured towards the railing. In the distance she could see a white boat that shimmered on the water. She gazed at the water as Amari talked to the limo driver. He came towards her.

"I thought we were just gonna talk," Raven said.

"We are. But I wanted us to talk in style."

"Okay."

He helped her onto the boat. "Is this a good idea? You know I can't swim that well."

"Then don't get in the water. Stay on the boat," he said, and then added, "You can wear a life vest."

She shook her head. Amari seemed prepared for every argument she could come up with to avoid getting on the boat with him. She realized she was wasting her breath. She allowed Amari to lead her on. She held his hands for support, but as soon as she felt steady on her feet she pulled her hand away. A man in a black vest handed them a tall glass of champagne. Raven took it then stood looking at the water.

"We'll take off in a few minutes," the captain announced.

"Thank you," Amari said. There were two chairs and tables on the deck and Amari noted the ice bucket and cheese and fruit platter. He was glad that everything had been taken care of.

"Whose boat is this?" Raven asked.

"I rented it for the evening," Amari said. "So for now, it's ours."

The sky looked beautiful as the sun was now making its way down. Amari liked how her skin glowed in the fading light, how lovely she looked, though he was seriously concerned about her weight loss. Still, she looked more fragile to him. So different. She liked it on the boat but she wasn't going to say it, he knew. In their two years of marriage they had hardly fought, and their first major fight was so difficult that he had no idea how to get things back on track with her.

The boat ride was about twenty minutes, and then they stopped in front of a white beach house. A table was laid out for two on the terrace.

"The house is ours for the evening," he said, pulling the chair for her. She looked towards the lake as she sat on the padded garden chair. The boat was still there waiting. Raven sat down and, before she finished pushing her chair in, their favorite chef, Kenneth Wallace, brought out appetizers.

"Here you are," Kenneth said, putting a plate of salad in front of her.

"Kenneth." She smiled and hugged him. "You cooked tonight?"

"Yes, Mrs. Thomas. I hope you enjoy what I have for you this evening. We'll start with this fresh garden salad with feta cheese and fresh fruit. After that I'll bring you your main course, which is an orange salmon with tender sweet potatoes and wild rice. For dessert I've prepared for you a peanut butter cake with cream and walnuts."

"Wow," Raven said. "My mouth's watering."

"I'll bless the food," Amari said once Kenneth left. Raven put her head down and listened as Amari began to pray. "Father, we thank you for this beautiful day. We thank you for forgiving our sins. Father, tonight we pray that you bless our food and our time together. Bless my wife, Lord. In Jesus' name. Amen."

"Amen," Raven said. She smiled at him. "This is a surprise."

"I wanted to impress you."

"You didn't have to."

"I know."

She picked up her fork and took a bite of salad. "Mmmh. Good."

"I know. It's got great flavors. Don't know how he does it, but Ken knows how to throw it down."

"He does."

"Do you remember what he made for our first Christmas dinner?"

"Oh, yes. I wanted to lick the bowl he baked in. I've tried to learn, but my stuff never comes out quite as good."

"It does, Ray. I think you're a great cook."

"You're just saying that because you want to . . ." She almost said it. She used to tease him. When ever he would compliment her she would say to him, "*You are just saying that because you want to get me to bed.*" She almost said it, too. He would always respond, "*I can get you to bed without saying a word.*"

It was strange how much had changed.

"I do."

He looked at her. His eyes were intent and focused on her. He could see the change come to her, a feeling she couldn't hide. He could read the desire in her eyes, but he knew that it wasn't going to be easy or maybe even possible to get her back into his arms again.

"Those days are gone," she said instead and looked away from him at the water. Just then Kenneth brought in the next course. It was delicious. The first bite melted in their mouths.

"So how's the center? Is Jalen still there?"

"Oh, yes. He's still there."

"That's good. I know he will do well."

"I haven't seen Esther in a while. How is she?"

"Fine."

Amari had no idea how difficult talking actually would be because of the elephant in the room. He couldn't talk about the movie, he couldn't even ask her about work because she was on leave of absence because of him.

"And you?"

She chewed her food slowly, regarding him. After swallowing she responded. "Fine. A mess. Fine."

"What can I do?"

Before she could answer, Kenneth brought out the dessert. "Here you go. I got the coffee started."

"Thanks, my man. I know it was short notice." Amari stood up and shook his hand.

"It's all right. You two enjoy your evening. I'll take off now."

Kenneth left.

"He doesn't need the boat?" she asked.

"No. You can come here by road or boat. I thought the boat might impress you a little."

She smiled. It was nice to see her smile. It was like a glimmer of sunlight from gray sky. She took a forkful of dessert. "It's good, but I'm full."

"I'll finish it." Amari took hers and polished off both their desserts in short order.

"We can walk on the beach if you like," Amari said. "Then we can come back for coffee."

"I don't know. Shouldn't we be getting back?"

No, no, Amari thought, but instead said, "If you like. I just want to walk this off and have some of Chef Wallace's coffee."

The walk was quiet, companionable, but Raven cut it short as she thought she had been bitten by mosquitoes.

"I didn't exactly come prepared for a night on the water," she said.

They got back in the house. It was very sparsely furnished, but with warm and inviting colors. The kitchen held the aroma from Chef Wallace's cooking and the brewing coffee. Amari poured their two cups then left to go upstairs. He came back with a tube of ointment.

"You sure know your way around this place," Raven said when she saw what he held. It was anti-itch cream.

"Do you want to put some on?" Amari asked and touched a spot on her back. "You seem to have a bump here."

"No thanks." She jumped at his touch and put the coffee down. "I think it'll be fine."

"I just wanted to help," he said.

"Amari, this is very awkward for me. I don't know if I'm ready to be talking to you."

"If you don't talk to me you'll forget how we felt about each other."

"Did you forget? I mean when you . . . did it with Lexie?"

"No. I made a huge mistake."

"Is she the only one? I mean, how do I know you are not making a fool of me every time you are on the road?"

"Because of this," Amari said, and reached for her hand. He put it on his chest. "Listen." His heart was going so fast he knew she could feel it. "Just look at me and tell me you don't see that I am not lying. That I regret hurting you more than anything else in my life."

She moved her eyes from his chest, where he captured her hand in his big strong fingers. She really looked at him and she knew he was sincere just as her breath caught in her throat. She didn't want to be a fool, but she was already melting. She had been trying so hard to hate him, but all she felt was love for him. He saw the tears before she broke down into sobs.

"Amari. I don't know what to do," she cried, and he pulled her close, holding her tight against him. She hit his chest gently. "I'm angry, but I miss you so."

"I miss you, too. I love you. I love you. Tell me you still love me, even a little."

She nodded and he captured her mouth, tasting her tears on her full lips. Their emotions were high and she knew the moment he kissed her that she was lost. It was a hungry kiss that brought her into contact with Amari's desire for her, sending fireworks through her body.

He stopped briefly and looked in her eyes, questioning, wanting to make sure that she was sure.

"Are you ready?" he asked and she nodded as a lone tear trickled down her face. She wanted this man and she was surprised by her desire. It went beyond logic as she surrendered to him and felt like she was coming home. They moved together towards the bedroom, kissed, held each other, removed buttons and flopped on the bed.

Once his shirt was off it felt incredible holding his strong body again, feeling his hands all over hers. She sighed and listened while he told her he loved her, drank in all his love and desire as they took each other high and higher, until the explosion of stars rendered them both crying out loud with release. Afterwards they collapsed into each other's arms, bodies languid and all the tensions of the past few months released into the air. She wanted to forgive her husband. She needed him. They would make it work!

CHAPTER 29

After the few days with Amari, cold hard life came back. Two pieces of news just took her back from the clouds and set her back to harsh reality. To say she was angry was an understatement. It went beyond anger and disbelief. She was being reckless, she knew, but she just couldn't help it.

"How long does this thing take?" Raven asked, her cellphone in one hand and the other holding the steering wheel.

"It shouldn't take long. As soon as Amari signs the papers, then your marriage will be over. I still wanted to talk to you about counseling. Amari seems to think that your marriage can be saved."

"No!" Raven screamed and made a quick turn in front of an oncoming red sports car. The car honked at her and the man in the car waved a fist at her. Raven barely registered him.

She had spent three days with Amari at the lake house, making love, talking, planning their future, but the moment she got back home to reality everything had fallen apart in stunning proportions.

"I never made love to Lexie. It was sex, and all it did was show the worst of me that I never want to see again. That weakness is what I am ashamed of. I take full responsibility, but I also want to forget about it. I always knew that God would never let us be tempted without providing an escape route. It was there, but somehow I was so relaxed I didn't take it."

She had listened to him, they had cried. She had screamed. It seemed that as hard as they tried to move on, Lexie was in bed with them. Now she understood why physical intimacy was so powerful. The joy and closeness it had given them was now being destroyed because he had shared what she thought was purely hers with somebody else. It was more than betrayal, it was sacrilegious. But forgiveness and love had won. Or so she thought.

If the tabloids had made her angry before, the article in *Challenge* had fueled her fire to volcanic proportions. Amari and Raven had gone back home after the idyllic three days by the water. She was excited to start over with Amari, and when they got to their house they had planned a second honeymoon together. They'd looked through the internet at exotic destinations like Bora Bora, Cancun and islands that she had never heard of. It was delicate but beautiful, being back together. Maybe the feeling could have lasted all week if she hadn't decided to go to the hair salon to get her hair washed and styled. Something fresh and new, to get her going with her new life with Amari. When she arrived at the hair salon she was surprised to find Candice there.

The hair stylist, Justine, was very happy to see her. Luckily she didn't bring up anything about Amari or the tabloids, so she took a seat by the washing basins. Then everything fell apart.

What made it worse was that Candice had brought the magazine to her when her hair was wet by the basins, the salon full of women she knew. "Hi, Raven," Candice said. "I see your husband's in the news again."

"He is?" Raven asked and received the thick fashion and beauty magazine Candice held out to her.

There were many things that made her heart stop. First the cover had Lexie, looking innocent and sexy at the same time, holding her stomach and a knowing smile on her face. The teeth seemed to mock her. Each one of her pearly whites spoke to her jabbing her and biting at her nerves.

The bold shout line on the cover read *LEXIE PREGNANT*.

That moment in that hair salon was the lowest point in her life. While Candice watched her face, Raven turned the pages and went to the article as if she was seeing a horrible accident in the street and was unable to look away. The big, glossy photographs were mainly of Lexie with her glowing, semi-transparent skin. There was one of her and her costars for her last movie, *A Lot Like Silence*. Amari stood there next to her, his arms around her.

They made such a good couple that bile rose in her throat. There were too many people watching her to allow the tears to fall, or to run away. If Candice or any of the clients and stylists in the salon saw, it would be all over the city. They would talk about how Amari had hurt her and left her for the stunning actress and how she had cried in the salon like a baby. It was better she swallowed the bitter pill and deal with the discomfort later, in private.

"Interesting," Raven said, closing the magazine and handing it to Candice. "But I brought a book to read."

I should leave, Raven thought, *I should just get up and walk out.* But she knew that she would not give Candice, or whoever was watching, the satisfaction of seeing her run.

She sat on the chair and opened up the book about missionaries that she had been reading. More and more leaving the country for a mission trip seemed attractive. Candice couldn't say more as it was her turn to get her hair shampooed, but the conversation turned to cheating spouses in no time. Nancy, who swept the hair from the floor and cleaned the salon, was very vocal in her assessments of men.

Raven listened to the monologue about cheating men as if it was the drone of a loud plane and she couldn't wait for it to take off into the sky. It looked like this plane was going to be stationary for a long time as Nancy stood center stage in the salon, holding her broom in one hand and a dust cloth in the other gloved one. Raven wanted to get up and run out but she told herself that if she survived that first major outing in the gossip-infested salon, then she would get stronger. God didn't want her running away as if she had done something wrong. She had to stay and listen. She had to get her hair done, and Nancy and her wild stories were not going to drive her away.

"What would you like me to do today?" Justine asked.

Raven looked at her face in the mirror. Her hair when blow-dried straight reached below her shoulders.

"Cut it."

"You want a trim?" Justine asked, measuring the length to cut with her fingers.

"No. Just chop it all off. As short as you can go. Just cut it, Justine."

Justine looked at Raven's face in the mirror. She saw something in her eyes that meant business. Justine, who usually had smart jokes about everything, didn't utter a word as she picked up the scissors.

Raven watched her hair fall off. It didn't bring relief, but it symbolized the end of something in her. Maybe the end of her marriage because Amari had failed to tell her about having a baby with Lexie. And maybe she had failed to see it, hoping that he wouldn't have a child with someone other than her.

Even though she had survived the trip to the salon and the encounter with her former best friend, she still knew that next time she would fork out the money to have the hair stylist come to her until the whole mess died down in about ten years or more.

After the salon trip she had to endure Clare asking about her hair. She was surprised when Clare said that it suited her. Philip looked at her and smiled.

"Wow. That's a nice hairstyle."

"What's wrong?" Clare asked.

"It's really over between me and Amari."

Raven watched both her parents look at her, shocked.

"You two have spent the past few days together. I thought things were getting better between you."

Raven didn't really want to admit that she also had high hopes for her future with Amari until a few hours ago. She didn't know if she wanted to show her mother the magazine, either. She remembered Amari saying that the magazines exaggerate but this was Lexie's own interview in her own words. She claimed that she was pregnant with Amari's baby.

"Did you talk to Amari?" Raven asked.

"I have. I know I was just as angry as you at the beginning, but now I'm beginning to see that he's going through a lot of pain. He has major regrets. He's hurting. I'm mad at him, but divorce . . . it's so easy to just give up when you can fight and make things work." Clare spoke to her daughter, but she would glance at Philip once in a while for his approval.

"It's over," Raven said resignedly. "It was too good to be true."

"Why do you say that, Rave?" Clare asked. Raven looked at her mother and father staring at her with concern. She shook her head, fighting the tears.

"Ma, you know . . ."

"Know what?

"I'm not that pretty," Raven said as a tear threatened to roll down one eye. She rubbed her eye ready to poke it out if she cried.

"That's ridiculous and you know it," Clare cried as Philip looked on.

"I'm dark. Why am I so dark, anyway? Both you and Dad are so light." Raven looked from her father's light brown skin to her mother's caramel complexion, so pale she could pass for white from a distance. As if a dream, Raven noticed the look that passed from her mother and father. It was so quick, but unmistakable. It seemed loaded with fear and something else Raven couldn't quite put her finger on.

Am I adopted? What was that all about?

"What?" Raven said, looking from one parent to the other. "What is it?"

"Nothing." Clare picked up her magazine, but Raven could tell she wasn't even reading it.

"Ma. You just looked at Dad as if you . . . you looked guilty or something. Like you know why I'm dark, which is ridiculous." Raven gave a nervous laugh when Clare wouldn't look at her. "Oh, my God. Am I adopted? Dad? Think about it. It's so obvious I'm surprised nobody ever talked about it. Everybody used to say I looked like Aunt Mildred, but how come Tahlia, Esther and PJ all look like you two, and me, well, I'm just the black sheep of the family."

"Don't say that," Clare said. Raven noticed that her mother's face was flushed.

Raven looked in her mother's eyes, really looked at her, and knew that she was about to discover something that could change her life. When she spoke now her voice had changed. It had an ominous quality that Clare had never heard before. "Ma. There's something you are not telling me. All my life I've never felt like I belonged. It wasn't just that I looked differently, but I just didn't fit in. I love you all, but I've never felt—special or beautiful, like all of you. That's why I'm not surprised that Amari would want something better. But, the reason I was different wasn't because I was just born different, was it? Am I adopted?"

Clare looked at Philip like a drowning woman reaching for a lifeline. There it was again. That look that made her blood freeze in her veins and her body tremble.

"No," Philip said. "You are our baby."

Raven shook her head. "I don't look like you. You can tell me. I can handle it. It's okay." Her voice sounded alien even to her own ears. It made so much sense. All those words people had said made sense.

"You look like me," Clare said. "I'm just lighter than you."

"No. It's more than the color of my skin. Even my build, even my temperament. I'm not a good Christian like all of you. I'm the only one not working in the church."

"Raven, it has nothing—"

"Philip! Don't say anything," Clare hissed at him, her eyes flashing. Her voice was raw like she had been screaming.

"What? What are you hiding from me?" Seconds ticked away like eternity as Raven stared at her mother and father like they were strangers, and then she demanded, "Tell me now!"

"There's nothing to talk about." Clare had that superior tone of hers that suggested that nobody could tell her anything. She knew that tone, and Raven had watched her mother use it countless times. She didn't yell but her silky voice, look and words could freeze the sun when she chose. This time Raven wasn't going to cower.

"I can always find out. I can insist on a blood test. I can announce it to the whole church unless you tell me!" Raven stood up, looking down at her mother with angry eyes.

"Raven," Clare said in that tone again. "We've been good to you. We never treated you differently. You went to the best schools and colleges. Why are you even saying this?"

"Clare," Philip growled. Clare glared at him, her eyes spitting fire. "Don't. It's time."

Raven looked at Philip's sad, resigned eyes and knew that her world would never be the same. She tried not to show the fear she felt. Inside she was unsteady, wanting to go to sleep and wake up and everything would be the way it was before this moment.

"It doesn't change anything, Philip," Clare said.

"Sit down, Ray," Philip said calmly. Raven slowly sat back on the couch but moved away from her mother.

"Raven. I want you to know that we kept this from you because we love you," Clare said, reaching her hands out to Raven. She put her hand on her daughter's, but Raven didn't respond to her touch.

"Kept what?"

Clare looked at Philip, wishing she could wake up from this nightmare. Raven could see in Philip's eyes that he wasn't going to say anything. It was all Clare's story to tell. Raven glanced at her mother with very little sympathy.

"When Philip married me I was already pregnant," Clare said simply.

"With me?"

"Yes." Clare practically forced the words out like she was pulling teeth.

"So . . ."

"Philip is your father, but not the biological one." Raven let the words sink in, going deep into her heart like ice going through rock. Her mouth opened but no words came.

CHAPTER 30

The last thing Amari wanted to do was to meet with Lexie. He wanted to focus all his energy on fighting for Raven. Pastor Philip Davies had asked him, man to man, "What do you miss about Raven? Why do you want her back so much?"

The images that passed through his mind had caused tears to form in his eyes. The image of her surprise when he proposed to her, or how she stood innocently in her wedding gown. Her silky, dark chocolate skin beneath his hands. He knew he had caused her a lot of pain and killed her trust in him, and that tortured him more than anything else. More than the fear that he might never be able to win her back. More than the dread that she would never look at him with that love and sweetness that he had come to rely on.

"I love her," Amari began, his voice choked up, but he couldn't pretend anymore. "She's pure, lovely, amazing. Being with her completed me, Dad. She—she's the best thing that happened to me. I knew I loved her before—before all this movie craziness. My life has no meaning without her."

Philip had nodded his head and still had to ask the next question.

"Then son, tell me this. Why did you sleep with that woman? Why did you do that?" Amari's face turned hot with embarrassment.

"It is and will always be the biggest mistake of my life. I've no excuse except I let my guard down," Amari said with anger. "I should've known. I've been in situations like that before. Women will even hide in your hotel room and wait for you. But I didn't think Lexie was that kind of woman. She seemed to have it all together."

"You didn't think she would be interested in you."

"I thought she was a friend, but I was wrong."

"What about this whole baby thing. Is that true?"

"I don't know."

Amari really didn't know. He had been avoiding Lexie, but now she had sent him an official letter to meet at her house. Amari didn't want to go there, but he knew that it was her house or a public place. A meeting in public wasn't going to help his case with Raven. Raven had been subjected to enough pictures of him and Lexie.

After their few days together, he knew he had to fly to California to finish up some business, but before he left Raven's lawyer had contacted him about the divorce. He thought that they had made up, but in two short beats he was back to square one. It was as if the time they had spent together at the lake had never happened. She wouldn't answer his calls and Philip told him to give Raven more time. When Amari boarded the plane he was angry, but not about to give up.

After he was let into the estate, Lexie opened the door herself. At the same time the twins came around to greet him. Madison put her arms around Lexie's bare leg. Lexie looked beautiful in the champagne-colored dress and gold slippers. Her soft, wavy hair framed her face. Her beauty was incredible but Amari wasn't moved. The kids around her added to the image she wanted to portray. Gorgeous, but warm and maternal.

"Hi, stranger," she said, then leaned in and gave him a hug with Madison still hanging on. "Come on in."

Amari followed Lexie into the beautiful living room. Unfortunately, being in Lexie's beach house reminded him of that time. The time he had done the unthinkable. Of course everybody else thought he was a hero, but he knew that God was not pleased with him. He wanted to fix the whole Lexie issue as soon as he could and get on with his life with Raven. If she would have him. Lexie's magazine articles were hurting him.

Lexie studied Amari as she sat down, and the girls clamored·around her like shields.

"How are you?" Lexie asked, her eyes searching his. Amari could barely look at her but he forced himself, keeping his hands on his suit pants.

"I'm fine. The kids seem comfortable," he said. Lexie looked at the girls.

"Did you say hi to Uncle Amari?" The girls giggled. "Come on, say hi."

"Hi," Madison and Morgan sang, their tiny teeth gleaming. Amari smiled.

"Hi, girls," he said.

"Do you play basketball?" Morgan said.

"Yes, I do," Amari said. "Do you?"

"I can play," Morgan said. "Madison can't play. She always drops the ball."

"But she tries," Lexie said, smiling at Amari. "A bit competitive." Amari nodded, then decided the time was over for polite talk.

"So, you said you wanted to talk to me about something important," Amari reminded her, looking pointedly at the girls.

"Why don't we just relax have a nice evening and then talk about it," Lexie implored. Her voice reminded him of that evening they had slept together. Friendly, but with underlying secret desires. Now he knew and recognized it. Amari looked at the twins then cleared his throat.

"I think it's important that you get to the point, Lexie, because I have some things to do before the premiere." Amari watched the irritation cross Lexie's eyes.

"Fine," she ground out, and then called in the direction of the kitchen. "Janice! Come and get the kids!" Janice ran in, dressed comfortably in sweats.

"I think you can have dinner with the girls. I'll dine alone with Amari. Tell the kitchen."

"I don't think I'll be staying for dinner, Lexie," Amari said quickly.

"What the . . . !" Lexie stopped herself. "Take the girls, Janice."

"Come Morgan, Madi," Janice said cheerfully, ignoring the flare of anger in Lexie's voice.

"I wanna eat with you!" Morgan said.

"I'll join you later. Just go, Morgan. Take your sister," Lexie said, the frustration evident in her voice. As soon as the kids were out of earshot she turned on Amari, her eyes flashing with anger.

"What's the matter with you? You're acting like we're strangers or something." She cursed under her breath, and Amari tried not to laugh. What was the matter with her? He had never seen her lose control like this. Lexie always acted cool and contained in public and at work.

"You said you had something to tell me in person. I just want to hear it and then go back to my place," Amari said.

"Oh, that's how it's gonna be now, huh? So what we did meant nothing to you?"

"What did we do?"

"I gave myself to you! I don't just sleep with any Tom Dick and Harry, but I let you . . ."

"No. I let you!"

"So what? It takes two, and we did it, didn't we?"

"Yes, and I'm sorry. That was a mistake," Amari said. He was sitting so calmly he didn't see the shoe come off and hit him in the face.

"Damn it!" He got up while Lexie stood up, too, her huge breasts rising and falling with her anger. "What's the matter with you?" Amari rubbed his face wondering if the gold stiletto had drawn blood.

"I'm nobody's mistake," Lexie said, walking up to him and pushing him in the chest. "I thought you cared about me!"

"I did, as a friend." He emphasized the word friend. "I didn't want anything more. I'm married!"

"To that ugly nobody!"

"Shut up!" Amari growled. "You don't talk about my wife that way. She's more beautiful than you'll ever be. Don't you dare talk about my wife."

"Well, where was she while you were busy doing me, Amari? You think you can just have your fun and leave me? I'm not a groupie! I'm my own woman, and I thought we could have a relationship together."

"Even if I wasn't married I would not have a relationship with you," Amari said, and caught her hand as she came to slap him. "This is not a movie and I'm not playing games. Stop spreading lies about me. I'm not in love with you, and I'm not leaving my wife for you."

Amari saw something in Lexie he didn't want to believe. Was that vulnerability? Her next words surprised him even further.

"Why can't you love me? What's wrong with me?" she asked. When she was honest like this he could almost feel sorry for her, but never love.

"We are from two different worlds."

"I can change, Amari," she beseeched, holding out her hands to him, but Amari didn't budge. "You could make me a better woman."

He knew she was acting. She didn't want to change. She liked her life just the way it was, playing with his life, playing games and not caring who got hurt in the first place. He had her number. He knew what kind of woman she was. "I'm not interested in digging through the muck to find your soul, Lexie."

"Oh, really?" Lexie snarled, her red lips curled angrily. The vulnerable woman was gone. "What about your baby, Amari? Is he or she going to be from a different world? What about that?"

"You've been hinting at some baby and nobody believes you. Why don't you just move on from that one-night stand so I can get on with saving my marriage?" Lexie snatched her hand away from him and rubbed it slowly where his hand had grasped her wrist.

"It's true, Amari. Raven knows it, too. All it took was that one time and I got pregnant," Lexie said calmly, a poker expert showing her ace. Her eyes filled with tears, and Amari could see the gears shifting in her head. "I never thought I'd be a single mother. I am one now with the twins, but I thought you and I could be a family."

"I don't believe you," Amari said quietly, staring at her stomach.

"That's what I wanted to tell you, Amari. I didn't come right out and say it to reporters because I thought you should know in person first. We're going to have a baby. A baby!"

Amari turned away from her, covering his head. He watched his life slowly drown beneath Lexie's words. Did Raven find out? Was that why she had suddenly changed?

"How do you know it's my baby? Lexie, you admitted that you had many lovers on national TV."

"I wasn't with anybody else for five months before I met you. I was too busy with Morgan and Madison, and I call them lovers but they were relationships that just didn't last," Lexie explained, still standing up. "This isn't how I envisioned this. Not at all."

"This isn't how I wanted to start my family, with a woman I barely know. Oh, God, what have I done?"

Lexie looked at Amari, great satisfaction in her eyes.

The next day they drove to see the doctor together. Amari wanted to find out first if Lexie was really pregnant, and, if so, if the child she carried was his or some other man's.

"Amari, have you thought about what you'll do about your baby and me?" Lexie asked.

"I've been too busy trying to get my wife back," Amari responded caustically.

"She doesn't want you, does she? Why don't you let her go? I heard what you did at her church. Speaking in front of everybody trying to win her back, and she still dumped you!"

"How do you know that?"

"News like that travels fast."

Amari was quiet, shocked and embarrassed. Her taunting voice was also making him very angry. "It's really none of your business."

"It is. Here I am carrying your child and yet you still stand in public professing love to a woman who doesn't want you. My family can't believe I let myself get pregnant with . . ."

"How did that happen, anyway? I know you have quite a colorful past, but I have never heard of you getting pregnant. Can you explain why now?"

"Did you use protection, Amari?" Lexie taunted, and Amari realized he didn't even like her.

After twenty minutes they arrived at the doctor's office, a luxurious-looking building in the heart of Beverly Hills. The meeting in the comfortable room was awkward, but the doctor spoke in a way that made Amari relax. Amari listened with a sinking feeling as the doctor explained that Lexie was already four months pregnant.

"I will be able to perform the scan today," the doctor said with a slight accent. She clearly wasn't born in the United States. Lexie looked at Amari, but he refused to meet her eye.

Finally, Lexie lay down on the bed and the doctor put some jelly on her stomach and ran a machine over the lubricated surface.

"You can take a look at the screen here," Dr. Simpson directed with her finger. Amari turned and looked, but all he saw was movement on the screen.

"Here is the head of the baby," she said while Lexie looked at the screen, tears in her eyes. Amari looked, too, and finally the puzzle became clear. He could see the body of the baby moving on the screen. A lump filled his throat. This was his baby. His baby was real.

CHAPTER 31

"Did Raven tell you what she was going to talk about?" Clare asked, putting the final touches to her makeup. Philip pulled his suit jacket from the bed where Clare had placed it for him and put it on over a white shirt.

"No, she didn't. Just that she needed some time to talk to the congregation and air some things."

"Philip," Clare cried, dropping her brush on the dresser. "What does that mean—what is she going to talk about?"

"I don't know."

"And you are just going to let her stand there and say whatever she wants? She could ruin me!"

"The truth never ruins anybody," Philip said. He was tired of the whole mess. Tired of the feelings of confusion in his family.

"I don't understand why you would let her do this. She hasn't really been a part of this church for so many years, and now she wants to go and stand in front of the congregation and say what? What!"

"Once again, Clare, I don't know," Philip responded calmly. He could see that the calmer he got the more worked up Clare became.

"I forbid it. Philip, I can't let you do that," Clare said, beseeching him with her eyes and voice.

"Many years ago you forbade me to tell anybody the truth about Raven's biological father. I didn't agree, but I did it. Today, I want to tell you that I regret it. I did it for you, but it hasn't served Raven well at all."

"I can't believe you. What good would telling her all those years ago have done other than make her feel even more alienated? What good, Philip?"

"I don't know, but the truth always has a way of coming out and it always sets you free." Philip took his wife's hands off his shoulders and walked out of the room. Clare fell on the bed, sobbing.

Raven read over her notes one more time while she sat in her father's office. For the first time she had arrived at church before him and spent a great deal of time praying. What was strange was that she didn't feel nervous. She felt strong, calm and focused. She felt like finally she was beginning to understand who she was, beyond what other people said, beyond how she looked.

Knowing that Philip was not her father was hurting more than she would like to admit. She had always felt that no matter what happened, she had the best father in the world. Now, well, he was still her father, and her mother's boyfriend certainly wasn't.

She had a long way to go but she knew that she was beginning to accept who she was. She was not going to let people hurt her anymore over things she could not change.

But there were things she could change. Her involvement in the church, her career, how she touched other people. She could change that.

The door to the pastoral suite opened and Raven looked up uncertainly. It was Clare. Clare looked on edge. Her eyes looked like she had been crying, and though she was perfectly dressed in a sky blue suit with matching accessories she didn't seem as composed.

"Hi, Mom," Raven said, standing up. Clare walked towards her, a determined look on her face.

"Raven. Your dad told me that you would be addressing the church." Clare's voice shook, and that scared Raven more than if she had been harsh and confident.

"Just something brief, Ma."

"What about?"

"You will find out along with everybody else, just like I did when Amari blabbed our business in front of the whole church," Raven said, and then picked up her purse to walk past her mother. Clare grabbed her arm.

"Is this about your father?"

"No, but which father?"

"Oh, Raven, don't be like that."

"Like what?"

"Are you trying to hurt me? Are you trying to hurt this family just because somebody else is your real father?"

"It has nothing to do with this, Ma . . ."

"I'm sorry I didn't tell you. I—I just thought it was easier on everybody if you didn't know, if nobody knew. I was ashamed of my behavior later in life. I felt bad, believe me."

Raven just watched Clare carry on, but she wanted to focus. She didn't want to listen to excuses, and she certainly didn't blame her mother that her father was some no-good high school basketball star who didn't amount to much and died from his lifestyle.

"I better go, Ma. I'll see you inside."

"Raven!" she cried, and as Raven walked out she could hear her sobs.

❧

Angelo and Esther led the praise and worship together as Raven sat with her family in the front row. She sang along with everybody else, and then it was time for Pastor Philip Davies to go up and introduce her. They walked up together. He held her hand up the steps and everybody applauded as they walked up. In all her thirty-two years, Raven had never done what she was about to do. The last time she had been on the stage was to get married, and before that it was when she sang in the choir with her sisters as pre-teens and had humiliated herself. Now she felt bolstered by her new way of thinking and understanding and her faith that God had not made a mistake in giving her life.

After a few words Philip finally said, "And today, my daughter Raven wanted to address our church family as part of our Sunday sermon. Please welcome Raven Thomas."

Raven flinched as he said her last name. This was not about Amari, this was simply about her. She took the microphone from her father, put her notes on the podium and glanced at the sanctuary. It was packed, and at the back there were some people still arriving and ushers showing them to their seats. The view from there was incredible. Her eyes traveled to where her mother and sisters sat. Angelo next to Esther, Tahlia and PJ, then Clare and Philip. Raven had been surprised when she saw Clare come in. It was rare for Clare to miss service, but she was so sure that after all the problems they'd had that Clare would stay away. Raven realized she should have known better. Unlike her, her mother never ran away from problems. Not Clare Marie Davies. Clare was made of much sterner stuff than that. Raven turned her attention to the congregation again, feeling a few butterflies flutter in her stomach. *All these people are going to hear what I have to say.* She swallowed the panic rapidly and began.

"Good morning, church. I am so grateful to my father for giving me this opportunity to speak to you all. Some of you know me as the oldest Davies daughter, but others may have never seen me here before. I've heard people say, 'Who is she? Oh, she is the Davies daughter. The ugly one.' " Raven waited for the collective breath taken by the parishioners. There were mutterings because everybody seemed shocked.

"I think as African Americans, we have a secret. It's this whole thing about color, the dark vs the lighter shades. The false perception that one is better than the other." Raven had let go of the podium and left her carefully prepared notes behind.

"I stayed away from the church not because I didn't love God or I didn't want to be in the comfort of my family, but because I let people's words get to me, making me feel less than worthy, inferior, and yes . . . ugly. Even after I got married I still thought I didn't deserve such a handsome man." Raven laughed and the church laughed, albeit uncomfortably, almost as if they were trying to suppress it. "He would tell me how beautiful I was and how much he loved every part of me, but I never, ever believed him. It was hard to completely love him when I didn't love myself. Do unto others as you would have them do unto you."

Raven looked down then up at everybody again, still confident, still sure of herself.

"What a fool I was. But anyway, that's all water under the bridge. I am getting stronger in my self-respect and love of who I am and the woman God created. I will continue to work on it, and God doesn't want me or anybody else to spend time on self-pity but to move on and help others. There are so many people right here in this church who have the same feelings I had. So many young girls who are ridiculed because of their dark skin. Some people are not hired because their skin is a richer chocolate and not light caramel. On the other hand, some darker-skinned people make fun of light people. I've seen some young people calling them white and so on. It's all there, this need for people to put others down, maybe to make themselves feel a little better.

"I'm not going to take too much time, but I hope in time to start a young people's forum or self-esteem camps to address these self-esteem issues that our young people have. They need to learn to accept who they are and also to learn to accept others. Not judge them because they are poor or rich or pretty." She held her hands up to show quotation marks around the word pretty. "Who decides what's pretty, anyway?

"So I am thankful to all of you for listening to me ramble on about my issues. I love you all, and, after my mission trip to Kenya for a few months, I hope to be back to start a program, help our young men respect women and help our young girls respect themselves so they can be all that God wants them to be. Thank you, Calvary Worship," she said. At this point Raven looked at her notes as she felt tears in her eyes. "Finally, I want to thank my mom. All these years she has always told me I was beautiful, that I was just a darker-skinned version of her, but I never believed her. I want to thank my father for being there for me, patiently waiting for me to accept who God made me. And I am grateful to my sisters who are strong women of God and my brother, PJ, a strong, respectful brother who I love dearly. Thank you all."

After church Raven excused herself from her family and drove to the home she had shared with Amari for two glorious years. It was time to say goodbye.

She stood outside the house for a few minutes, just staring, trying to remember the good times with Amari and to forget the searing pain of his betrayal.

Before she went in a bright red car pulled into the driveway. Raven couldn't believe it when she saw Candice step out of the car. Raven stayed where she was as she watched Candice pull a baby from a car seat. The infant was dressed warmly in a miniature pink jogging suit. Her curly hair was pushed back by a pretty white band with pink flowers. She looked so pretty as she smiled at Raven. Raven couldn't help smiling back. She hadn't met Candice's daughter. What a sight she was, a miniature version of her beautiful mother.

"Hey, Ray. This is little Aisha," Candice said as she approached her.

"Hi, Aisha." Raven briefly touched the little girl's garment, forgetting for a minute to ask why Candice was there as the baby gurgled delightfully. "Where's Junior?"

"He's with my mother. Sometimes I need a break from the two of them," she said. Raven nodded, feeling the lump in her throat. *Was Amari with Lexie right now, shopping for their new baby? Would she ever have kids? Would she ever get married again? Would she even want to?*

"You must be wondering what I'm doing here, after all this time," Candice said, looking at the house.

"Do you have some magazines of Lexie to show me, or maybe something juicy to tell me?"

Candice laughed humorlessly and shook her head. "No. I don't know why I did that before. I'm sorry, Raven."

"I'm sorry for bringing it up," she apologized quickly and gestured towards the house. "Want to come in?" Candice followed behind her and stood by while Raven opened the solid oak door. Inside the hall Candice glanced around.

"It's a beautiful house," she said, looking up at the high ceilings and the living space ahead. Raven led the way to the formal living room and then Candice put Aisha down. She immediately crawled to the table and tried to stand up. Raven tried to figure out how old she was, but couldn't remember.

"I've never been here," Candice said. "It's nice."

"Thanks," Raven said. She wasn't going to elaborate on the fact that the house would soon be on the market, or say that Candice is the one who ended the friendship and not her.

"That's a beautiful picture." Raven followed Candice's eyes to their wedding photo. She realized she didn't know what she would do with the wedding photos now that their marriage was all over and done with. What did people do with things like that when the marriage was over? She turned her eyes back to Candice questioningly. She had really wanted to be in the house alone without anyone to witness her grief, but here was Candice, sitting opposite her obviously with a lot to say.

"I just came to apologize. I've been feeling really guilty," Candice began. Raven looked at her, not sure what she was apologizing for. For disturbing her private grief? For ending their friendship and acting childish afterwards?

"What are you talking about?"

"First for not coming to your wedding," Candice continued, keeping her eyes on her daughter as she moved around the lounge, exploring. Raven didn't know what to say. She had completely given up on ever being Candice's friend again. It seemed like there was no hope for them, but here she was apologizing to her.

"I never understood that, Candy. I mean you just turned on me," Raven pondered aloud. "I was very shocked and . . . hurt."

"I'm sorry for that. I was going through a hard time when your life was all about Amari and your wedding. I was mad with jealousy. I was so used to being the one who had everything, and frankly you didn't. I was the one with the husband and the kids and my life was on its way up, but then in a few short months you had met and married a man who everybody wanted. Suddenly you were no longer 'poor Raven' but somebody with a life and a great catch for a husband. Your life was better than mine because Amari was such a good man, unlike my cheating husband."

Raven nodded at what she was saying, taking the insults in just as she did in the past. "Well, now you are back because now I have nothing again I guess," Raven interjected, feeling bitterness she could not hide. Candice looked at her, surprised. "I mean you only started talking to me when news of Amari and Lexie broke. Now that my marriage is completely over and I'm humiliated you feel that you can be my friend again?"

"No! It's not that. I was wrong to feel that way and wished there was a way I could get rid of the jealousy."

"So what do you want now? To gloat?"

"No!" Candice yelled and her daughter turned to her, surprised. She had been entertaining herself with the small face sculptures from Kenya. Raven couldn't bring herself to stop the child from banging her precious possessions on the floor.

"Then what is it?"

Candice sighed, touching her face and then her neck. "I just want to say I'm sorry. I admit I'm a bad person, but I miss you and our friendship."

Raven stared at her. She didn't know what to feel. She regarded her friend of so many years. She wasn't a bad person, just self-centered and spoilt. She had been so jealous it had poisoned her actions. She felt her heart melt, though she didn't want it to.

"I missed you, too," Raven finally declared. She did miss some aspects of the relationship, but she still wondered how healthy the friendship had been. She wanted to start her life anew, and Raven wasn't sure if Candice had a place in it. Only time would tell. Candice stood up with tears in her eyes and walked towards her. Raven stood up and they embraced. Raven didn't cry. She was glad that she was able to forgive and let go, but she wasn't sure if their friendship would ever be the same. It had been broken, and even if they glued it back together the cracks would still remain.

CHAPTER 32

Raven made up her mind to leave the US for Kenya a mere month after she learned that Pastor Philip Davies was not her father. A memory of him came to her mind as she watched the plane glide to a stop outside the Nairobi International Airport in Kenya. She had been about nine or ten at the time and the girls in her class were all so into their looks and boys it was sickening to watch. Best friends would fight over the cutest boy in the class and would miss class just so they could go and kiss in the bathroom. At least that's what they said. At that time, some of the girls just decided to pick on her, calling her names because of her dark skin. She had been so distraught and cried to her father. The next day Pastor Philip took all his children to a center for orphaned children.

What they saw when they entered the building broke their hearts. There were children playing in one of the rooms, and though it was clean and warm it wasn't like home. Some of them looked sad and one little girl was crying.

Her father had taken her to that orphanage to save her from her self pity even at such a young age. Now, almost twenty years later, Raven was doing the same thing to get out of the pit of despair that was threatening to engulf her. It was an easy decision for her. She needed to get away, as far away from Amari and Lexie as possible. From comments made on television shows about them. Far away from her lying parents so she could work through some things on her own.

Though she felt empowered by the speech she had given to the church, she still had work to do in her heart, to forgive, to gain strength, to build her self-worth.

As she walked off the plane she recalled her last trip and noticed how the atmosphere seemed different. Maybe it all seemed different because six years before she had come alone, and then two years ago Amari had been with her as they went on their honeymoon to Mombasa. It seemed in the two years since she had visited Nairobi the airport had been renovated. She walked off the plane with many people from all over the world and some returning Kenyan residents. After waiting for her bag she walked out of customs. Her weariness faded when she saw Josh standing among all the waiting family and business partners outside the arrival lounge. She smiled widely as he walked towards her.

"Raven!"

She walked towards him and they embraced. She felt relieved to find him waiting after so many hours on the plane.

"Dr. Hardin! Here I am, finally!"

"Here. Let me get your bags," Josh said, taking her part from her. "And please call me Josh."

"Even at the clinic?" Raven asked, looking at his handsome, clean-shaven face. He was dressed very smartly for a man who worked in the middle of nowhere outside Nairobi.

"Even at the clinic. It's very relaxed there. You'll see."

"I'm excited," Raven said.

"Good. We can certainly use some enthusiasm."

As they drove out of the airport towards the city and then on to Mombi Village in Josh Hardin's white pickup truck she asked questions about the clinic.

"As you are aware most of our cases nowadays are HIV cases and advanced AIDS. On top of that, we do everything there from delivering babies to removing warts and treating burns. People walk for hours to come for treatment."

"Wow. There are still no new clinics where they live?" Raven asked, watching the scenery.

"Not yet. Just us."

After driving for two and a half hours in the January heat they took off on a crude road where the car was jostled from side to side. Raven watched the scenery like she was watching an absorbing movie. It wasn't humid, but just a dry heat that made her thirsty. When Josh slowed down the car she realized they had arrived. Naturally there were no signs to show when they actually arrived in Mombi, but it felt good to read the sign that said "Calvary Clinic."

The clinic was bigger than the last time she saw it and with its white-painted brick walls and metal roof blended in with the rugged environment. Three ladies came to greet Raven.

"This is Rose, Aziza and Zahara," Josh introduced her to some of the nurses who worked at the clinic.

"Jambo," Raven said in Swahili, remembering the greeting from the last time she had visited.

"Jambo," they responded, smiling. They looked so young and excited to meet her. Josh spoke to them in Swahili and they nodded.

"You'll learn it very quickly." Josh turned to her. "I told them I'm going to show you to your house because you are very tired."

"That's true," Raven said. The fourteen-hour flight was taking its toll. There were three other buildings that had doors leading to separate rooms, and Joshua led Raven into one of the them and told her it would be hers. There was a single narrow bed made up ready for her. The shiny cement floor gleamed and she could see that somebody had tried to make the place as comfortable as possible. She turned to look at him gratefully as if he had just shown her into a penthouse suite of a five star hotel. It was as far away from home as possible, and that was all Raven needed.

❧

The sun would shine and then the rain would fall, hitting the soil until it turned dark. Joshua employed three other nurses, and a few weeks after Raven arrived in Mombi Village two medical students from Canada arrived to help with the treatment and running of the clinic. It was hard work, dealing with the sick children, the people on their death beds and their need for more and more supplies.

With the rain, the surrounding area was filled with tall green grass and bushes. The land around the clinic was used for growing corn and ground nuts by the villagers. Behind the biggest building Josh had worked with everybody at the clinic to plant a garden with local vegetables, herbs and spices. They had tomatoes, cabbage green beans, peas and carrots.

Joshua worked tirelessly and Raven was amazed that such an intelligent, educated black man would give up life in America with all the money he would have been earning to come and help people in Africa. She had always admired him, but now as she saw his dedication firsthand and his great relationship with people, she was in awe of him. There was very little time to have discussions as he had patients lined up from sunup to sundown, but one weekend they drove to the bank together.

"How are you finding it, Raven?" he asked.

"It's tough but I can handle it," she said.

"I know you had some problems with your husband, I'm sorry about that," Joshua said awkwardly. Raven felt her heart constrict, and Josh must have felt the force of her emotions.

"I didn't mean to pry. I just sensed that you had something weighing heavily on you."

"No, Josh, it's okay." Raven turned to him as he drove. "I'm fine. My divorce became final in December just before I left. It's over."

"That must be tough. If you need to talk you know I'm there. Well, sometimes I'm there," Joshua said trying to make light of the situation.

"Thanks. I'm really grateful. You know being here makes all my problems seem like nothing. That is what my . . . father taught me. To look to those in need when my life is unfair. He always taught us to focus on other people other than our own problems, you know."

"That's why you came here?"

"Yes. To focus on more than me. What about you? Why are you really here?"

"I came here when I was in med school, just like those Canadian young men. I really felt God speak to me about going to Africa. I ignored that voice for many years, and eventually I came when your dad decided to open a clinic. I don't know if anything else I do will ever give me as much satisfaction. God provides all our needs here, and sometimes when we least expect it we get a delivery of medical supplies and donations of even a million dollars at one point. The next thing we are thinking of is building a church and a school."

"That's amazing," Raven said. "You are amazing." Joshua had stopped at the yield sign and turned to look at her. The look in his eyes made her come alive just a little. She turned away and looked at the cows grazing on the farm outside her window.

That night Raven lay in bed staring at the wooden planks on her roof. The full moon sent a shaft of light through the flimsy curtains. Her body was sore from standing all day assisting Josh with two surgeries that they had to perform soon after coming from the bank and helping the nurses to clean and disinfect the bedding. She took a bath in the bathroom she shared with the other nurses and now, instead of falling asleep, her mind kept going round and round in circles.

She imagined the man who had fathered her and thought about the father who had raised her. If anything, because of the way Clare treated her she expected to find out that Clare wasn't her mother, not that Philip wasn't her blood. She didn't tell her sisters or her brother, and Clare was happy to leave it that way, too. Not telling them meant that she had no one to talk to.

She turned over again and punched the hard pillow. She had to admit, running away had been as vital as breathing when she left but whatever she had wanted to leave behind was right there when she arrived on Kenyan soil.

As she lay in her bed, Amari wasn't far from her mind. The pain was still too fresh. She wondered if there would come a time when thoughts of him wouldn't send shards of unbearable misery through her heart. *Would that day ever come?*

Early the next morning, her day off, there was a knock on her door.

"Who is it?" Raven asked groggily.

"You have a call from the U.S. It's your sister," Josh said through the crack. Raven scrambled out of bed and grabbed her robe from the crude closet on one side of the tiny room. She opened the door to see a beautiful sunrise over the mountains and breathed in the fresh morning air. A tiny breeze like a whisper brushed against her cheeks as she made her way over the damp grass towards Josh's two room home. The door was slightly opened, and she walked into the living room and kitchen towards the phone.

"Thanks," Raven said, looking at his kind face. Josh nodded and then left the room to give her privacy.

"Raven here," she said, sitting on the chair.

"Hi! It's Esther. How are you? How's Africa?"

"Kenya is fine," Raven replied, not wanting to lecture her sister about how Africa was a continent, not a country. "It's been raining a lot."

"Wow. We are now just experiencing some sort of spring, but it's been so cold," Esther said. "We miss you." Raven put her free arm around herself, sadness washing over her. She missed them, too.

"Me, too. How's Angelo?"

"Fine. Fine. He says he wants to plan a mission trip to your clinic, and I told him he needs to focus on his music and giving me a baby instead of going to some African country," Esther said, and Raven could hear the teasing tone in her voice. Even though Esther could laugh about it, they had been having problems conceiving.

"It will happen," Raven said.

"I know. Sometimes I wonder how it can be so easy for people like Lexie. I know she's not your favorite person or mine, but she sleeps with Amari once as he claims and boom, she's had his son."

"What?"

"Oh, Ray. I thought you knew. I always forget that you don't get this kind of news over there," Esther apologized. Raven was quiet, catching her breath. She didn't know that she could feel any more pain, but now it was there. She could feel herself sinking, sinking into a dark bottomless pool of desolation.

"Ray," Esther called.

"I'm here," she said in a voice she could barely recognize. "When?"

"Two days ago. It's all over the news like a prince is born or something. I think the baby was early. Called him Hart Lamar Thomas. I think she wanted to keep her name in his, too."

"That's nice. How's Tahlia?" Raven asked, looking at the ceiling, similar in structure to hers. It kept the water in her eyes instead of sliding down her cheeks.

"Getting ready to graduate. Are you going to try and come? It's next month, you know," Esther said. Clare had been asking her the same thing the last time she called. She'd only been in Kenya for three months and already they wanted her back home.

"I can't promise. They need me here. In fact, I have to go to work. Thanks for calling," Raven lied. She had to get off the phone and tend to her throat that now felt like she had swallowed a sharp, frog-sized object.

"Ray. I'll call again soon. I've found a good phone plan to keep in touch with you since you don't even have email," Esther said.

"I'll talk to you soon. Bye, Esther."

"I love you," Esther said.

"Me too. Bye," Raven croaked and put the phone back on its cradle as a sob escaped her hurting throat. She got up and ran from Josh's room as if it was on fire then ran across the small field and threw herself on the floor of her room, crying like she had never cried before in her life. She heard a knock on the door but ignored it.

"Raven," Josh called and knocked again.

"I'm fine," Raven wailed, and looked up from the floor where she crouched holding her stomach. The door opened and Josh looked in, concern on his face. His forehead was creased with worry as he approached her.

"Is everybody okay at home? What is it?"

His gentle voice and the need for comfort brought fresh tears to Raven's eyes. Josh saw a box of Kleenex on the side of the bed and he strode over there and grabbed a few. He held them out for her and Raven took them, wiping her eyes and nose. She turned bloodshot eyes on him.

"Thanks," she croaked and winced again as her heart constricted with pain, sending tears rolling down her face. Josh crouched by her.

"Tell me. What is it?" he coaxed. Josh watched Raven take deep, shuddering breaths and let them out. He waited patiently.

"Everybody's fine. Ma, everybody. It's silly. I—I thought I was over it. I thought I could handle it—but . . ." She paused, and this time Josh leaned over and brought the whole box of Kleenex to her. She grabbed a wad of them, holding on tight. Josh regarded her, still puzzled.

"My husb—ex-husband has a son now. Esther just told me," Raven spluttered. "We wanted a baby. We were getting ready to try when—when. Well, it's ridiculous. I don't care."

"It's normal to be upset," Josh disagreed. Raven turned to him.

"Thank you," she said, and then impulsively reached to hug him. It seemed to take him by surprise, but he recovered and put his arms around her.

"It's gonna be fine, Raven. You'll get through this," he said over the top of her head, rubbing his strong, capable hands on her back. Raven felt a little of the agony recede as she held on to him. If she let go she felt like she might drown, so she held on tight.

CHAPTER 33

"Amari. You have to make up your mind. The shoot is next week and if you want to be a part of your son's life then you get here and show that you are his father!" Lexie yelled. The phone was on speaker as she lay on her bed. The new nanny for her son was about to bring the baby in, but when she heard the yell she walked back out with the boy bundled up in a pure white blanket. Lexie watched her leave as she listened to Amari.

"Don't threaten me, Lexie. I don't have to be in some ridiculous tabloids to show that I care about my son. I'm not going to do it."

"Then don't bother coming to see him again! He'll grow up just like you did, fatherless!" she yelled and slammed the phone down. She got up from her bed angrily. Her hair was wild around her face and her eyes were red from crying. This had never happened to her before. Men didn't leave her. She left them! Amari was the father of her son! Lexie Hart's son and she had to beg him to come and be with her on the day he made his public debut as a celebrity child. *People* magazine was actually willing to pay for those pictures and also put her on the cover. They wanted a six-page spread of her and Amari. How could she do it without Amari? America would think he didn't want to be seen with her.

Amari listened to the dead phone after Lexie's words cut through him. He attributed her recent ravings to the hormones. No woman could be that crazy. And not the mother of his child. Lexie had screamed at him when he insisted that they have a paternity test. It didn't take long to get the results. Hart Lamar was his.

Amari was instantly filled with love for his son and the need to be there for him. It meant spending a lot of time on planes flying from Detroit or wherever he was at the time to go and see Lexie when she claimed she was sick, and of course when Hart was born he had to miss a playoff game. Headlines had run that story, from the sports pages and the tabloids, speculating on their relationship and impending marriage. He had never talked to Lexie about marriage. The only person who had talked about marriage was his mother, Gloria.

"Give my grandson a family, Amari. You and Lexie can do that for him. You can give him stability, teach him about God and show him how to be a man. I always wanted that for you, and felt you missed something growing up without your father. I hated how other kids teased you about not having a father. Don't let your son go through that."

"I don't want to, Ma," Amari replied. "I love Hart and will always be there for him. I'm not sure marrying Lexie is the best answer."

"What's the alternative, son? Seeing him every couple of weeks? That's not what I wanted for you."

"That's not what I wanted for my life, either. Raven and I were planning on raising three kids together. Boys or girls, it didn't matter. I messed it up."

"No, baby," Gloria disagreed vehemently. "Raven messed it up. She just couldn't take one mistake. She had to run so fast you couldn't even catch her. She has a hard heart."

"I did it. I'll never blame her for any of it."

"She's gone now. All the way to Africa. She made you sign divorce papers you didn't want. She abandoned you. I say you move on. Make a family for your son. He's innocent and deserves a home with a mother and father."

Amari felt the pressure building in him. The loss of his wife, his new son, Lexie's demands, Gloria's appeals and his career. All of them were pulling him in different directions. One thing he knew he had to do was to appease Lexie, if only temporarily. He would do the shoot with her, not for her but for his beautiful, innocent son that he loved beyond words.

In Kenya, the air around Raven and Josh was beginning to change just as the weather was starting to cool off. It started off the day she got the call. Josh Hardin, who had always been kind and helpful, began to show more of an interest in Raven. When he went to Nairobi for meetings or fundraisers, he took her with him and they would explore the markets, eat at local restaurants and sometimes grab a Big Mac at the MacDonald's in the city center.

Raven had been in Kenya for almost six months, and she now knew the language. She knew where to shop and had made several friends in the city. Working on the clinic was rewarding though challenging, but she also enjoyed the times they would leave the clinic and go to the city or take vacations at game parks. That's how life was in Kenya, the poor were extremely poor and the rich got to enjoy the game-viewing and stunning beaches. Raven felt fortunate to be able to see all aspects of Kenyan life.

It was when they were staying at the famous Giraffe Manor that Raven managed to check her email and also read some news from the US. She couldn't resist typing in Amari's name. The first page had headlines of Amari and Lexie's photos with baby Hart. She stared at the gorgeous infant for long minutes, trying to see Amari in him. Amari holding the baby brought the tears to her eyes. She could see the love in his eyes as he looked at his baby. In that moment, she knew that he was lost to her forever and it was time to close that door of her life, like it never happened. There was nothing tying her to him except his name, and she would change that as soon as she got the chance.

Raven Thomas no longer existed.

The sting was there, but she quickly shut it off and took a walk around the grounds, where she spotted a giraffe over the trees. She didn't want her vacation to be spoilt by what she had seen on the internet. As she walked she focused on the beauty of the land. The rustic mountains and the possibilities of seeing different animals. She stood there remembering the words to a song she hadn't sung in a long time. That she was not skilled to understand what God had willed or why she was now standing here in Kenya, but she trusted Him. She wanted to trust Him more to heal her heart.

She was about to turn back and go to the hotel when Josh came and put his arm around her shoulders. Raven looked at his arm, surprised, but decided not to say anything.

"Good news," Josh said, squeezing her shoulder.

"You can expand the clinic now?"

"Oh, yes. And with the extra funding we'll be able to employ some of the local physicians to come out for a few weeks at a time. Right here in Mombi. And a huge Christian organization wants to come and help build a school. Sort of make that whole area an oasis in the village for education, medical supplies and even nutrition."

Raven couldn't help being caught up in his enthusiasm. Josh worked so hard to get poor and sick Kenyans all the help they needed. It was his life's work. She hugged him impulsively, joyously laughing with him.

"Great, Josh. Your dream is closer to coming true," Raven said on his shoulder.

"It's God's plan," Josh said simply, his dark eyes sparkling. "Nothing will stand in His way if that's what God wants for his people."

"What about the food that those politicians won't release? Will that affect us?" Raven asked, stepping back from his embrace, suddenly aware of him as a man. A strong, handsome man who sometimes seemed just too angelic to be of this earth.

"That's another battle. The tribes further north have been warring for years and there are other missionaries out there helping, but it's not safe. I wouldn't want you to go there," Josh said, his expression suddenly serious. "Having you around has made a huge difference in my life."

"Josh. I'm not even a doctor or nurse. I just help . . ." Raven said, looking down, embarrassed. She pulled her sweater against her as if she was cold, though it was warm and sunny outside.

"It's not that," Josh said, then glanced over at the chairs by the pool. "Can you come and sit with me for a second?" Raven followed his eyes, and then nodded. Josh pulled a chair for her and she sat down on it, sensing a critical discussion about to unfold.

Josh cleared his throat as he sat opposite her. His dark brown eyes seemed to pin her down with their intensity.

"Raven. I'm forty years old, dated a few times before moving here. Nobody I dated wanted to come and live in Africa, especially where the clinic is, with no hair salons, TV, cable and all those things. Besides, I was just too busy with this mission to even care."

Raven nodded looking at him. She didn't respond.

"I had come to accept that I would be a bachelor forever and spend my life serving unless God sent someone to me. But having you here . . . it's just made all the difference. I know you've gone through a horrible divorce and you've been hurt and I didn't want to say anything until maybe a year . . . until you . . ."

"Josh . . . I . . ." Raven wanted to speak but the words caught in her throat and Josh stopped her.

"I don't want you to make any decisions now, but I'm falling in love with you. You complete my mission. I see us spending maybe six months here in Kenya before traveling to South Africa and Namibia and get involved in policies in the UN and then I could also work in the States for some time, but it will all mean so much with you by my side."

"Josh. You are an incredible man," Raven began, and reached for his hand on the table. "I feel so unworthy."

"Don't," Josh growled out. "Don't ever think that you are unworthy."

"If I'm honest, my reasons for being here are not all that noble. I came here to run away from my father, my failed miserable marriage and to seek a new perspective . . . you came here to give hope . . ."

"Don't compare us, Raven. This is not a competition. I want to love you and protect you. But at the same time I know that you can't answer anything now, anything about a future together. You're still healing from your past. I won't even propose marriage to you. Just know that I promise to be there for you, to love you." He grabbed her hands and held them tightly in hers. She returned his grip tears in her eyes. He leaned towards her and their foreheads touched.

"You are an incredible man. I'm always amazed at your drive, your desire to help people. I sometimes think you are an angel," Raven said with tears in her eyes. Josh kissed her cheek shaking his head.

"No angel. Just a man. I know everything I just said sounds ridiculous and we do work together but I want you to know that I'm there for you."

"It's not ridiculous, Josh," she whispered. God was giving her another chance at love when she thought that she was always going to be alone.

❧

Raven went to her hotel room opposite Josh's, letting the warmth of his words wash over her. He had, in a roundabout way, proposed marriage to her. Josh offered her a life of travel and love with one of the most honorable men she had ever known. Amari was like a piece of burnt trash compared to Josh. She slipped out of her dress and boots and got into her pajamas. The hotel room was cool at night. She was going to need the extra blanket.

She picked up the phone and looked out at the view of beautifully lit gardens, pools and the dark forest beyond remembering the time Josh took her and all the staff from the clinic to a safari. She had been spending a lot of time with Josh, and even though she was hurting it was not difficult to see how attractive Josh was, how kind and how genuine he was. His words had confirmed what she had seen in his eyes when they were on the safari trip. She had seen it, but he hadn't said a thing.

She dialed her home number. Michigan was about six hours behind Kenya, so her parents were already up and about doing their business.

"Raven," Philip sounded excited.

"Hi," Raven said. "I'm sorry I missed Tahlia's graduation."

"She understood. We missed you, too. You are my daughter."

"I know, Dad." Tears filled Raven's eyes. "I miss you. I'm really happy here, though."

"How is Mombi Village? Is Josh taking good care of you?"

"Yes, he is. Dad, do you think it's too soon for me and him?" There was silence on the other side. Raven knew her father was surprised.

"What's going on?" Philip asked. "Josh is one of the most incredible people I've ever come across. I know you can trust him."

"He says he loves me," Raven said. "I think I love him, too."

"But you think it's too soon?"

"He thinks so, too. I think we are engaged but not engaged."

"That's excellent news. I wish I could be there to talk to you in person," Philip said.

"Me, too. You always knew what to do and say," she said with smile.

"Can I ask you something?"

"Sure, Dad."

"Are you over Amari? Are you healed enough to start another relationship?"

"Amari was out of my life the moment he did what he did with Lexie. I don't respect him, I don't love him, sometimes I hate him . . ."

"That's what I mean. If you still feel anything for him, be it hate . . ." Philip cautioned.

"No! He chose Lexie, Dad, and he hurt me. I never want to have anything to do with him again. I don't want to see him or hear from him."

"You made that perfectly clear, my child. I'm glad you and Josh Hardin are taking your time with your relationship. Your mother will be very happy to hear that. She always hoped that Josh would marry one of her daughters."

"Really?"

"Oh, yes. We used to plan, but Esther fell in love with Angelo, you married Amari. Tahlia was always too young."

"That's funny. Well, don't tell Mom anything yet until we send invitations out."

"I won't. You be careful out there. Don't go too far away from the clinic on your own. Be safe."

"I will, Dad. Thank you." She yawned. "I better go to bed. Besides, the phone bill might be ridiculous."

"Good night. So you are sure about Amari? You are over him, right?"

"I'm so over him, Dad, I can't even spell his name anymore."

After Philip put the phone down he wondered about Josh and Raven. He would do one more thing for his daughter, and after that it was up to God. He picked up the phone and dialed Amari's number.

CHAPTER 34

Amari arrived in L.A three days later after having a serious talk with his mother. Gloria wanted him to forget about Raven and try and make a life for his son with Lexie. Amari had told his mother that he was looking for a home closer to them but didn't want to share where his heart was leaning with his mother until he was sure. Gloria had heard news about Raven and Josh in Kenya and wanted her son to move on, too.

Lexie didn't look like someone who had just given birth to an eight-pound baby. Her figure was svelte and she looked beautiful.

"Hi, Amari," Lexie greeted him after he had been sitting waiting for half an hour. "Hart is sleeping."

"How's he doing?"

"He's fine. So now you are concerned about him?"

"I've always been concerned about him. I had the playoffs, remember?"

"So what's the plan now that you finished playing?" she asked with hint of mockery behind her sultry voice. She talked like a woman who held the trump card in her hand. That ace in her hand was Hart, safely upstairs where Amari couldn't even see him.

"I would like to spend some time with my son," Amari said.

"Our son," Lexie interjected, crossing her legs as she leaned back on the white embroidered love seat.

"Yes."

"You can't have one without the other, Amari. He's a part of me."

"I would like to see him," Amari said. He watched Lexie's eyes light up with glee. To her way of thinking she had him cornered. The tabloids had hinted at marriage between them and a start of a beautiful family with Morgan, Madison and their own biological child, Hart. One thing he had learned about Lexie was that she would do anything for publicity. It was the fuel that drove all her actions.

With Gloria's help he had started tracking all the magazines that had them together. He didn't realize how many lies they had printed. They basically wrote articles as if Lexie and him were about to get married. Maybe he should have set the record straight, but he didn't want his son reading later that his father didn't want him or his mother. During the première of *A Lot Like Silence* Amari had refused to answer any questions about his relationship with his wife or Lexie, but the reporters had obviously unearthed his divorce papers and published them. Now he was in the house of the woman who had helped mess up his life, but also give him a son that he loved with all his heart. He looked at Lexie, who regarded him with contempt.

"He's sleeping," Lexie repeated more firmly.

"I haven't seen him in a long time, Lexie, and I just want to see that he's all right."

"And wake him up?"

"I won't wake him. Just take me to him, Lexie. What's the matter with you?"

"You don't even know anything about him. He cries a lot, and when he gets an opportunity to sleep I don't want to disturb him. The nanny needs a break, too."

"I understand all that. Just take me to my son."

Amari's tone tolerated no arguments. After glaring at him angrily, Lexie turned and led the way upstairs. Amari followed a few paces behind her, trying to ignore her swaying hips and fragrant hair. He was still a man and Lexie exuded power and sexuality packaged in her confident aura. This was the mother of his child.

The nursery was on the first floor, decorated with painted murals, stuffed animals, and a mobile hanging over his crib. The furniture she bought for him had been talked about on *Entertainment News* as if she was now the expert on baby products.

Amari approached the crib slowly, carefully, and looked down on his son. He put his hands in his jeans pocket to resist the urge to pick him up. Hart lay on his back, facing sideways, and seemed to smile from dreamland. Amari felt Lexie come and stand next to him, looking down at their child.

"I'm sorry, Amari. I act crazy at times because I want so much for us to be a family," she whispered, placing her fingers over his arm. "Sometimes I feel so alone without you. At night it's just me and him, and we need you."

Amari continued to look down at Hart, seeing his innocence, purity and blamelessness. He felt his heart constrict. What was he thinking? At that moment, Hart opened his eyes and turned to look at them, his hazel eyes focused on them as questioning as they were sleepy. Lexie leaned over the crib and picked him up. Then, gently supporting his head, she placed him in Amari's arms. When he held Hart in his arms his heart felt at peace, like nothing else mattered except being there for his son. He would do anything to protect him, to make sure his son knew that he was loved. That he had a father who loved him more than anything on earth. When he turned and looked at Lexie he knew what he was going to do. It was time to have a serious talk with his agent. The time had come to take serious steps to move his life out of limbo.

Clare read over the letter she had written to Raven. It was the most difficult thing she had ever written, but she knew that Raven was old enough to know her mother, warts and all. When she refused to tell Raven the truth about her conception she had done more to protect herself than Raven. Clare knew Philip was disappointed in her, but that hadn't stopped her from keeping the truth from Raven a little longer.

She reread the letter, wondering if she should add anything else.

Dear Raven,

I'm sorry for the heartache you felt when you found out that Philip was not your biological father. We never meant to hurt you. Everything we did was to protect you. But we were wrong.

When you were conceived I was in my last year of high school. Just sixteen. I was a young naïve girl who made all the bad choices children tend to do at that age. But out of my bad choice you, my miracle, came along. My firstborn baby. I can't say I was that happy when I found out I was pregnant. Naturally it was a shock. I know I always told you to save yourself for marriage, but I didn't lead by example because nobody had ever told me any different. I was surrounded by people who slept with boys as naturally as going to the movies. A date with a boy usually involved going all the way. That's what they considered dating. Especially when I was dating the popular guys in the school.

You see, your biological father. Well, he was the popular captain of the basketball team. He was dating me and other girls, too, but I didn't care. I just wanted to be with the in crowd. But when I got pregnant it was like waking up from dreamland to reality. Nick, your biological father, didn't want anything to do with me. He was that cold and callous, but more than that he was just a child himself. He was trying to act cool when all he really wanted was some stability in his life and a family that didn't let him down time and again.

Philip saw me crying one day after school when he walked up to me. He was brave to do that because I didn't talk to boys like him. He also told me that he was afraid of girls like me. The pretty girls who always had an entourage following them. We talked that day, and for some reason I felt safe with him and told him my whole story. I told him

SHOW ME THE SUN

how I had not told my parents about the baby. He said he would do anything to help me and said he would even marry me. I couldn't believe it. He walked me home, and each day he would walk me and we would talk. He was already so mature even though he was my age. God sent him to me because he even agreed to be your father before he even met you.

My parents yelled at him, but eventually they accepted him. His parents were not happy with him, either, but they eventually came around and accepted our relationship. They didn't believe that your father would have slept with any girl. I think Mama Davies always knew that you were not really his biological child. She fought our relationship but Philip was determined to stay with me, no matter what. Eventually Mama Davies had no choice but to accept her only son's wishes. They blessed our union. They were happy to help us raise you from the beginning. Your grandparents were incredible, helping us with a place to stay, and you had all the things a baby could ever want. I fell in love with Philip very fast. What I had with Nick had been nothing but I thank him for giving me you. He was killed in a car accident on his way to college. I'm sure he would've been a basketball pro like Amari. You inherited his passion for life, his strengths, his beautiful dark chocolate skin and long lean body. But you also got my stubbornness. And as Philip raised you, you got his gentleness, his caring heart. Nobody can be around Philip for long and not develop a love for God's work and moving the Kingdom forward.

So my dear child, my Raven, my firstborn, after you read this letter I pray that it'll bring you peace and help you accept yourself as this wonderful daughter to us and incredible big sister to Esther, Tahlia and Phil Junior. You are a part of us and always have been.

   Love, Your Mother,
   Clare.

Clare read over it one more time and put it in an envelope. She decided that the next time she would see Raven, she would give her the letter. It was something she wanted Raven to read right in front of her. Clare knelt down and prayed for peace.

CHAPTER 35

Raven felt the cold so much more in Africa because there was no central heating. Some hotels had heated floors, but most offices utilized space heaters and some homes had wood burning fireplaces. June and July were very cold at night, but during the day the sun was sweet. Though she still worked at the clinic with Josh, she had also become very useful for the clinic working at a non-governmental agency in Nairobi, securing aid and more physicians to come and help with the clinic and other desperate areas. Josh and Philip both wanted to expand the clinic, build a real operating theatre and get more physicians. He had once told her that there were very few doctors for every thousand people. It shocked Raven when she realized the kind of illnesses people died from that could have been cured so easily in the United States. The infant mortality, the women who died giving birth, the AIDS deaths. It was overwhelming.

The arrangement that had Raven spend time in the city had been working well for them for two weeks. She was just finishing off her report on the computer when she felt someone cover her eyes from behind. She squealed with surprise.

"Guess who?" It was Josh.

"What are you doing here?" Raven asked, turning around in her swivel chair. Her hair was now done in tiny micro braids. She couldn't believe how inexpensive it was to get her hair done in Nairobi, and they were so artistic about it.

"I came to pick you up. I thought we could go visit this new market and maybe find some pieces for your collection of African art."

"Is there a point in collecting African art if you live in Africa?" she asked, getting up from her seat and hugging him.

"It can be put in our house in the States. We should have a home there for when I go back and work there to renew my certifications and raise money for our kids." Raven laughed at his enthusiasm.

Their relationship was chaste and he was patiently giving her time to heal but everybody at the clinic had noticed the warmth between them, the gazes they shared when they thought nobody was looking. Zahara and Aziza would tease her about it in Swahili and she would answer back saucily. She was now almost fluent in Swahili.

"I like your way of thinking," Raven said, shutting down her computer.

"I thought you would." Josh took her work bag from beside her desk while she picked up her purse.

She closed up her office and went to join Josh in his new truck. The new, white SUV had been donated and worked better than the old pickup Josh had been using when he arrived. She sat in her seat and Josh closed the door. She rubbed her hands.

"It's so cold." Raven's teeth chattered.

"I'll turn on the heat," Josh said starting the car and turned on the heat.

Raven loved the market and being there brought back the memory of her apartment in Detroit and the closet where she had kept all her artifacts. She tried not to remember when Amari had opened the closet and everything had tumbled down and his look of surprise. She looked at a gorgeous tie-dye fabric to distract her from thoughts of Amari.

"Look at these," Raven cried, walking through the outdoor market. "Josh, how did you hear about this market? I thought I'd been to all of them."

"This one is not frequented by most tourists. Here you can actually barter."

They spent two hours there. Then, as it was getting dark already, they started the long drive back to the clinic. They talked and laughed all the way back home and Josh put on one of the hats she bought at the market. She laughed at him as she got out of the car as the last vestiges of the sun shone over the mountain ahead of them. Josh walked around the car and opened her door for her and she adjusted his hat, laughing. Her laughter froze when she saw a figure of a man walk towards them from behind the clinic. She felt fear at first.

With the sun behind she couldn't see who it was but there was something about him that looked familiar, something that caused her heart to almost jump out of her body. He stepped closer and her eyes widened with shock. It was Amari.

CHAPTER 36

"Hello," Amari finally said after the few moments of stunned silence. Josh moved his packages to his left hand and held out his hand to Amari.

"What a surprise! When did you get here?" Josh asked, shaking his hand. His voice sounded calm and in control. Josh never lost his cool while she shook with shock.

"About four hours ago. I arrived in Nairobi two days ago and drove out here today," Amari replied, then looked in Raven's direction. She smoothed her black pants with hands that were suddenly sweaty. She stared at him, her heart still beating fast. She could barely hear what he was saying as a million thoughts went through her head. "Hi, Raven," Amari said, his eyes on her. She was staring at him like he was some strange animal. She couldn't tear her eyes away, and it took her a while to find her voice. When she finally spoke her voice sounded strange to her ears.

"Ummh, Amari. What are you doing here?"

"I came to see you," he said, then looked at Josh as if asking for permission. "I just wanted to talk to her."

"Raven," Josh said, and she looked at him.

"Josh. I didn't ask him to come here," she said, looking from Josh to Amari.

"I know, Ray," Josh said. "I think he wants to talk to you. I'm going to go and visit my friend Amos at the farm. I'll give you two some time to talk, okay?"

Raven and Amari spoke at the same time. He said thanks and she said no vehemently. Josh touched her gently on the shoulder.

"It's fine. I'll be back soon, all right. I'll just put this stuff in my place." Josh walked towards Amari and stopped just by him, thumping him on the shoulder. "Amari. It's good to see you." Raven watched Josh walk into his house. She turned to look at Amari in the now-fading light.

"It's okay, Raven. I won't bite," Amari said, still standing a few feet from her his hands on his side. "I just came so we could talk."

Raven folded her arms, looking down. She looked at him in confusion and then turned to look as Josh came back. She wondered what kind of picture the two of them made standing there facing each other like adversaries instead of former couples.

She knew he found this whole situation more than awkward. *Who wouldn't?*

"You look good," Amari said, and Raven walked past him towards the house.

"You could've called," she grumbled, her confidence still ebbing. She ignored his compliment. She did not look good. She was living in the country and here nobody cared about what you wore or what hairstyle you had. Still, she wished she had worn her black and white pants that fitted her better than the black slacks she had on and quickly chastised herself for even caring. She was almost near the door when she heard Amari's voice behind her.

"I can't believe you are living here."

"A lot of people live here," she murmured, then spoke louder. "I can't believe you are here!"

"I should've called, but I just thought surprising you would be good."

"You thought wrong. How did you even know how to get here? We don't have Mapquest here." She stopped outside her door, key in hand, looking at him.

"I did some research. I've actually been in Nairobi for three days. I had to build up my courage to come here." His words made Raven stop and look at him. Through the faint light she could see the sincerity in his face and her heart melted a little. His presence had certainly stolen all her words from her mind. After a while she said, "And you waited here for four hours. What if we had stayed in the city? What then?"

"I don't know. Is it safe here? It's kind of in the middle of nowhere."

"There are villages all around and a farm farther north. It's quite safe," Raven declared, and then looked around. She didn't know where to take Amari to talk to him. The clinic didn't have space, and it was too cold to stay outside. Her room was so tiny Amari would practically fill it up with his height and those big feet.

"What's wrong?" he asked.

"This is my place," she said, opening the door. It creaked a little as she stepped in. "I guess we can talk here. It's too cold out there."

Amari bent his head as he walked into the room. It still held the same bed, but Raven had tried to make it homely with a few framed pictures of her family and a new duvet on the bed. Her clothes still hung on the makeshift closet that Josh had now put doors on. She had purchased a hand-carved wooden chair that was opposite her bed. She turned on the light, glad that the solar panels had gained enough power to light her room.

"You have electricity?" Amari asked, looking at the flickering bulb.

"We use solar. The electrical generator is mainly used for the clinic and the surrounding areas rely on the solar panels. The rest of the villagers use firewood for cooking and candles for light."

Amari nodded. She glanced at him as he stood awkwardly by, looking around the tiny room. Raven tried to see it through his eyes but she was too nervous to look around.

"Should I sit here?" Amari asked, pointing to the chair.

"Can you fit?" Raven asked, sitting on the edge of her bed. She felt very crowded in the room all of a sudden and the fading light of the evening made everything seem like a dream to her.

"I'll try." Amari sat in the chair, looking very uncomfortable. "It's a nice chair."

"Thanks." Raven tried to smile back, but it was hard. She took a small blanket and covered her legs. Amari looked at her and their eyes held. She smiled shyly. His eyes still had a hold over her. How often had she dreamed of them?

"How are you?" Amari asked after a few seconds.

"I'm all right. I'm getting used to life in Kenya. Different pace. Less to worry about," Raven said.

"I'm proud of you," he said. "You've always cared about other people, and now you are here helping the most helpless."

"Josh is the amazing person. Everybody here loves him. He is the most selfless person I've ever known." Raven looked at Amari, hoping for a response, but none was coming. She smiled.

"What's so funny?" Amari asked when he caught her smile.

"You. What has brought you here, thousands of miles from home?" she asked. "This small talk?"

"No. I came to see you. Wanted to see why I couldn't get you off my mind," Amari said, looking at her. Raven moved back to the wall like a cornered mouse.

"That's all very well, but how is your son?" Raven asked. That was harder to say than she had imagined. Well, she never imagined Amari actually being in her tiny bedroom.

"He's fine." Amari stood up and reached in his pocket. He took out a tiny photograph of his smiling son and walked towards her. He sat next to her and showed her the photograph. Her heart stopped when he sat next to her and practically dipped her bed to the ground, but she had to pretend that he wasn't affecting her and causing her heart to race. She kept her focus on the photograph of the boy. "I can't pretend he doesn't exist and he hasn't changed my life." Raven nodded, unable to say anything more.

She suddenly had an urge to cry, but it was quickly replaced by nervousness at Amari's closeness. She was momentarily confused. Swallowing hard, she wished she could be stronger and not have her body and heart betray her so quickly. He was showing her a picture of his son. That should make her angry, but the boy was so adorable and innocent.

Amari continued, unaware of the effect he was having on her, "I want us to help raise him together, Raven. I know it's too much to ask of you, after all this time and the divorce but . . . He's here and I love him, but I want you in my life, too." Amari's voice seemed to float to her, deeply penetrating her now foggy brain.

"What about Lexie?" She turned to look at him, his eyes increasing the tempo of her heart.

"She's Hart's mother, but she and I can never be together. Not when I'm in love with somebody else," Amari said, and she looked at him and their eyes locked. He seemed to take a breath before continuing. "I only ever wanted to marry for love. I love you. I loved having you as my wife, Ray. You made coming home exciting with the sweet things you would do to make me smile after a loss. The trips you would plan and just sitting in our house with your feet on my knees. I know many people got married for different reasons, especially in my profession, if you can call it that." He was so serious. He was hypnotizing her, working his magic on parts that used to hurt. She had forgiven him, but . . . Josh.

Raven jumped off the bed and Amari stood up and held her arms from behind. Suddenly the room felt so hot, as if there were ten fireplaces blazing red in it. She couldn't breathe, her body deeply aware of his. She was melting as his breath came close to her ear.

"I'm in love with you, Raven. God joined us together and we became one. I never stopped loving you," he whispered and her eyes closed. She was surrendering to the memories, new desires that she had never felt before. It was all so new and yet so familiar.

"I can't," she breathed back, though her voice was so weak she could barely hear herself.

"A part of you must still love me. Come back to me," he groaned and turned her around. His hand went to the back of her neck and, slowly gauging her lack of resistance, his lips touched hers. She whimpered, amazed at how she had lost all sense of place and time as he drank from her lips like a hungry, thirsty man in the desert. Her hunger seemed to match his as her hands went around his body, much leaner but stronger to her touch. Her body was answering Amari's call.

Josh's image flashed through her mind. Kind. Loving. Loyal. Godly. She fought hard to resist Amari, and it took so much willpower she screamed as she pushed him away.

"No!"

Amari stepped back, stunned, his eyes smoky from the same longing that she felt. He was breathing hard and she was also breathing like someone who had run a marathon without training.

"We can't."

"Yes, we can. As far as I'm concerned you're still my wife. There's no divorce in the Bible," Amari said. She remembered him saying that before.

"Depends on what you do!" Raven moved away from him and leaned against the wall, trying to slow her heart. Her hand covered her throat as shivers went through her body like tiny earthquakes. "Josh and I are getting married." Raven watched Amari's reaction. He winced, but somehow he didn't seem all that surprised. "You knew?"

"Your dad told me," Amari admitted after a minute of silence.

"So that's why you are here. Just to mess up my life? Dad is still telling you things about me! Still thinks you are a gift from Heaven!"

"He knows we should be together, Raven. You loved me once, and I love you."

"Love is not enough," Raven protested. "I've moved on with the most wonderful, caring, perfect man under the sun. I trust him. I don't trust you."

Raven could tell that her words had a huge effect on him. He visibly flinched.

"Raven. I know I messed up, but you can trust me again. I'll never let you down again."

"How's that possible? Lexie has your baby. Your first-born," Raven said, her hand gestures wild around her face. "She'll always be in your life. Always."

"Can't change that. But—I know who I want, and it's you." His voice rasped with powerful emotion. It resonated with her heart, her body.

Raven stared at him and pressed herself deeper against the wall as he moved towards her. His face was filled with pain, but also with a certain determination that took her breath away. He took one of her long braids in his fingers.

"Lexie manipulated me and I should have been smarter. She's still playing games, but that's beside the point. Let's get back together, Raven."

Raven shook her head but didn't say anything as a tear rolled down her cheek. Amari reached over and gently caught it on his thumb.

"I'm gonna go back to Nairobi," he said, and Raven's eyes opened wide. She could feel her heart race.

"It's so far. I mean, it's too late."

"It's fine. I'll be fine. Goin' to be at the Intercontinental Hotel in Nairobi. Here are the details." Amari handed her a note with his address, phone number and room number. She scrunched it up in her hand after a quick glance. Amari grimaced, and then straightened his face out again.

"I'm there until Friday evening," he said, looking deeply into her eyes. "I'm hoping you'll come before I leave. I promise you, if you don't come, I'll never bother you again. I'll wish you and Josh the best. No matter what you choose, Ray, I wanted to make sure you were happy here. I couldn't live with myself if you weren't. He's a better man for you."

They stared at each other and Raven's breath caught in her throat and she released it in a rush. His words had gone to places that evoked emotions so deep they could make her float away. She was speechless.

He brought her limp body close and held her in a long embrace with her face on his chest, breathing him in taking him in even as she fought for control. She put her arms around him, realizing that that could be the last time she would ever see him, or hold him.

"Where's your car?" she asked after he released her and rubbed her arm.

"Out there. You didn't see it, you were too shocked to see me," Amari said.

"Just be careful," Raven said. "Be careful on the road."

"I will." He opened the door, then looked back at the tiny room and back to Raven's concerned face. He touched her face. "I worry about you here. It's so dark out there."

"It's okay. Josh'll be here soon."

"I'll be waiting for you." He turned and kissed her on the lips one more time before walking off into the dark. Raven saw his car next to the clinic and watched him sit in the car when the lights came on. Everything seemed surreal.

The powerful engine started a dark four-wheel drive. He reversed, turned the car around and drove right by her. He waved at her and she waved back. Raven watched until the car disappeared.

CHAPTER 37

On Sunday morning Raven and Josh went to church together. The service was quintessential as they sang Swahili songs. The pastor, a young, energetic man, spoke in Swahili while another man translated into English. The drive to the church was far, about an hour away from the clinic, but they attended as often as they could. After church Josh took her to the game park where they drove around in open trucks looking at the wild animals, something they liked because each trip revealed new and wonderful wildlife. Some days they would see baboons, called *nyanis* or *pofu,* or *eland,* which were the largest of the antelopes. They enjoyed seeing the impala jump high when they were disturbed. They saw these often and were just as common as the monkeys on the sides of the road.

They had lunch at the game park hotel, watching rolling coffee fields and forests. From the top of the mountain they could see the coffee plantation stretching as far as the eye could see, a solid green cloud.

"So what did Amari talk to you about?" Josh asked after the waiter poured their cups of coffee. The fire blazed in the hearth of the comfortable spacious restaurant that the hotel guests used.

"He was worried about me," Raven said, her eyes down.

"He's gone back to the States?"

"On Friday. He says he leaves on Friday," Raven said and then took a sip of her coffee. "This is good. Tastes even better from up here. You know soon they will be picking coffee. We should go and see that, don't you think? You know all the coffee has to be picked by hand. I would love to try it."

Raven looked out at the view, lost in thought. They had taken a tour of the coffee plantation a few weeks back, learning the history of Kenyan coffee production. She was amazed at the unique process. Now that she had met some small-scale farmers of the plant, she was even more fascinated about its growth.

"Ray," Josh called. "What do you think?" Raven turned to him, realizing he had said something.

"Oh, sorry. What did you say?" Raven asked. Josh looked at her with a knowing look in his eyes but did not repeat himself.

On Monday they worked side by side in the clinic and even visited a young woman in the village who was having twins. It was hectic and busy, but many times Raven would be distracted, causing Josh to repeat his instructions to her. On Tuesday she was supposed to go to Nairobi for a meeting with a recording artist who wanted to help in Kenya, but she convinced Zahara to go instead as she stayed and worked with Josh. On Wednesday they looked over the plans for the extension and the planned school. Friday morning she woke up early, washed her clothes and hung them up on the wire line before work.

"Working hard," Josh said, walking towards her. He was dressed in khaki pants and a dark blue shirt and looked like a game ranger to her. She smiled at the thought then turned back to her clothes. Raven was hanging her last white blouse. She clipped it with the clothes hangers and turned to him.

"This is one thing I'll never get used to around here. No washing machines, no dryers. Painful hands." Raven blew into her fingers to warm them up.

"Here," Josh said, and took her hands into his and rubbed them. She smiled at him.

"It's freezing out here," she said, blowing vapor from her mouth.

"Yep," Josh said. "So it's Friday, Ray. Don't you have to be somewhere?"

Raven looked at him questioningly. "Did I forget something?"

"I've watched you mope around the place all week. You can't hide it. I wasn't sure you would hold out here until Friday while Amari sits alone in some luxury hotel pining for you and you sit around this rural place, wanting him."

Raven laughed and pulled her hands away from his grip.

"Josh. Please."

"Ray. What are you waiting for?"

"What are you talking about?" Raven shook her head. Josh had lost his mind.

"If you hurry, you can catch him before he gets on that plane," Josh said. "The minute I saw Amari standing here I knew I lost you, and it's all right. You ran away from him, but his love stayed with you."

Tears filled her eyes so quickly it was like a waterfall of pain. He was right. She had fought so hard. Tried so hard to forget him. And poor Josh had been a part of her charade. A part of her wish to forget Amari.

"Oh, Josh."

"Ray. Be honest with yourself. I can see it. When you think I'm not looking I can see you are lost, thinking about him. Or trying to forget him but sometimes when you wake up your dreams of him are still in your eyes but you deny it."

"Josh, what have I done? You must think the worst of me."

"No, Raven. I always knew that I had to be careful. That I could lose you."

"I tried. I thought I could forget him," Raven cried, tears filling her eyes. "It was all I wanted to do. But . . . I couldn't do it."

"It's all right. You have to rush. Don't worry about anything here. Just go."

"What if I'm too late?"

"Here, take the car. You know the way."

Raven took the keys and dropped them as her hands trembled. She bent down to pick them up from the ground. "Thank you."

She hugged him quickly then let go. She looked at his face, thanking him, wondering how she was so grateful for having had him and his guidance all these months.

"I'm sorry, Josh," she said. Josh took her hands in his.

"There's nothing to be sorry about. You need to move fast."

Raven gave a small teary smile and turned away from Josh into the tiny room. She grabbed her purse and coat. She was about to step outside when she remembered the note Amari had given her. It had fallen on the floor behind her chair. She panicked when she couldn't find it and eventually found it under the bed, hidden behind one of her bags.

Raven picked up the paper and opened it up. With trembling hands she read the name of the hotel, his room number and phone number, all in Amari's huge messy writing.

She still had many questions.

Where would they live? Would Hart like her? Who would continue her work in Kenya?

Despite all that, she knew clearly that she was doing the right thing. She felt the peace wash over her like a soft cloud of sweetness as her heart settled on Amari, for better or worse. Though she drove carefully on the bumpy road she wanted to be in his arms that second. Raven was impatient to see his eyes. She was going to get the man God had intended for her all along. And she was going to enjoy being loved by him and loving him fully in return.

The End

Show Me The Sun Discussion Questions

Why do you think people are so concerned with outward appearances?

What could Raven have done to defend herself against people who made fun of her skin color?

What do you think of the way Clare treated her daughters?

Have you experienced certain treatment from your own race about the darkness or lightness of your skin?

How can a man or woman choose the right person without being influenced by outward appearances?

Who determines what is attractive and what is not?

How do you deal with family's expectations of you and those of your own?

What challenges do children of pastors face?

Why do you think Amari fell in love with Raven when she was not the perfect ten all his teammates talked about?

What, if anything could Amari have done to avoid the situation with Lexie?

What, if anything could Raven have done to protect her marriage?

How do you handle jealousies from friends? Do you keep the friendship or remove yourself?

Can a person be more dedicated to their cause than their own marriage?

What does God say about adultery and forgiveness?

Did Raven make the right decision? Why or why not?

What challenges will her relationship face after she makes her decision?

ABOUT THE AUTHOR

Miriam Shumba has had several short stories and articles published in Zimbabwe, South Africa, and the United States. She earned her teaching degree at Rhodes University in South Africa and continued her education at Walden University. Miriam has taught elementary school in several countries. She moved to the United States from Zimbabwe in 2001 and now lives in Michigan with her husband. *Show Me The Sun* is her first novel. You can read more about her writing and life journey at *www.miriamshumba.com*.

SHOW ME THE SUN

2010 Mass Market Titles

January

Show Me The Sun
Miriam Shumba
ISBN: 978-158571-405-6
$6.99

Promises of Forever
Celya Bowers
ISBN: 978-1-58571-380-6
$6.99

February

Love Out Of Order
Nicole Green
ISBN: 978-1-58571-381-3
$6.99

Unclear and Present Danger
Michele Cameron
ISBN: 978-158571-408-7
$6.99

March

Stolen Jewels
Michele Sudler
ISBN: 978-158571-409-4
$6.99

Not Quite Right
Tammy Williams
ISBN: 978-158571-410-0
$6.99

April

Oak Bluffs
Joan Early
ISBN: 978-1-58571-379-0
$6.99

Crossing The Line
Bernice Layton
ISBN: 978-158571-412-4
$6.99

How To Kill Your Husband
Keith Walker
ISBN: 978-158571-421-6
$6.99

May

The Business of Love
Cheris F. Hodges
ISBN: 978-158571-373-8
$6.99

Wayward Dreams
Gail McFarland
ISBN: 978-158571-422-3
$6.99

June

The Doctor's Wife
Mildred Riley
ISBN: 978-158571-424-7
$6.99

Mixed Reality
Chamein Canton
ISBN: 978-158571-423-0
$6.99

2010 Mass Market Titles (continued)

July

Blue Interlude
Keisha Mennefee
ISBN: 978-158571-378-3
$6.99

Always You
Crystal Hubbard
ISBN: 978-158571-371-4
$6.99

Unbeweavable
Katrina Spencer
ISBN: 978-158571-426-1
$6.99

August

Small Sensations
Crystal V. Rhodes
ISBN: 978-158571-376-9
$6.99

Let's Get It On
Dyanne Davis
ISBN: 978-158571-416-2
$6.99

September

Unconditional
A.C. Arthur
ISBN: 978-158571-413-1
$6.99

Swan
Africa Fine
ISBN: 978-158571-377-6
$6.99$6.99

October

Friends in Need
Joan Early
ISBN:978-1-58571-428-5
$6.99

Against the Wind
Gwynne Forster
ISBN:978-158571-429 2
$6.99

That Which Has Horns
Miriam Shumba
ISBN:978-1-58571-430-8
$6.99

November

A Good Dude
Keith Walker
ISBN:978-1-58571-431-5
$6.99

Reye's Gold
Ruthie Robinson
ISBN:978-1-58571-432-2
$6.99

December

Still Waters...
Crystal V. Rhodes
ISBN:978-1-58571-433-9
$6.99

Burn
Crystal Hubbard
ISBN: 978-1-58571-406-3
$6.99

Other Genesis Press, Inc. Titles

Other Genesis Press, Inc. Titles (continued)

Other Genesis Press, Inc. Titles (continued)

Other Genesis Press, Inc. Titles (continued)

Other Genesis Press, Inc. Titles (continued)

Naked Soul	Gwynne Forster	$8.95
Never Say Never	Michele Cameron	$6.99
Next to Last Chance	Louisa Dixon	$24.95
No Apologies	Seressia Glass	$8.95
No Commitment Required	Seressia Glass	$8.95
No Regrets	Mildred E. Riley	$8.95
Not His Type	Chamein Canton	$6.99
Nowhere to Run	Gay G. Gunn	$10.95
O Bed! O Breakfast!	Rob Kuehnle	$14.95
Object of His Desire	A.C. Arthur	$8.95
Office Policy	A.C. Arthur	$9.95
Once in a Blue Moon	Dorianne Cole	$9.95
One Day at a Time	Bella McFarland	$8.95
One of These Days	Michele Sudler	$9.95
Outside Chance	Louisa Dixon	$24.95
Passion	T.T. Henderson	$10.95
Passion's Blood	Cherif Fortin	$22.95
Passion's Furies	AlTonya Washington	$6.99
Passion's Journey	Wanda Y. Thomas	$8.95
Past Promises	Jahmel West	$8.95
Path of Fire	T.T. Henderson	$8.95
Path of Thorns	Annetta P. Lee	$9.95
Peace Be Still	Colette Haywood	$12.95
Picture Perfect	Reon Carter	$8.95
Playing for Keeps	Stephanie Salinas	$8.95
Pride & Joi	Gay G. Gunn	$8.95
Promises Made	Bernice Layton	$6.99
Promises to Keep	Alicia Wiggins	$8.95
Quiet Storm	Donna Hill	$10.95
Reckless Surrender	Rochelle Alers	$6.95
Red Polka Dot in a World Full of Plaid	Varian Johnson	$12.95
Red Sky	Renee Alexis	$6.99
Reluctant Captive	Joyce Jackson	$8.95
Rendezvous With Fate	Jeanne Sumerix	$8.95
Revelations	Cheris F. Hodges	$8.95
Rivers of the Soul	Leslie Esdaile	$8.95
Rocky Mountain Romance	Kathleen Suzanne	$8.95
Rooms of the Heart	Donna Hill	$8.95
Rough on Rats and Tough on Cats	Chris Parker	$12.95
Save Me	Africa Fine	$6.99

Other Genesis Press, Inc. Titles (continued)

Secret Library Vol. 1	Nina Sheridan	$18.95
Secret Library Vol. 2	Cassandra Colt	$8.95
Secret Thunder	Annetta P. Lee	$9.95
Shades of Brown	Denise Becker	$8.95
Shades of Desire	Monica White	$8.95
Shadows in the Moonlight	Jeanne Sumerix	$8.95
Sin	Crystal Rhodes	$8.95
Singing A Song...	Crystal Rhodes	$6.99
Six O'Clock	Katrina Spencer	$6.99
Small Whispers	Annetta P. Lee	$6.99
So Amazing	Sinclair LeBeau	$8.95
Somebody's Someone	Sinclair LeBeau	$8.95
Someone to Love	Alicia Wiggins	$8.95
Song in the Park	Martin Brant	$15.95
Soul Eyes	Wayne L. Wilson	$12.95
Soul to Soul	Donna Hill	$8.95
Southern Comfort	J.M. Jeffries	$8.95
Southern Fried Standards	S.R. Maddox	$6.99
Still the Storm	Sharon Robinson	$8.95
Still Waters Run Deep	Leslie Esdaile	$8.95
Stolen Memories	Michele Sudler	$6.99
Stories to Excite You	Anna Forrest/Divine	$14.95
Storm	Pamela Leigh Starr	$6.99
Subtle Secrets	Wanda Y. Thomas	$8.95
Suddenly You	Crystal Hubbard	$9.95
Sweet Repercussions	Kimberley White	$9.95
Sweet Sensations	Gwyneth Bolton	$9.95
Sweet Tomorrows	Kimberly White	$8.95
Taken by You	Dorothy Elizabeth Love	$9.95
Tattooed Tears	T. T. Henderson	$8.95
Tempting Faith	Crystal Hubbard	$6.99
The Color Line	Lizzette Grayson Carter	$9.95
The Color of Trouble	Dyanne Davis	$8.95
The Disappearance of Allison Jones	Kayla Perrin	$5.95
The Fires Within	Beverly Clark	$9.95
The Foursome	Celya Bowers	$6.99
The Honey Dipper's Legacy	Myra Pannell-Allen	$14.95
The Joker's Love Tune	Sidney Rickman	$15.95
The Little Pretender	Barbara Cartland	$10.95
The Love We Had	Natalie Dunbar	$8.95
The Man Who Could Fly	Bob & Milana Beamon	$18.95

Other Genesis Press, Inc. Titles (continued)

Order Form

Mail to: Genesis Press, Inc.
P.O. Box 101
Columbus, MS 39703

Name _____
Address _____
City/State _____ Zip _____
Telephone _____

Ship to (if different from above)
Name _____
Address _____
City/State _____ Zip _____
Telephone _____

Credit Card Information
Credit Card # _____ ☐ Visa ☐ Mastercard
Expiration Date (mm/yy) _____ ☐ AmEx ☐ Discover

Qty.	Author	Title	Price	Total

Use this order form, or call 1-888-INDIGO-1	
Total for books	_____
Shipping and handling: $5 first two books, $1 each additional book	_____
Total S & H	_____
Total amount enclosed	_____
Mississippi residents add 7% sales tax